The Final Contract

The Black Ledger Billionaires

Rebekah Sinclair

This novel contains **mature themes, explicit content, and dark romance elements** that may be **disturbing or triggering** for some readers.

This book is **intended for adult audiences** and **reader discretion is strongly advised.** If any of these topics are sensitive for you, please proceed with caution.

- Sex Work / Escorting
- Sexual power dynamics & coercion
- Explicit sexual content, kink & masturbation
- Explicit language & derogatory / degrading terms
- Toxic relationships & power imbalances
- Physical violence, aggression & murder
- Emotional trauma, manipulation & abandonment
- Revenge, stalking, blackmail & captivity

- Knife play, weapon use & threats during intimacy
- Kidnapping, gagging, restraints & sedation
- Fire, explosions & entrapment
- Near-death situations & life-threatening injuries
- Past death of children by fire (referenced)
- Past graphic death of drunk driving victim (referenced)

The Black Ledger

Welcome to The Black Ledger

An elite, highly exclusive escort service where billionaires strike discreet deals, and escorts set their own terms.

- ~ No complications.
- ~ No attachments.
- ~ Just business.

But desire is never that simple.

Here, control turns into obsession, rules are meant to be broken, and the one risk no one dares take—falling in love—may be the most dangerous deal of all.

Because at The Black Ledger,
contracts are final...

But hearts were never meant
to be part of the deal.

Each book is a **standalone** with interconnected characters. ***No cheating***, ***no cliffhangers***—just powerful men, the women who bring them to their knees, and spice that will leave you breathless.

**Thank you for choosing The Black Ledger
and we hope you enjoy your contract.**

Lucian Vale

*For the ones who like their billionaires ruthless, their escorts
reckless, and their endings filthy.
You made it to the final contract.*

May it ruin you in all the ways you secretly wanted.

Chapter 1

The chandeliers glitter like a thousand captive stars, throwing fractured light over silk gowns and masks lacquered in gold. For one night, New York pretends it's the Palais Garnier. The final curtain call of *Phantom of the Opera* has turned into a requiem and a celebration all at once—the fortieth anniversary marked by a masquerade ball that feels more fantasy than real.

My arm is tucked into Maestro Levant's, the celebrated conductor of the production. He insisted on making an entrance, and I am his carefully chosen ornament for the evening. The Black Ledger delivers nothing less, after all.

My gown weighs more than I do. Layers of silver tulle and embroidered lace cascade around me, swallowing my frame until I feel less like a woman and more like a stage piece. The mask pressed against my skin is delicate, feathered along the temple, meant to soften.

Smile. Tilt your head. Keep your eyes warm even when the rest of you is screaming to breathe.

The orchestra swells, strings curling around the room like smoke, and the crowd arranges itself around the dance floor.

A waltz designed for spectacle—partners rotating, no longer people but a painting in motion.

I let Maestro Levant guide me, my steps light, my chin tilted just so.

When the dance ends, the Maestro will share the announcement everyone has been waiting for. Next year's fortieth anniversary of *Phantom* will be marked by a grand flourish, and then the guests will travel to the veranda to watch as fireworks split the skyline.

But as the champagne flutes lift and laughter roars, a shiver crawls down my spine.

It's the masks. Too many faces covered in gold and bone-white porcelain, expressions fixed into something alien. Every smile looks painted on. Every laugh echoes too loud. I press closer to my date, the perfect Companion, listening when he speaks, laughing when he expects it.

Still—at the edges of my vision, shadows move wrong.

Maybe it's the heat, the crush of bodies, or the suffocating weight of my gown. Maybe it's the eerie beauty of the night.

Or maybe it's instinct.

The one I've never ignored.

Not since I realized I had a phantom of my own.

He isn't an apparition from the stage but a man made of obsession. A stalker. A fanatic who lingers in the cracks of my life, haunting me in ways the play could only romanticize.

My one comfort is that Killian is here. Somewhere.

I can't see him through the glittering crowd, but I feel him the way a tether feels its anchor. He's been watching over me for the past year—ever since the night everything changed. When I was abducted by a paying client, pulled along as collateral for a debt I had no part in. When my boss, Lucian Vale, had to bloody his hands to get me back.

And when Killian became my shadow. My bodyguard.

At an event like this, I never know exactly where he is, only that he's somewhere watching. That knowledge is the only reason I can draw breath beneath the weight of this gown.

The dance is second nature. I've trained in studios for twelve years, and though I left that world behind, my body remembers. The steps are ingrained in my muscles, as familiar as the taste of my own name.

The gown—an homage to the screen adaptation's *Think of Me* dress, all satin weight and jeweled embroidery—clings like memory and moves like water. Every twirl makes the fabric ripple, every step a careful echo of a role I was never cast to play.

I let myself fall into it. The music. The movement. The endless blur of masks. Faces slide past like shifting cards in a deck, each one painted, feathered, jeweled. The waltz turns into rhythm, rhythm into instinct—until something stills me.

A flower.

Not just any flower. A white rose, dipped at the tips in red.

It peeks from the lapel of a passing mask, and my pulse spikes.

The room keeps spinning, the dance keeps pulling me along, but my heart stutters because I know what that rose means. He's here.

My stalker.

Since this began, he's made himself known only by this calling card. A white rose, tainted with red paint. Silent reminders that he's watching. Waiting.

I only know one thing about him—one detail I've clung to, prayed to forget.

One brown eye.

One ice-blue.

A gaze that sees straight through me.

Sometimes he vanishes for months, as if he never existed at all. Then—without warning—he reappears. A rose on my doorstep. A shadow where no shadow should be. Never violent. Never close enough to touch. Just near enough to remind me that he can.

When it first began, we tried to catch him. The police. Private investigators. Lucian. But he slipped away, a phantom in his own right. Untouchable. Unseen.

The waltz carries me, steps ingrained into muscle memory, but my heartbeat is uneven. The Maestro spins me gracefully, and my skirts flare like pale smoke across the floor. I use the turn to scan the crowd, searching past jeweled masks and champagne smiles, desperate to pin down that rose.

Nothing. Only strangers, glittering and false.

Perhaps I imagined it.

The pressure in my chest tightens, panic clawing its way up—until my gaze lifts and I find him.

Not my phantom. My shadow.

Killian stands on the second-story balcony, half in shadow himself.

No mask.

He'd never hide.

His tuxedo cuts a severe line against the golden light, and his presence alone swallows the space around him. He's already seen the shift in me, already read the panic I thought I hid. There's something relentless in the way he watches—steady, unblinking, as though I'm the only movement in the room worth tracking.

Even from here, I feel the coiled readiness in him. A predator on the edge of pouncing. One signal from me, and he'll bring this ballroom to its knees.

And relief loosens something inside me at that thought.

Five years. That's how long the shadows have followed me—sometimes loud, sometimes silent, always there. Long enough that I've learned to live with it, to tuck it away like a background hum. Everyone else moved on when he went quiet, and I let them. Easier to pretend it was nothing than risk drawing blood by admitting it still lingered.

But Killian... he doesn't know. Not the way it is now. If I told him, he'd never rest, never stop until he flushed the bastard out of whatever hole he's crawled back into. That's who he is. Unyielding. Consuming. And maybe that terrifies me more than the stalker ever did.

I give the smallest nod. A quiet command in our language of glances we've perfected. *No. It's fine. Stay.*

His posture doesn't change, but he stays rooted. Watching. Waiting.

The final measures of the waltz crash through the air, sweeping me back into the movement. I let the music carry me, finishing each step with practiced elegance, though my pulse still thunders louder than the applause.

Maestro Levant offers his arm again, guiding me up the grand staircase. We ascend together, my skirts heavy against each marble step, until the spotlight finds us at the far left. Behind us, tall, gilded doors wait to open, promising the night sky and fireworks.

The Maestro clears his throat, his voice swelling into the microphone with the pomp and grandeur of the announcement. Forty years of history. One final farewell. His words are drowned in applause, but my focus isn't on him.

It's on them.

Every mask. Every tuxedo. Every gleaming boutonniere.

And there—movement where everything else is still.

A man in the middle of the crowd, drifting toward the right. His mask is gold, molded into the half face of a phantom.

My breath catches.

My eyes lift instantly to the balcony. To Killian.

He never stopped watching, steel-gray eyes locked on me. He saw the shift in my posture. Reads me like no one else can. His hand brushes to his ear, activating the earpiece, murmuring something low to our driver stationed nearby.

"No," I mouth, almost imperceptibly. My chin dips just enough to give him the signal. *Not now. Not here.*

Too many cameras. Too many eyes. This is not my stage,

not my announcement. The Maestro is still speaking, and if Killian storms the ballroom on my word, everything erupts into chaos.

Besides, my phantom has never been this direct before. Never brazen. Just...present. Lurking.

Applause surges, and a child—barely ten, dressed like a cherub from the chorus—approaches with a bouquet of roses.

Red. Beautiful. Perfect.

She holds them up to me with both hands, and the crowd claps again, charmed by the gesture. I smile, take them gently into the crook of my arm, and give her a gentle bow.

I don't hear the Maestro's final words. I don't even register the applause rising like a wave.

The double doors swing open. The night explodes in light as fireworks scream against the skyline.

And then—something warm trickles over my hand. Wet.

I glance down.

Scarlet smears my palms, staining the pale satin of my gown.

My heart lurches into my throat.

The roses aren't red.

They're white.

Each one dipped in crimson paint, still dripping like blood, soaking into my skin.

The crowd gasps at the fireworks. I can't hear them.

All I can hear is the rush of static in my ears.

Because this isn't a gift.

It's a message.

The crowd swallows me.

Bodies press in on every side, bumping my arms, brushing the roses that drip red down my hands. I can't move, can't breathe. My chest tightens, panic clawing up my throat. Masks glitter and shift, gold flashing everywhere I look.

Which one is him?

I turn too quickly, skirts tangling, vision blurring—until I see him.

Ten feet away. Perfectly still. A tuxedo. A gold phantom mask.

And the eyes.

One brown. One glacial blue.

They lock on mine. And he smiles. Slow. Sinister. Certain.

My stomach drops, fear carving me hollow. For years he's been a ghost, a nuisance. But this...this is the first time I believe he intends to harm me.

Then the roses are torn from my grip. An arm bands around my waist, hauling me backward against a wall of muscle.

I don't need to see him to know it's Killian. The sheer force of him radiates through every inch of contact—unyielding and dangerous.

He doesn't hesitate. He shoves us into the current of people, cutting a path as if the crowd itself senses better than to resist him.

I stumble against the weight of my gown, nearly topple, but Killian doesn't slow. He simply sweeps me up, skirts and all, as though I weigh nothing. His stride quickens, cutting through the tide of bodies, down a side staircase, and out into the night air.

The music fades, replaced by the slam of a door as he barrels us into the night. Cool air slaps my face, sharp, bracing.

The limo waits at the curb. Felix stands stiff beside it, holding the door open, eyes scanning the street.

"Killian—put me down," I gasp, shoving at his shoulder.

He doesn't. Not until he's reached the car. He stuffs me inside, gathers the mountain of gown after me, then climbs in close, the door sealing us off from the world.

Felix slides behind the wheel. The city lurches forward.

Killian doesn't say a word.

But the iron set of his jaw, the barely leashed violence in every line of him, is louder than any promise.

He's ready to spill blood.

Chapter 2
Killian

Blood.

It's everywhere.

Across my hands. Smearing her dress. Glazing her arms up to the elbows.

"Where are you hurt?" I growl, dragging her against me as my fingers search frantically. Neck. Ribs. Waist. I don't care if I have to rip every inch of this fucking gown apart to find it.

Her protests are noise. I don't hear them. I only see red.

My Irish brogue thickens the way it always does when I'm at my limit—pissed or drunk or buried deep in a beautiful woman.

But that's not what this is. This is panic clawing at the edges of me.

"Tell me who the fuck did this, Seraphina. Now."

She shoves at me, twisting, and when I don't stop—when I pull my knife and get a fistful of satin—her palm cracks against my cheek.

"Killian Shaw!"

The sound rings sharper than the strike itself. It barely stings, but it halts me. Shocks me enough that my grip loosens.

Her chest is heaving, eyes blazing through the mask still clinging to her face until she rips it off and flings it across the limo. "I'm not hurt, you giant bulldozer."

For a beat, the limo hums with nothing but Felix's steady driving and her ragged breaths. Mine are worse.

I put my knife away, drag my hand through my hair, and look at her properly. No pain in her face. No tremor in her voice. Just fire in those blue eyes.

I clamp my hands around her wrists—not soft, not cruel, but firm enough to still her. Her skin is sticky—red smeared against pale.

"Then explain this," I snap, holding her hands up between us. The bloodstains look like evidence. Proof of something I can't yet name.

Because if she's not bleeding... then whose blood is this?

"It's just paint, big man." She fights with the endless amount of fabric, settling herself further into the black leather seat. "It's not a big deal."

"Paint?" I grind the word out like it's poison. "You expect me to believe this is nothing?"

She twists, trying to push me back with that cool façade she wears when she wants the world to think she's untouchable—calm, collected. But I've spent a year with her. Almost every fucking day.

I've spent too many hours with her—watched every twitch of her mouth, every tightening of her shoulders. I know when she's telling the truth. And I know when she's lying through her teeth.

She's doing it now.

"Stop actin' like I don't know ya," I snarl. My brogue cuts sharper than I want it to, but I don't reel it back. "I've been at your side for a year, Seraphina. I've seen you terrified, I've seen you broken, and I've seen you fight your way back from hell. And this—" I hold up her dripping hands, "—isn't nothing."

Her eyes flash, chin tipping up. Defiance. It's always defiance with her.

And Christ, it stirs every demon in me.

Lucian and I flew halfway across the world to drag her out of the deranged clutches of a madman.

That bastard's gone now—ashes in the ground. But I remember the night too clearly. Some wannabe king's little brother knee-deep in drugs, drowning in debt. And not just any debt. Debt with the Irish.

And an Irish debt is a life debt. No questions. No mercy.

As soon as I heard my old family was involved, I knew what it meant. They wouldn't hesitate to shoot her down on their way to their target.

Collateral damage, they'd have called her.

And I would know better than anyone.

I've kept her close ever since. Because I don't trust the world not to take another bite out of her.

So no, I don't believe her calm little act. I don't believe in coincidence. And I sure as hell don't believe roses dripping red into her hands are just fucking paint.

The fight doesn't stop when Felix pulls up to her building. It climbs with us in the elevator, follows into her kitchen, spilling over marble countertops and the wreckage of that ruined gown.

The kitchen lights are too bright after the chaos of the ballroom. I strip off my jacket and toss it over the back of a chair, then roll my sleeves to the elbow. The sink hisses as I scrub the red off my hands, water running pink down the drain. Paint, she says. I'm not convinced.

Behind me, the fridge opens. She pulls out a bottle of water, panting faintly as she twists the cap. From the fight? From the panic? From me? I don't ask.

"You want to tell me the truth now?" I say without turning.

Her silence stretches, then breaks. "I have a stalker."

I freeze, hands braced on the stainless steel. Slowly, I shut off the tap and turn.

"Do you remember?" she asks, voice softer now. "Years ago. When Lucian tried to find him."

I remember. How could I not? Back then, I thought it was handled. Dealt with.

"Five years," I murmur, the pieces slotting into place. "Five fucking years you've been looking over your shoulder?"

She shrugs, sipping her water like we're discussing the weather. "It stopped for a while. He was mostly quiet for a bit. I thought he had moved on and it was not worth making a fuss."

Not worth making a fuss? A fucking stalker?

She walks away like that settles it. Like we're finished.

We're not.

Not even fucking close.

I follow her down the hall—every step of her penthouse already memorized. I know where the floor creaks, which door sticks, how the curtains leak light in the mornings. There's not an inch of this place I don't know.

In her bedroom, she sets the bottle aside and unclasps her earrings, placing them neatly on a tray. "You don't need to get worked up, Killian. It's nothing."

"It's not nothing," I snap, trailing after her.

She disappears into the bathroom. I go too.

She sets her necklace down with careful hands, avoiding my eyes in the mirror.

"Quiet?" I repeat, bracketing her against the counter with both palms flat on the marble. My reflection looms behind hers. "That's your excuse? Quiet?"

Her jaw tightens, but she doesn't pull away. "He's left a flower here and there. Three times this year. That's it. I got rid of them before you could see."

The words hit like a gut punch. "You've been covering for him."

"I've been handling it."

"No." My voice drops lower, heavier. "You've been living with it. There's a difference."

She finally looks at me—steady, stubborn.

I have to force myself not to stare at her mouth, at the pale-pink gloss catching the light, making me wonder how soft she tastes. To keep my eyes on hers, away from the corset that shoves her tits together, the way they bounce just so when she walks—like they're begging for my hands.

I push the anger forward so it's all I can feel.

Anger—at her for hiding it, at Lucian for not crushing this bastard years ago, at myself for standing at her side blind while she pretended it had gone away.

Never again.

I lean in, crowding her back against the counter. "This ends now. You hear me? Not another flower. Not another text. Not another ghost at your shoulder that you hide from me."

The bathroom goes still. My voice is low, steady, meant only for her ears. And despite the fight still simmering in her, I catch something else in her stare—something dangerous.

Because I'm here to guard her. Not to fuck her.

"You hear me?" I press, my mouth just inches from hers.

She nods once. Silent. Then her tongue flicks across her bottom lip, and it nearly fucking kills me. Thank God for the way I'm standing—hiding the hard-on straining against my trousers.

Her eyes shift, sliding past mine to the mirror. She turns slightly, hands braced on the counter beside mine, gaze locking with mine in the glass.

Christ.

This position. The swell of her breasts spilling from the corset, the faint looseness in the bodice where the dress is fighting to keep up. Her blonde hair, pinned high, a few strands falling to brush her neck, trailing over her bare shoulder like temptation itself.

I could press into her now. Let her feel what she does to me. Tear this goddamn dress off her and take what I've wanted for months—years, if I'm being honest.

Instead, she whispers, "Help me out of my dress?"

Quiet, but loaded.

Her brow arches, the smallest twitch, and I know she's aware of every thought in my head.

My jaw tenses as I force myself upright, but I step closer all the same. "Just pull the string out," she instructs.

My fingers—too big, too rough—find the delicate satin laced tight down her spine. I tug one loop free, then the next, unraveling the crisscross pattern inch by inch.

She never takes her eyes off me. I look down only when I need to. Like this is some silent standoff. Like she can use this to make me drop this whole stalker revelation.

Not a fucking chance, angel.

Near the top, the fabric slackens, and she holds it to her chest, modest in gesture but not in effect.

The string finally gone, I retreat a step. But she isn't finished with me.

"There's a zipper too."

Her voice is lighter now, almost casual. But when she glances back over her shoulder, her eyes catch mine, and I know she's baiting me.

I reach again, fingers brushing the warm line of her skin as I find the zipper. Goosebumps ripple under my touch, her body betraying her even if her face doesn't.

I could lean down, kiss that spot. Warm her with my mouth, taste the heat of her pulse.

But I don't.

Because I can't. Because the one rule—my cardinal rule—is never—fuck the woman you're meant to protect.

And then the zipper drops.

The dress loosens. Fabric slides. And what greets me steals the air from my lungs.

A pale-pink thong, nothing more. A tiny bow at the waistband like it's a gift waiting for me to unwrap.

I want to slide my hand beneath it. Feel her wet and ready for me. Drop to my knees and taste what I've only imagined.

But I don't.

I take one step back. Then another.

She turns, eyes tracking me, sharp as blades and soft as sin all at once.

A third step. A fourth. Until I'm clear of the bathroom, standing in her bedroom doorway.

"I'll be out here if you need anything," I say.

My voice is steady, controlled.

Even if I know one day she'll be the death of my control.

Chapter 3
Seraphina

I've always loved it here.

Anastasia's house has a way of wrapping around me like a memory I never earned—warm, sunlit, permanent. Even the air feels softer, salted with the Atlantic breeze, carrying the distant call of gulls and the lull of waves crashing against the shore. We're only a short drive from Manhattan, but it feels like another world. Her world.

My twin's life looks nothing like mine.

Stasia is a wife, a mother. She's built this picture-perfect home with the white shutters, the trimmed hedges, the kind of laughter that sticks to the walls.

She stuck with being a nurse while I quit the hospital to play house in penthouses that don't belong to me.

I dine in the finest restaurants wearing dresses someone else paid for and sail across the world on the yachts of men who want nothing more than a beautiful distraction on their arm. My life is polished, glittering, enviable—yet none of it feels like it belongs to me.

But this? Sitting here in my sister's backyard, fading golden sunlight filtering through the branches while the sea hums in the background—this feels like peace. Like breathing for the first time in weeks.

Stasia sets down a tray between us, the delicate clink of porcelain teacups breaking the quiet. "Tea with lemon," she says, sliding one toward me. "And lemon cookies. Still your favorite?"

"Always," I murmur, grateful for the sweetness of something that's real.

Across the yard, Aurora runs barefoot through the grass, her sundress billowing behind her like a banner. Oliver crouches low, mud smeared on his hands, too proud of whatever creature he's just dug up.

"Ollie, don't you dare tease your sister with that worm!" Stasia calls, her voice carrying the edge of practiced authority.

Too late. Aurora shrieks, darting toward the porch with wild blond curls streaming behind her. She darts behind a post, clutching it like a lifeline, cheeks flushed pink.

From the corner of my eye, I catch Killian—lounging on the back steps with his phone. He hasn't moved in half an hour, eyes flicking over the screen like he's actually reading the news. But I know better. He's scanning. Hunting. Waiting for my phantom to appear in the shadows.

For half a second, his lips twitch into the faintest smirk as Aurora dives for cover. Almost human. Almost soft. But then he looks up at me, and just like that, the smile is gone. As if I'd only imagined it. His eyes harden, his attention sinking back to his phone.

Stasia leans back in her chair, lifting her teacup with a pointed look. "So," she says, far too casual. "Care to explain why my darling sister was splashed across the Friday papers?"

My stomach dips.

She pulls her phone from her pocket, scrolling until she finds the headline. She turns it toward me, and there it is, bold across the screen: **The Jewel of the Phantom Is Carried Off After Fainting at Gala.**

Stasia arches a brow. "Did you really faint?"

I hesitate, toying with the edge of my nail polish like the answer might be written there. "No."

Her eyes narrow. "Then what really happened?"

I look away, pretending to sip my tea, but she's not buying it.

"My twintuition is screaming at me," she says flatly. "So I'll just go ahead and guess. The stalker?"

The word hits harder than I want to admit. I've never hidden anything from my twin. It would be impossible to try. She's always known everything going on in my life, always supported me—even when she wants to scream at me and shake me by my shoulders.

I don't answer right away. I can't. But after a moment, I nod. Just once.

Stasia exhales slowly, her gaze shifting toward her children, her expression softening as Aurora edges back out from behind the porch post, still wary of her brother.

"I hate that this is your life," she says, her voice low but fierce, like it's meant for me alone.

My throat tightens. Because she doesn't mean the job—

never has. Stasia was the one who held my hand when I finally told our parents what I really did for a living, the one who patched the fallout as best she could. Needless to say, Mom and Dad weren't exactly thrilled to learn their darling daughter was a professional escort. But over time, they learned to pretend—to smile like they believe I'm still a nurse working alongside my sister.

Ignorance is bliss.

But not for Stasia. She's never wanted the façade. She's always been my partner in crime, the one who asks about my clients, the yachts, the cities I pass through like postcards. She doesn't hate what I do—she hates the shadow that follows me, the stalker who turned the fantasy into something sharp and ugly.

And maybe, deep down, she hates that I didn't stay in the life we started together—two sisters in scrubs, fresh out of nursing school, pulling shifts at the same hospital. She chose a steady future with Daniel. I chose freedom and the Ledger.

"I thought he was gone," she murmurs.

I toy with the rim of my teacup. "He just … backed off. A little."

Her breath hitches, a long drag through her nose as she watches Aurora giggle again, safe in the sunlight. Oliver crouches low, plotting his next ambush, as if worms could solve everything.

Then her gaze slides past me. To him.

"Does this have anything to do with the giant iron mountain currently sitting under my porch?" she asks.

I can't help it. A laugh slips out, soft and unsteady. "Stas—"

"Uh-huh." Her tone is pure triumph, her mouth twitching into a knowing grin. "That's about what I thought."

I wave her off quickly, heat crawling up my neck. "He's just my bodyguard. From the ... other incident."

Her brow arches. "Sera, you've had so many life-threatening events lately I'm losing track. Which one was this again?"

I groan, sinking deeper into my chair, but she doesn't let me off the hook.

Her eyes sharpen, voice dropping into that tone she only uses when she's about to give me the truth I don't want to hear.

"So, tell me," she says, leaning closer, "when are you going to think about moving on? About getting out of the Ledger? Maybe going back to nursing? Or something else?"

The words hang there, heavier than the tea between us.

And I wish I had an answer.

I've thought about it. More than once.

Never nursing. I could never put on a pair of scrubs again, no matter how badly Stasia wants me to. And she knows exactly why.

Every time I think about life after the Ledger, this is what I see—this backyard. Lightning bugs flickering like fairy lights, the sound of children's laughter trailing across the lawn. My children. A slice of peace that belongs to someone else but always feels close enough to touch.

The only part that's always missing is the husband. My mind never conjures him. Maybe it's the wall I've built around relationships; maybe it's the truth I don't want to admit—that I don't know what it looks like to belong to someone without it costing something.

But Stasia and Daniel ... they're different. Fifteen years married, and they're still disgustingly in love. The kind of love that hasn't faded or fractured.

I hear the slam of a car door and glance up just as my sister does. Her face lights. She's already heading for the gate before he even rounds the corner. And when he does, she's the first thing he sees. His arms lock around her waist, pulling her in, her arms twining around his neck as she rises onto tiptoe for a kiss that still makes her blush.

Every time I watch it, I feel that pull. That rope tightening around me, tugging me farther from the Ledger. Slowly. Steadily.

But I still don't know what waits on the other end.

That thought gnaws at me as my eyes flick toward the porch.

Killian is watching me watch them.

He's leaning forward now, forearms braced on his knees, his phone forgotten. Even from here, I can feel the storm building behind his gray eyes, the tension carved into every line of his body. He lifts his scarred brow, just slightly, as if asking a question only I can hear. *Ready?*

And I think I am.

I rise slowly, brushing crumbs from my dress, and drift toward him. Behind me, my sister's laughter twines with

Daniel's, the sound a warm counterpoint to the restless energy tightening in my chest.

"You about ready?" I ask as he pushes to his feet.

But before he can answer, Stasia's voice cuts across the yard. "Killian, if you two don't stay for dinner, I'll take it personally."

I whip my head toward him. *No,* I mouth, sharp enough to cut.

"We've got to get going," I say firmly—at the same time Killian says, "I'd love to."

My sister smirks, already triumphant. I glare at him, trying to burn the warning into his thick skull, but he doesn't so much as flinch. If anything, his mouth twitches.

"We really can't. I've got an early day tomorrow," I press, trying to salvage it.

"No, you don't." His tone is flat, but there's a thread of humor beneath it.

My eyes narrow. I lean closer, my words a low growl. "I will end your bloodline."

He chuckles, maddeningly unbothered. "Easy, little killer. It's just dinner."

"Exactly why I like him." My sister betrays me as she heads inside.

"Kill!" Daniel grins as he steps under the porch, Aurora perched easily on his hip. He reaches out a hand to Killian. "Always good to see you, man."

Aurora's wide eyes blink up at the giant beside her father. "Are you a real killer?" Ollie asks in fascination.

"Oh, Daddy! Can the killer come to my birthday party?" Ro nearly screams in excitement.

Killian's scarred brow arches as Daniel inhales a deep breath and holds it. I leave the two men to field those questions and follow my sister inside.

***

And that was the beginning of several hours of interrogation.

Exactly the reason I didn't want to stay.

The kids never stopped—question after question, relentless as only children can be. How many people had Killian killed? Did he think unicorns were real? Had he ever been to prison?

For some reason, they weren't buying it when he claimed to be an accountant.

That excuse made me roll my eyes so hard I nearly saw my own brain.

The man was about as much an accountant as I was a nun.

With those calloused hands, that scar running through his brow, and shoulders broad enough to block out the sun? Please. I know he has killed people—with nothing more than his bare hands. The image of him hunched behind a desk filing someone's taxes was so absurd it was comical.

But then Oliver tilted his head and asked, "Are you and Killian boyfriend and girlfriend?"

I nearly choked on my iced tea. My cheeks burned hot as I stumbled over myself, blurting some incoherent denial. Meanwhile, Killian leaned back in his chair, stretching one arm across the back like he owned the space, casually wiping his trimmed dark beard with a napkin—probably to hide the smirk tugging at his mouth.

He was enjoying every second of my humiliation.

Thankfully, Stasia swooped in with a cheerful, "They're just friends, honey."

And with the way Killian cleared his throat, I wasn't sure which one of us that answer burned more.

***

After dinner, Daniel took over the dishes and, to my surprise, Killian rolled up his sleeves and joined him at the sink. The sight of the Irish mountain washing plates beside my brother-in-law was enough to make me blink twice. Meanwhile, Stasia and I wrangled the kids into their playroom.

Which mostly meant Oliver painstakingly organized his army of figurines while Aurora presented me with every single toy she owned, demanding my opinion on which she should keep out for her birthday party.

Killian appeared in the doorway, knuckles rapping against the frame twice. "You ready?"

"Oh, now you're ready?" I shoot back, standing with Aurora still clinging to my neck.

"Mm," he hums, unbothered, as I carry her over. Her tiny frame looks even smaller when I shift her close to him. He's not just tall—he's solid. Every inch of him built from muscle and quiet menace. And there is not a single part of him that strikes me as small.

I shove the thought down before it can detonate.

Killian lifts a hand to my niece. "High five."

Aurora grins and slaps his palm. "Next time you go kill someone, can I come?"

"Aurora Williams!" Stasia's voice cuts sharp from down the hall.

Daniel, Killian, and I all burst out laughing.

"No, you may not join a murder," Stasia calls, sweeping her daughter away toward the bath. Oliver trails after, calling over his shoulder, "So he is a killer, then?"

Their voices fade down the hall, leaving me and Killian to see ourselves out.

"Let's go, big man."

The drive home is silent but not empty. His sleek car hums beneath us, the leather cool against my skin. One of his hands rests steady on the wheel, the other shifting gears with effortless precision. And, for reasons I cannot explain, the movement looks sinfully sexy.

My mind drifts the entire way back—sliding into dangerous places I don't let it linger often.

The first thought came to me when Killian tried and failed to discreetly adjust his jeans. I wondered if there would be enough room in the driver's seat for me, if Killian were to pull this car over and pull his cock out for me to ride. Because with the hard-on he was trying to ignore, my earlier thoughts of nothing being small were absolutely correct.

I lean my head against the rest, closing my eyes as the dark road hums beneath the tires.

I push away that naughty image and instead picture that family. The backyard. The children's laughter that cuts the night. And for the first time, I don't see myself alone.

I see someone standing beside me. A particular Irish mountain, cut from iron and storm clouds, who smells of rugged sandalwood and pure stubbornness.

A dangerous image.

One I can't quite make myself banish.

Chapter 4
Seraphina

The walls of The Black Ledger are made to impress. Floor-to-ceiling windows overlooking the city skyline, marble floors polished to a sheen, and furniture so sleek it feels like no one actually uses it. But underneath all that gloss and control, there's an edge to this place—like you can hear secrets breathing in the walls if you're quiet long enough.

Today it feels sharper than ever.

Killian strides in beside me, every step radiating iron-willed determination. I've argued, cajoled, even threatened, but nothing would dissuade him from this. He demanded we tell Lucian about the stalker. Demanded, as if I'm on his payroll.

Lucian Vale sits at the head of the long obsidian table, immaculate as always—dark suit, steel-gray eyes, the kind of authority that doesn't need to be spoken to be felt.

He owns The Black Ledger and every Companion in its employ. I've seen firsthand exactly what these two men are capable of, and somehow the button-down dress shirts suddenly add to the menace they exude rather than mask it.

Sienna is already perched in one of the side chairs, legs crossed, sipping her espresso like this is brunch and not a potential inquisition. Her eyes flick from me to Killian, one brow arching. "This should be entertaining."

Lucian rolls his eyes at his girlfriend's intuition. His steely look shifts to Killian, sharp and unyielding. "What was so urgent it couldn't wait until the morning briefing?"

Killian leans forward, elbows braced on the table, the knife he carries everywhere twirling between his thick fingers. "It's about—"

"It's nothing," I cut in quickly, waving a hand before he can build momentum. "Really, Lucian, he's being dramatic. The stalker hasn't been a problem for weeks."

Sienna chokes mid-sip. "Seraphina." My name cracks across the room like a whip. "You're telling me you've got a stalker and said nothing?"

Heat creeps up my neck. "Not a new one," I mutter, wincing. "The same one."

Killian grumbles under his breath, low but audible. "At least she's kept it from everyone and not just me."

My glare snaps to him, but Lucian's voice cuts the air clean. "Details." His tone is final, heavy. "Now—and leave nothing out."

The room stills. Even Sienna goes quiet, watching me from the corner of her eye.

So I tell them. About the flowers, the notes. The feeling of being watched. How it all quieted—until the opera gala. How I'd brushed it off before, called him harmless, just a fanatic who liked the fantasy too much. But when I saw him in that crowd—the smile, the way his gaze pinned me like a specimen, the way my body knew before my mind did…

Lucian leans forward, his jaw taut. "You felt like he wanted to hurt you."

The words scrape across my skin. I swallow hard, then nod.

Killian's knuckles crack, the sound sharp and violent in the silence. Fury coils in him like a storm barely chained.

He doesn't ask permission, doesn't soften his voice. "Who do you have who can help me hunt this bastard down?"

Sienna sets her cup aside, resting her chin on her hand. "Oh, you know exactly who would love to get his nosy little hands on this."

Lucian's mouth twitches, almost a smile. "Do me a favor. Next time you see Jaxon, tell him you called him 'little.' Please make sure I'm there to watch the meltdown."

Sienna snorts. "Noted."

"Jaxon Kane," Lucian says, turning back to Killian. "He'll have eyes where we don't. Get anything and everything you can to him. I'll let him know what's happening."

Killian nods once, sharp and decisive. "Good."

Lucian holds his gaze a moment longer, the air between them a heavy agreement. Then, quietly, "And when we find him—he's all yours."

Killian doesn't blink. He just slides his blade back into the holder strapped around his thigh. "Wasn't even going to ask."

The dangerous promise lingers in the room long after the conversation moves on.

Killian leans back, satisfied; Sienna swishes her espresso like she's watching a thriller; and for a moment I think that's it. That we're done.

But we're not.

Because if I let them end it here, I'll never get the words out.

I clear my throat, shifting in my chair. "Actually ... there's something else."

Three pairs of eyes land on me.

I force myself to sit taller. "I've been giving this a lot of thought. The Ledger has been my home for years. My family. But ..." I pause, swallowing the lump in my throat. "I think it's time to move on."

Lucian doesn't flinch, though I catch the faint crease of thought at the corner of his brow. He has always respected when Companions are ready to transition—whether it's to their own businesses, quiet retirements, or entirely new lives. His rule is unshakable: once Ledger, always Ledger.

"I thought this would be coming soon." His voice is calm, steady. "What do you have in mind?"

"This," I say softly, "is where you may be able to help me. With one last thing. My final contract."

Silence presses in. Sienna straightens slightly in her chair. Killian looks at me like he's trying to predict what I'll say next.

Lucian's hard gaze doesn't waver. He studies me, the wheels turning behind his eyes.

"A marriage," I say.

Sienna blinks, then narrows her eyes like she's already racing through a million logistical thoughts. Killian's brows draw low, thunderclouds already forming.

But Lucian—Lucian just watches me. I can almost feel him weighing the words, turning the shape of them over in his mind.

The Ledger has always provided Companions to the world's elite—temporary arrangements, carefully brokered deals where intimacy and power are transacted in equal measure.

But what I'm proposing is something entirely different. Not a contract measured in weeks or months. Not companionship for a season.

A partnership. A marriage.

My final contract.

Killian's voice cuts first, rough as gravel. "Do you really think that's safe with everything going on? A stalker still on the prowl?"

I meet his storm-colored eyes. "Companions take a risk with every contract. I know that better than most."

The air shifts, the weight of memory pressing between us.

After my abduction, Lucian tore down his old policies and rebuilt the systems, the security, the tech. Jaxon had come in like some boy-genius billionaire from another world, inventing trackers for every Companion—devices that could measure heart rate, speed, even altitude.

Tiny. Unassuming. But powerful enough to ensure no Companion could ever vanish again.

I rub my thumb over the polished nail hiding my own

tracker, mindlessly tracing the glossy curve. I've worn one since the night I came back. Quiet protection. A secret anchor if my phantom ever did decide to reach for me again.

But this isn't about him.

"This is my life," I say, steady now. "And I want more out of it. A family. Children."

"This," Sienna starts, nodding slowly, "is going to be epic. Hell yes. Let's do it."

A laugh slips out of me, but it rings a little empty. Especially with Killian sitting close, fury radiating from his silence. I hadn't mentioned this to him. Hadn't wanted to look him in the eye when I said it. I'm not even sure why.

Lucian's gaze pins me. "How do you envision this working?"

I lift my chin. "Put out a query. Build a catalog of suitors. There have to be billionaires out there looking to buy a bride—someone to give them an heir. A strong prenup, of course."

Lucian studies me for a long beat. "This wouldn't be a love match."

My mind flickers to Stasia and Daniel—their love is real, rare, once in a lifetime. But that kind of bond doesn't grow on trees. I've seen the other side of it too many times. I've been the secret escape for married men who slip away from their wives, who hand me diamonds or first-class tickets in exchange for pretending they're still capable of feeling something true. I know how men work. I know what love looks like when it rots.

And that's not what this would be. An agreement. Nothing more.

"Love," I reply quickly, firmly, "is not in the cards for some of us. I know that."

Something flickers in Lucian's expression—the smallest softening, at least as much as a man like him allows. "You never know. Love may surprise you."

His hand travels to Sienna's thigh under the table, and she smiles at him—the one woman who managed to pierce his armor.

"Don't lock that door before it's even opened," she adds quietly.

Across the table, Killian hasn't spoken for several minutes. His leg bounces in steady rhythm under the table, his gaze fixed on one point in the polished obsidian like he could burn a hole straight through it.

Killian finally breaks his silence, his voice all business. "I'll need a few extra guards to rotate shifts if she's going to be dating. Until this stalker is found."

Lucian nods in agreement.

Of course. Straight to logistics, straight to planning ahead. That's Killian. Always practical, always a step ahead. It shouldn't sting. But it does.

Not as much as his next sentence.

"And when she's not my assignment anymore, we'll talk about plans for tightening security at events. Galas. Operas. No Companion should be vulnerable like that again."

The words slice sharper than they should. *When she's not my assignment anymore.*

Sienna's gaze flicks to Killian, then slides deliberately to me. I cut my eyes away quickly before she thinks she's caught something that isn't there—before she guesses that comment landed like a bruise. That I hadn't let myself think about a future without Killian shadowing me.

Lucian nods once, decisive. "Good."

Killian rises to his full height, tugging his jacket straight. "I'll get Jaxon started."

"And I'll get Eve started on pulling your prospects, Sera."

The door shuts behind him with a finality that makes me flinch, though I try not to let it show.

Chapter 5

Killian

The door shuts behind me, and for the first time in hours, I can finally take a breath.

Not that it helps. The air is still thick with the echo of her voice. *Marriage. A family.* The words circle in my head like vultures—pecking, gnawing, refusing to leave me be.

I don't know why it bothers me. It shouldn't. Seraphina's life isn't mine to shape. My job is simple—keep her safe, eliminate threats, keep my distance. And yet the thought of her in someone else's house, in someone else's bed, wearing someone else's ring—

My jaw tightens until it aches.

I've sat through every contract she's taken this past year. Seen the way she smiles, the way she plays the role, the way it's all just performance. I know better than anyone it's a transaction, a mask she slips on and discards when it's over. But this? A final contract isn't a part she can step out of.

A husband isn't a client. He wouldn't just hire her—he'd

own her. Body. Name. Every fucking breath. And for reasons I refuse to name, the thought makes my blood burn hotter than it should.

I force my focus forward. The hallway outside the Ledger's boardroom stretches wide, lined with glass and steel. A janitor whistles a tune while mopping the black marble floors, the sound echoing off the ceiling.

I'm halfway to the elevators when footsteps sound behind me. Controlled. Heavy.

Lucian.

"Killian," he calls. Not a request. A command.

I stop, shoulders stiffening, and wait until he comes alongside me.

"Files are on their way," he says. "Everything we had the first time. I've already looped Jaxon in." He cuts a glance at the staff cleaning the hall. They hear a lot. See a lot. But we all know some things can't even be whispered about in the open.

Right on cue, my phone buzzes in my pocket. Lucian doesn't waste time.

I grunt my acknowledgment. "I'll find him."

Lucian studies me as if measuring every ounce of my tension. His stare doesn't waver. "What do you think about her proposal?"

My teeth grind. "Not my place to think about it."

"Still," he presses, "you have thoughts."

I shrug, making it look easy when it feels anything but. "It complicates things. That's all. Guarding her during a marriage contract... different logistics, different risks."

His brow lifts slightly, like he's waiting for more, but I

give him nothing. "If it's what she wants, it's her choice. My opinion doesn't matter."

Lucian doesn't buy it—I can see it in the way his mouth twitches, like he's a second from calling me a liar. But he lets it slide, for now.

"Come up," he says, jerking his chin toward the elevators.

The ride is silent except for Lucian's voice filling it, low and sharp as he takes a call. Orders, barked quick and precise. Not Ledger business. The other side. The newer empire he's been rebuilding piece by piece since the Italians burned themselves down.

I stare at the polished floor, jaw locked, pretending I'm not listening while every word brands itself into my skull.

When we step into his office, he shuts the door with a click.

Through the window, I catch the silhouette of stone rising just above the trees—what's left of the old cathedral. Most wouldn't notice it at all. I do. Ghosts of my past are buried there, and maybe we stirred them when Lucian and I spilled Irish blood that day.

I cut straight to anything but Seraphina. "How's it going? Rebuilding the Italians."

Lucian drags a hand down his face and lets out a humorless laugh. "It's a fucking shit show."

No surprise there.

Seraphina's abduction had been the spark that lit the whole war and reduced half of Manhattan's underworld to ash. Lucian against the Italians. His old friend Lorenzo—like a brother to him. That was a long time ago. Before Lucian walked away from that life. Same as me. Different story, same ending.

And when the Irish decided to stick their nose where it didn't belong, both their heads ended up bleeding out the day we ended that war.

The Irish had a successor. The Italians didn't.

So Lucian took the throne. Not to play king, but to do it the right way.

Lucian sinks into his chair, shoulders heavy, expression carved in stone. "The Irish aren't doing so hot either. Blood at the top always rots the roots. You ever check in on the old family?"

I shake my head once. "No."

He studies me, but he already knows. I cut them off cold. All of them.

Everyone except my mother.

She'd left long before I did—divorced my father when my brother and I were still boys. Walked away from the O'Malley legacy, took her name back, became Shaw again. Everyone called it betrayal. Cowardice.

But I knew better. It was survival.

She couldn't take us with her. That would've been her death sentence, and she wasn't stupid. So she left us in the lion's den, and we stayed. Learned to fight, to bleed, to survive under O'Malley fists and rules.

I'd always wished we'd gone with her. Both of us. Me and Cormac.

But when the time came, when I finally broke free, I did exactly what she did. Walked away. Took her name. Left the O'Malleys bleeding behind me and never looked back.

Lucian's gaze lingers on me, sharp as ever. "You might want to rethink that. The Irish are shaky right now. Some of your old allies could still be in place. Might be useful to pull on a few strings while we hunt this stalker."

The answer comes out clipped, final. "No."

His brow ticks.

"Whatever I do," I add, "I'll do it without the Irish."

That's a wound I won't reopen.

I shift in my chair, restless, ready to drag us off this subject before he digs deeper. My eyes rake over him, taking in the faint shadows under his eyes, the tight line of his mouth. "You look like shit, Vale. Go take your old lady to bed and stay there a week or two."

For the first time this morning, an actual chuckle rumbles out of him. He turns toward the espresso machine tucked into the corner, dark roast filling the air a moment later. "You're not wrong." He offers me one with a tilt of his chin.

I wave it off. "I'm wired enough."

Lucian takes the cup for himself, leans against the counter, and exhales. "It's getting to be too much. I can't keep my attention where it needs to be. That's why I'm looking for someone to run the Italians for me."

My head lifts. "Step down?"

"Not completely." His eyes glint over the rim of his cup. "They'll still be under me. Under the Ledger's shadow. But the day-to-day... someone else can bleed for that throne."

He shakes his head, almost smiling to himself. "And I think Sienna will sic her dog on me if I don't pick someone soon."

The mental image of Sienna's oversized mutt tearing through Lucian's marble halls nearly drags a laugh out of me, but I rein it in, rubbing my jaw instead.

"She's turned your attack dog into nothing but a cuddle monster."

"Fuck if I don't know it." He cocks a brow and tips his cup to me before taking a sip.

But he would tear this world down for her—and that cuddle monster—if it came to it.

And that's my cue to get the hell out of here. Because the longer I sit in this office listening to Lucian Vale play house, the more I start admitting dangerous things to myself. Like how I'd do the same for one very particular, very challenging Companion.

Only because I'm charged with her safety. That's all.

Even as the thought forms, I know it's bullshit.

I push up from the chair, rolling the tension out of my shoulders. "I'll check in with Jaxon. We'll have this fucker flushed out soon enough."

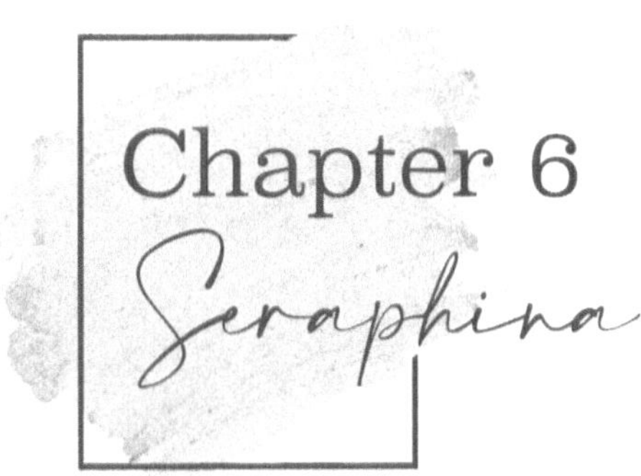

Chapter 6
Seraphina

"I'll admit it," I murmur, sliding another glossy profile across the table. "I didn't think there would be this many."

Eve smirks, her red lips curling around the rim of her teacup before she sets it down. "You're surprised? Please. You're the Black Ledger's crown jewel. Half these men would sell their souls for a night with you. A marriage contract?" She lifts a brow, sifting through another folder. "That's a feeding frenzy."

I roll my eyes, though she's not wrong. The stack in front of us is a mountain—files, photos, summaries of backgrounds, wealth, influence. Every one of them a man with too much power and not enough warmth in his life. Every one of them looking for a bride.

We wade through them together, Eve flicking her fingers like she's shuffling a deck of cards. "Too old. Too boring. Definitely a serial killer."

I snort, pushing a candidate into the discard pile. "What about this one?"

"Prospective," she decides, tapping the page with a scarlet nail. "He's handsome enough to keep you entertained at galas, and his net worth makes my eyes water. That's a maybe."

Eve has been at this game a long time. Loves what she does, just like me. But I think she'll probably be a lifer. Even if she stops taking contracts one day, she'll do something else for the Ledger.

Lucian would hand over pretty much anything to her to run if she asked for it.

We poke fun at some, laugh at others, and slowly build a small pile of men who might actually fit. It feels strange, staring at my potential future on paper, clinical as a shopping list.

But it feels strangely freeing too.

Across the room, Killian looks like he's trying to bore a hole through the wall with nothing but the daggers in his gaze. He hasn't said a word since we started this, hasn't protested the process. Not a whisper of the *too risky* argument he threw at me in the conference room.

But I can feel his storm brewing.

It doesn't matter. It can't.

Because I know it's time. I can't let a phantom dictate the rest of my life. Can't let fear keep me pacing the same cage while the world moves on without me. If anything, maybe this will draw him out. Maybe this is what finally forces him into the open where Killian can do his job.

A shiver snakes down my spine as I think about the

opera gala—the most direct interaction I've ever had with him.

Why now? Why make himself known in such a public way?

Is it an anniversary to him? Some twisted moment in his mind that tied me to him forever? Or is it a warning—that he's coming to claim me at last?

I don't know. And maybe I never will.

But I know this: I'm done waiting.

I won't sit still in the dark, wondering when the knife will fall.

It's time to live.

Eve flips to the next file, her eyes lighting up as she scans the page. "Ohhh. Now here's a contender. Six foot five, former football star. Apparently, he's working sponsorships like a stripper pole and investing every dime. Net worth's climbing so fast it might break orbit." She fans herself with the folder, grinning. "And look at those shoulders. You could build a house on them."

I lean over to glance at the photo. Handsome, big, polished smile. A little too polished, maybe, but he checks enough boxes. "Okay," I say, sliding him into the pile.

Across the room, Killian exhales. No—sighs. Like his entire life depends on it.

Eve cuts him an amused look, lips twitching. "How tall are you, Irish? Six three?"

His glare flicks her way. "Six six."

"Mhm." She smirks, clearly getting to him. "That with or without your platform boots there?"

He pushes off the wall, arms folding across his chest.

"How much longer is this going to take? I've got new security coming to her penthouse for a walkthrough and instructions."

"It'll be hours yet," I answer, deliberately breezy.

Eve waves a dismissive hand. "Doesn't have to be. I can draft a profile based on the ones we've flagged already and filter the rest out from there. Save you both some time. I'll send the final list to your cell."

"Perfect," I say, turning to her. "Go ahead and get started scheduling dates with the ones that make it through."

There's a beat of silence.

From Killian's corner, I catch the low rumble of his voice —so soft it almost blends into the hum of the air system. But I swear I catch the words.

So eager.

Heat flares under my skin, and I pretend I didn't hear it.

The lights flick on as soon as we step inside my penthouse, the glow spreading across sleek marble floors and glass walls. Killian's voice is steady, all business. "The new guards will be up in a few minutes to—"

I stop dead.

He notices immediately, his head snapping toward me, then following my gaze to the counter.

A white rose with blood-red tips lies there. Perfect. Waiting.

Killian's gun is in his hand before I even breathe. He moves in front of me, solid, unyielding, his other hand clamping around my arm to pull me behind his body. My fingers instinctively curl into the thick muscle of his bicep, holding on as he backs us both up.

He maneuvers me into the corner of the entryway, then releases me, already tapping the comm in his ear. "Finn—get up here now. Urgent. Bring the sweep kit. Everyone else stays in the lobby, lock the exits. Nobody in or out." His voice is sharp, practiced, the tone of a man who's done this before. Too many times.

"I'm sure this is not necessary," I whisper, but it sounds weak even to my own ears.

He cuts me a look, cold steel. "Stay here. Don't open the door—I don't give a fuck who it is. You do nothing. You say nothing."

I bristle. "I'm not some—"

"Try me," he growls, low and lethal. "I'll lock you in a closet if I have to."

My mouth opens, shuts. He's not bluffing.

Then he's moving, gun raised, steps precise, body coiled like a predator. He sweeps the space in slow arcs, eyes never still, muscles taut beneath his dark shirt.

And God help me, I can't stop watching.

The way he moves—controlled, lethal, like the entire room bends to him. He disappears around a corner, and suddenly I feel exposed without him in sight.

I wait. Listen.

The silence stretches, broken only by the faint hum of the city beyond the glass. My pulse thuds against my ribs.

I wait some more.

Then—restless—I edge a foot forward, careful to make

no sound. Then another. Like sneaking in the house after curfew, praying the floorboards won't give me away.

Three hard bangs rattle the door behind me.

I yelp, jumping nearly out of my skin—just as Killian rounds the corner, gun going back into his holster, eyes blazing, and sees me exactly where I swore I wouldn't be.

"Christ, woman," he snaps, fury crackling off him. "Do you ever listen?"

Three bangs again, controlled this time, and he steps past me to unlock the door. "That'll be Finn." The Irish coming out a touch in his words.

He swings it open to reveal his second-in-command. Broad-shouldered, sharp-eyed, slight gray at the temples of his near-black hair and already carrying gear.

Killian jerks his chin. "Inside."

Finn nods once, calm but quick, moving past him into the penthouse while Killian's attention cuts back to me, hard enough to pin me against the wall.

Killian shuts the door behind Finn and turns on me, voice low and clipped. "Who has access to your penthouse?"

I blink at him. "You know this already."

His jaw tightens. "Humor me."

I exhale. "Only you, the building attendants, and my cleaning lady."

"Yeah," he mutters, sharp as broken glass. "Fucking dozens of people."

I step closer to the counter, eyes narrowing on the rose. Up close, I see the red tips are dry now, curled slightly at the corners from the paint. It's resting on top of a small stack of envelopes.

"One of the stewards must've brought it up with my mail," I say. "It had to have been in my box."

Killian doesn't waste a second. His hand taps his earpiece. "I want the name of whoever delivered the mail to the penthouse today. Now. And get me the security footage of the mailroom—every angle. We're looking for someone delivering a white flower to her mailbox."

While he barks orders, I'm already moving, thumbing open the app for my own cameras stationed around the penthouse interior. I scroll back through the notifications until I find the right timestamp. "Here." I tilt the screen toward him. The feed shows the steward walking in with the mail, setting it on the counter, and leaving again through the service elevator.

Nothing unusual.

"It's just the steward," I say, giving him the name.

He takes the phone from me without asking, flicking through, sending the clip to himself. Before I can protest, a sharp ping breaks the silence. A new text.

Killian's expression hardens as he glances down at the preview. His stare darkens, like storm clouds rolling in over a harbor. His lips press into a thin, furious line.

"Seems Eve has already lined up a date for you." His voice is flat, dangerous.

He hands the phone back, brushing past me with a controlled stride. "...For tonight."

Chapter 7

The penthouse is quiet now.

Hours ago, I had the team up here, running them through the space—cameras, hallways, staff routines, security choke points. They've all got the files, but paper doesn't tell you everything. You've got to stand in the space, breathe it in, feel the angles pressing against your back before you really know it.

Now it's just me, waiting on Seraphina.

Usually, my job ends once she's on Ledger grounds or within the walls of her penthouse. I guard, I escort, I walk away. But this stalker changes everything. If he can get a rose onto her kitchen counter, he can get closer. And I'll be damned if he gets close enough to leave something worse.

Which means someone has to be with her every minute. No gaps. No mistakes.

I keep my own place, and I'll need some things over here if we're doubling down on security. And tonight was supposed to be someone else's shift.

Yeah, not happening.

No way in hell am I letting another man shadow her while she steps out with her first suitor.

The thought turns sour in my gut: a stranger sitting across from her, smiling at her like he knows her. Touching her hand. Whispering something in her ear.

For all we know, the bastard we're hunting could slip into the mix—pretend to be a contender, get her alone, do whatever sick thing he's been planning since he started this.

That image alone makes my trigger finger itch.

I open the Ledger app, scan the name of tonight's date at the top of the profile, and it hits me like a wave of annoyance.

Elijah Fucking Carter.

Of course.

Ledger auction regular. He shows up every year, loud with money, louder with ego. Always buys a Companion for the prestige, like he's purchasing a piece of art he'll never bother to hang. It's never about the woman—it's about the brag. The clout.

And now he thinks he wants Seraphina.

The Ledger's crown jewel.

My jaw grinds as I picture him walking her into a room with his hand on her back, introducing her like she's nothing but a trophy he finally snagged. The thought makes my vision blur red.

Of course Elijah threw his name in. Because marrying Seraphina Wilde wouldn't just be a contract. It would be a fucking coronation.

Not if I can help it.

I'm still looking over the app when her door opens.

The vision of her nearly takes me out.

Seraphina steps into the hall in a Ledger-red dress that clings in all the ways that make my pulse kick. The color turns her eyes sharp and bright, like polished sapphires. Her blonde hair falls in long curls, bouncing against her shoulders, and her perfume hits me in a slow wave, wrapping around my ribs like a chokehold.

For half a second, I forget to breathe.

I force myself to clear my throat, to grip the counter tighter, to remind myself she's not mine to look at like this. She's my assignment. Nothing more.

Still, something shifts under my skin, restless and dangerous, as I drag my gaze back to the phone in my hand.

Professional. Focused. Untouchable.

That's the line. And I can't afford to cross it.

She doesn't look at me as she walks out, head high, chin tilted just so. No shy glances, no waiting for my approval.

She doesn't need it. Seraphina knows exactly how beautiful she is—always has. She doesn't need puppy eyes or compliments to remind her.

And it's not my line to give her anyway.

That privilege belongs to her date.

The thought makes my jaw grind.

"What is the stalker protocol for a girl to get a repair done around here? My toilet is running."

I darken my phone, force my eyes away from her curves, and keep my voice flat. "I can look at it for you. Probably an easy fix."

She folds her arms over her chest and—fuck me sideways—I want my mouth on those tits so badly.

"I pay a fortune for building maintenance, you know. Do you need to perform a lie-detector test on the repairman, or can I just schedule it, big man?"

Big man. Something else I'd like from her in a different context—like hearing her breathy moan when I push my cock into her. Instead, I just clear my throat.

"The car is ready."

Then I move for the door without waiting for her answer, because if I stand here another second, I might forget where the line in the sand is.

I might pretend it's me taking her out. That I have the right to slide my arm around her narrow waist and pull her into me.

That she does look at me, ready to hear me say how she fucking ruins me with this dress. How we might not make it to the date because of my need to have her right this second —claim her so every cocksucker in New York knows she's mine.

But she's not. So when the elevator doors open and we step in, I leave those thoughts behind, letting the doors slide closed and lock them away for good.

I didn't sit in the back this time. Couldn't. Something about seeing her walk out of her room dressed like that —ready for him—knotted my stomach tight. So I stayed up front, silent, staring straight ahead, pretending the passing buildings were more interesting than the woman who smelled like heaven in the back seat.

The car slows to a stop outside the restaurant. I'm out first, scanning, then opening her door. Eyes sweep the street, the valet, the windows above. Nothing unusual. Nothing I don't already have covered.

She steps out without looking at me and adjusts her dress. My hand is usually there to help her, but I don't extend it and she doesn't reach for it.

Something about that burns in my chest. All I can do is check my holstered gun and the blade at my waist.

The maître d' is waiting, smile polished and professional. "This way, Miss Wilde."

We head upstairs, the faint hum of violin music floating down the hall. A private room—candlelit, table set for two.

And there he is.

Elijah I'm-a-dickface Carter.

The schmuck is sitting in his chair reading a newspaper, wearing jeans, a blazer, some blinding patterned shirt, and Converse sneakers. Christ. Here she is—looking like a fucking siren—and he couldn't even bother with a tie.

What burns worse? He doesn't even stand when she enters. Doesn't greet her. Doesn't pull her chair.

Patience frays fast. I take a few quick strides forward, grip the chair, and draw it out for her.

Her hair brushes against my arm as she turns, the clean, sweet scent of her shampoo assaulting me in the best way. She tilts her face up, a soft smile curving her lips. "Thank you," she whispers.

The words cool the furnace inside me. For about half a second.

"Oh, yeah—I was going to get that," Elijah says, a lazy grin plastered on his face as he nods at me like I'm the help.

I want to deck him.

He whistles, low, and my fists clench.

"Sera-fine-as-hell," he drawls. "That dress is amazing."

This motherfucker wants to die.

I look up—prayer to the angels I don't believe in—that I make it through appetizers without breaking his jaw.

"Seraphina—Fi Fi," he starts, like he's going to nickname her.

What the actual fuck?

"Seraphina will be just fine," she cuts in, voice polite but firm. "Elijah? Or Mr. Carter?"

"Elijah, of course. Or L.J., if you prefer. You know I met the president at the White House—he coined that nickname. Everyone calls me that now."

Right. Sure they do.

I retreat to the wall, stance wide, hands clasped in front of me, watching.

Elijah leans back, smirk widening. "So does your hound dog have to be in here, like... the whole time?"

Seraphina draws a breath, ready to answer, but I cut in first—my voice flat, absolute.

"Yes."

Elijah leans back, spreading his cloth napkin over his lap like he's about to give a speech. "Well... won't this be cozy."

Then, without even glancing at her, he snaps his fingers twice over her shoulder.

What a prick.

A server appears like magic with two whiskey sours.

Seraphina's hand lifts before the glass can be placed in front of her. "Water for me, thank you."

She hates whiskey. And Companions almost never drink on a first meeting—sometimes a small glass of wine, maybe, but never whiskey.

Elijah shrugs, grinning like an idiot. "More for me, then." He snatches both glasses, claiming them without a second thought.

It makes my blood burn. If he gave a damn about her, he'd have asked what she liked.

Fuck, he'd *know* what she liked—asked in advance, had the Grey Goose and cranberry with pineapple juice cocktail ready for her. Because that is her favorite.

He would try to impress her, show some kind of care. Instead, it's all about him—and his next line seals it.

"I knew as soon as I saw your contract hit the Ledger app, I had to jump on it. Offered triple the rate to snag the first date."

He says it like she should be impressed.

Seraphina doesn't react. Grace wraps around her like armor, her smile soft, her tone smooth. "I'm honored by your eagerness. I'd love to hear about you."

And with that, a black hole opens up.

Elijah starts talking. And talking. And talking. He never shuts up. He never asks her a single thing about herself. She barely gets more than a hum, a "that's interesting," or a polite nod between his monologues.

The courses come one after another—curated by him in

advance. Each dish is something she won't touch. I watch her pick at the food, polite but detached, hunger buried beneath etiquette. I know her well enough now to read it in the subtle downturn of her mouth, the way she sets her fork down too quickly. She's going to be starving after this.

So will I.

It seems holding yourself back from committing second-degree murder really works up an appetite.

The date's on a clock, like all of them. Companions have signals to cut things short or let them play out. Seraphina gives the one that says she'll end right on time—no early escape, no dragging it out longer.

I shift my stance just enough so she sees me. My promise in silence: I'll be ready when you are.

I glance at my watch and sigh. Fifteen more minutes of this circus.

Elijah's still talking, already droning about their "second date." Paragliding.

Perfect. Just what you want to do with a woman you've known for exactly an hour—throw her off a cliff and hope the straps hold.

I grit my teeth and slide my phone out, pulling up the Caviar Black app.

It's the kind of delivery service only billionaires bother with—exclusive, invitation-only, the sort of thing where anything you order shows up plated like it belongs in a Michelin-star kitchen. No hassle. No wait. Just the delicacies of the world at your fingertips.

And the Ledger has one of the top accounts. Nothing but the best for our Companions.

I put in an order—more than enough for Sera—then send the instructions to Finn. Delivery window. Placement. Setup. Exactly where I want it waiting and a few extra directions.

Then I slide the phone back into my pocket, lean against the wall again, and count down the minutes until this shit parade is over.

T his isn't the worst date I've ever been on.

But Elijah Carter? He's easily in the top three for douchiest men I've had to endure. And that's saying something.

In my line of work, I'm paid to cater to men—to fluff their egos, make them feel big, brilliant, powerful. But Elijah is doing all of that for himself, puffing his own chest without any help from me. Of all the rich and elite men I've crossed paths with, he may be the most self-centered.

Nine o'clock can't come soon enough.

The last ten minutes, he hasn't shut up about some rival tech entrepreneur he's about to surpass with a new development. I know from Eve he's referring to Jaxon Kane, and hearing Elijah talk so confidently is almost comical.

Jaxon isn't just another tech entrepreneur. He's it. He sits leagues above the world, shaping it with every idea. If he hasn't produced something, it's probably because he already handed the concept off to someone else, bored of its simplicity. After Jaxon, all the other tech leaders fight among themselves for scraps. And Elijah? Elijah isn't even near the top of that list.

So I sit there, nodding in polite agreement while my mind drifts. I daydream about being home, scrubbing off this makeup, curling into my pajamas with my fireplace on. I'm starving, and the thought of food from Hearth—the sleeker, residents-only version of Ember & Ash—makes my stomach clench. One of Manhattan's best steakhouses, worth every outrageous dollar Damien Wolfe charges to live in one of his buildings.

A soft throat clearing behind me snaps me back. Killian.

I feel the warmth of him at my back as he takes hold of my chair. "I'm afraid it's time for Miss Wilde to go."

He pulls it out gently, and I rise, folding my linen napkin onto the table. Killian steps back but keeps his eyes locked on the two of us, giving Elijah the chance to play gentleman and say goodbye.

Instead, Elijah catches my hand and lifts it, pressing his mouth to my knuckles. "You are even more lovely in person, Seraphina."

Then he leans in, voice dropping low, breath too close. "I thought we could ditch your big, scary bodyguard and perhaps get to know each other more privately at my place with a nightcap."

My stomach twists. He's close enough now that I can see a faint ring around his irises—colored contacts.

And suddenly, a thought drops like ice water through my veins.

What if he's wearing colored contacts to hide it? The ice-blue eye that makes my stalker stand out above everyone else.

I stumble back, tripping on the leg of the chair. Elijah lets go instantly, unconcerned, but Killian isn't. His arms catch under mine, pulling me tight against him, solid and sure, keeping me from hitting the floor.

"Whoa," Elijah says with a grin, clearly thinking himself clever. "Didn't mean to sweep you off your feet on the first date."

He's not clever. He's desperate. Pathetic.

I can feel Killian vibrating behind me, his fury restrained but barely. If I don't end this now, he might.

I ease out of his arms, smooth down my dress, and extend my hand. "Thank you for the lovely evening, Mr. Carter."

His mouth tightens, and I can see it in his stare—the offense, the realization that the night is over and nothing else is coming. But with Killian standing a few feet away, looking like a caged beast waiting for someone to unlatch the door, Elijah swallows it down.

"Likewise," he says stiffly.

I try to walk normally to the waiting limo, my heels clicking across the pavement, Felix sitting tall and steady behind the wheel. Killian keeps pace at my side, a silent shadow, his presence heavier than the night air.

He reaches for the door handle, opening it in one smooth motion, then extends his hand.

Instinct takes over. Muscle memory. My fingers slip into his before I think better of it.

His hand feels warmer than usual—not the kind of heat from an overheated body, but something else. A steady, grounding warmth that sinks through my skin and steadies the tremor Elijah left behind.

Maybe it's just the shit show of the evening. Maybe his familiar touch feels like a tether because I've spent the last two hours enduring Elijah Carter's endless bragging. Or maybe it's because when we arrived, Killian didn't offer me his hand at all. He always does.

And I'd bitten back the sting of it. Because I can't let myself forget why I'm here. I'm here to find a husband. A future. When I do, Killian will be reassigned. I won't need him anymore.

But for now, I cling to that moment of contact.

His hand is firm, his palm calloused, so much larger than mine that it swallows my fingers whole.

I can feel the tension in him, like he's on the cusp of saying something—about Elijah, about my ridiculous date, about the way I tripped on a chair leg like a nervous schoolgirl.

So I slide into the limo without looking at him and cut him off at the pass. "Don't even say it."

"I wasn't going to say anything."

But the faint curve of his mouth, the ghost of a smirk, betrays him completely.

Killian shrugs out of his suit jacket before sliding into the back seat with me. Another deviation. On the way here, he'd sat in the front with Felix, a deliberate wall between us. Now he's back in his usual spot, close enough that I can feel the air shift with him.

And I hate to admit it, but I feel better for it. If something happened, at least I'd see him, know he'd face it with me.

The car eases forward, headlights cutting through Manhattan's night. Killian's fingers tap against his knee in a steady rhythm before he stops, tugging at his cuffs, rolling one sleeve with deliberate precision.

By the time he starts on the second, I catch myself watching—the flex of his forearms, the hard line of muscle that no fabric could disguise, the curve of his biceps shifting under his shirt.

"You want to tell me what that was about back there?" His voice is quiet, but it cuts.

My brow furrows. "What do you mean?"

"When you tripped over the chair. You weren't clumsy. You were startled. Like you were about to bolt straight through the wall."

I glance out the window. "It was silly, really."

"Nothing is silly when it could help us figure out who's harassing you."

The intensity in his gray eyes catches me when I finally look back at him. It holds me there until I let out a breath.

"I thought..." My voice lowers, almost embarrassed. "What if he's wearing colored contacts? What if Elijah's the stalker? It was just the thought, and then I—reacted. It was dumb."

Killian doesn't blink. "That's not dumb. You've been pretending this doesn't exist because that's how you survive it. But tonight made it real. And now it can't be ignored."

His words settle heavy in my chest.

"Why him?" he presses. "Why'd you think he could be the stalker?"

"Because..." My throat tightens, but I force it out. "He's a similar height. A similar build."

Killian nods once, then pulls out his phone, thumbs already moving across the screen.

I frown. "What are you doing?"

"Building a profile. Everything we know goes in. Every detail. It'll go into Ledger files—and Jaxon's system."

I nod slowly, leaning back against the leather seat. "Right."

The car hums on, city lights sliding past, but I don't speak again. The rest of the ride, I just stare out the window and try to piece together how quickly this all spun out of control. How a few flowers, a few notes, became this.

And how crazy it feels to know that, for once, I can't just walk away.

The elevator ride up to my penthouse is quiet, only the low hum of the cables filling the space. Finn will be posted at my door tonight, and Killian—well, for all intents and purposes, he's moving in.

Guest room, most nights. Rotating guards at the door. And one day a week, Killian will be off duty, and someone else will be my shadow.

That's the plan, anyway.

When the doors slide open, we walk the short stretch of hallway to my door. Finn straightens from his post, sharp suit fitting his tall frame perfectly.

"Finn," I nod in greeting.

"Ma'am," he replies, his Irish accent wrapping around the single word. Stronger than Killian's, unmistakable. Killian's is faint, slipping out here and there in certain words—but Finn's? Full and rich.

And it makes me think... if Killian's accent ever bled through like that, paired with his already dangerous good looks and that lethal body?

Deadly.

As it is, Manhattan's women are already in trouble.

I'm about to suggest food, already halfway to saying it aloud. "I was thinking of ordering some—"

The thought dies in my throat.

The moment the door swings open, a scent greets me. Rich, decadent, mouthwatering. And the warmth of flames flickering from the fireplace, casting the room in soft amber glow.

My steps slow as I take it in—the low lights, the fire, and a lavish spread of dishes arranged carefully in my living room.

My living room.

The place where I always end up. Not the table, not the stools at the bar. The couch. The deep, overstuffed couch that swallows me whole while I eat and read, while I let the world fade away.

It's exactly what I wanted after tonight. Exactly what I daydreamed of during Elijah Carter's never-ending mono-logue. And it's already here.

Already waiting for me.

I glance over my shoulder. Killian is standing a few feet

back, speaking low to Finn, pretending like none of this has anything to do with him.

I can't help myself.

"Finn," I say sweetly, "did you do this?"

The look on Killian's face is priceless—staring straight ahead at the blank wall, like he wasn't expecting me to throw the bait.

Finn's mouth twitches. He cuts his eyes toward Killian, already catching on, and smiles. "Aye, well, I might take the credit for it, but I reckon he'd sack me straight away. Kill took care of ye, ma'am."

Killian's glare could burn a hole straight through him. "That'll be it for the night, Callahan."

Finn chuckles, shaking his head as he steps past. "Night, Shaw. Night, ma'am."

"Night, Finn," I reply with a smile, watching him go.

The door shuts behind him, leaving me alone with Killian.

And the spread he pretends he didn't arrange for me.

"Surely you didn't plan for me to eat all this by myself." I glance at the lavish spread again, arching a brow at him. "Will you be joining me?"

Killian looks at me, and for one dizzying second my stomach nearly drops to the floor.

I've been in this penthouse alone with him before, plenty of times. But tonight feels different. Heavier.

Like if I blinked, he'd already be crossing the room, wrapping those strong arms around me, pulling me into a kiss that would tear down every wall I've built. One that would change everything.

But then he blinks instead. And the moment—the gravity of it—vanishes in an instant.

"Sure," he says easily. "I wouldn't mind a bite."

He strides into my living room like he belongs there, like this is our place and this is what we do—coming home from a night out together, sharing food, slipping into a routine that's never existed but feels dangerously natural.

"Why don't you freshen up?" he suggests, already moving toward the wine fridge. "I'll open a bottle."

My lips curve into a small smile. "That would be great. The Sancerre? There's an aged one in the wine fridge."

"I got it." He glances at me over his shoulder—and winks.

A wink.

He's never winked at me before. My mouth goes dry, my pulse quickening, and I have to force myself to turn away before he sees the flush creeping up my neck.

In my room, another surprise waits.

Laid out neatly on the bed are my favorite pajamas— silky, the shade of deep wine, with flowing pants and a thin cami, paired with the matching robe. Beside them, my ridiculous pink fuzzy slippers.

My smile beams, wide and unguarded, knowing no one's around to see it.

I wash away the night at the sink, scrubbing off makeup, letting the tension drip down the drain. My hair slips into a side braid. I slide into the pajamas, loving the way the fabric whispers against my skin.

But just before I leave, I pause.

I untie the robe, letting it hang loose, and unclasp my

bra. Tossing it into the hamper, I take a deep breath and let the robe fall open around me, thin silk draped lightly over my shoulders.

And then, with my heart knocking a little harder than it should, I step back toward the glow of the fire.

Chapter 9
Killian

I stand in her living room, one hand braced on my hip, the other lifting a glass of wine to my mouth.

Her space is... light. Airy. Very much Seraphina. Not the polished, poised Ledger Companion she wears like armor. This is the Sunday-morning version—rolling over with a sleepy smile, asking to go to brunch, the side of her hardly anyone else gets to see.

Books line the wall, floor to ceiling. A gas fireplace flickers low, throwing shadows across the room. And then there's the couch. Big, deep, soft enough to swallow me whole. Most furniture never fits me, but this? There's room. Plenty.

I can almost see it: me stretched out, her curled against my chest, her laugh muffled against my shirt while some movie drones on in the background.

I take a long breath and blink that away, dragging my attention to the wide windows and the sun catchers fixed on them. Even at night, the glass gleams. By day, I think of the sun catching them, scattering colors across the floor. I think about what she looks like standing in that light.

I raise the glass to my mouth. And choke.

She's standing there in pajamas—thin silk the color of wine, pants flowing loose, a cami clinging tighter. Her nipples are hard beneath the fabric, her breasts practically on stage, and I've got the front-row seat to a show for one.

Smirking, the little minx did this on purpose. It's attempted homicide, trying to kill me.

And I'd fucking let her. Little killer.

She walks toward me, breasts bouncing freely without a bra, and drops into her oversized armchair like she owns the room—and me.

I sink into the couch, forcing my muscles to stay loose, and hand her the glass I already poured.

"Killian, this is..." Her words die as her eyes widen, taking in the spread on the table.

The caviar service catches her first—Osetra and Beluga presented in silver pedestal dishes set on ice, surrounded by all the fixings. Buckwheat blinis, toasted brioche points, crème fraîche, chopped egg yolk and whites, lemon wedges. Mother-of-pearl spoons catching the firelight.

Her whole face softens. "It's perfect."

Her eyes find mine, bright and grateful, and for a second I can't look away.

"Thank you." Then she tips her head, teasing to ease the weight of it. "Are you sure you aren't my stalker?"

I scoff as she helps herself to the caviar. "Pretty sure I'm a tad larger than Elijah. If he matches your stalker's build, I don't think you'd confuse us in a lineup."

She laughs softly, but I watch the way she relaxes as I sit here, how her shoulders loosen, her breaths come easier. I know what she feels when I'm close. Safe. Untouchable.

The same way she exhaled when I slid into the back of the limo tonight. The same way her gaze lingered on me when I rolled my sleeves up, thinking I wouldn't notice.

Oh, I noticed.

And yeah—that was for her.

We eat. We talk.

Mostly, we make fun of Elijah.

The spread's simple but elegant, exactly what I knew she'd want after a failed dinner. Truffle-mushroom risotto —velvety, indulgent but not heavy. Seared scallops with champagne beurre blanc—her kind of refined, delicate bite. And for later, a pistachio crème brûlée with a caramel crust begging to be cracked.

Every time she leans forward, that flimsy little cami threatens to give me a full show. She props her elbows on her knees, pushes her arms together, practically serving her cleavage on a silver platter. It's all I can do not to keep my eyes glued to her chest the entire time. She knows exactly what she's doing.

Halfway through the scallops, her robe slips from one shoulder. My fork stalls halfway to my mouth.

And suddenly I'm gone—lost in a vision of dragging her into my lap, that robe falling away, the thin straps of her cami sliding down her arms. Her breasts bared. My mouth closing around one of those stiff peaks, tongue swirling until her head tilts back and she moans, grinding against me—

"Is Killian still in the building?"

Her voice slices through the fantasy.

I blink, cock aching hard against the zipper of my pants.

She's smirking. Teasing. "I asked—what will the profile do to help catch the stalker?"

I clear my throat, forcing my voice steady. "It'll flag any Ledger clients who fit. We'll vet every one of them. Make sure none of your suitors match."

She nods, moving on to dessert. And I almost lose it all over again.

The way she dips her spoon into the crème brûlée, slides it past her lips, eyes fluttering shut as she hums. A soft, sultry sound that lands straight in my gut. My fantasy brought to life, and it kills me.

I need out of this moment, before I do something that burns us both.

"Sadly," I say lightly, beginning to clear the empty dishes, "Elijah would match the profile now. So no second date. Shame about the paragliding—I know how much you were looking forward to it. Will you be okay, Sera-fine-as-hel?"

Her gasp is sharp, scandalized. "How dare you?"

Then her eyes narrow, dangerous. She plucks up the tiny caviar spoon, brandishing it like a dagger.

"I'm pretty sure I could kill you with this," she says sweetly. "How macho would that be? Irish giant bludgeoned to death by mother-of-pearl spoon."

I grin despite myself while she grabs some dishes too.

I catch her eye as she brushes past me. "I think you just wanted an excuse to get your hands on me." My voice is low in her ear, and I swear I see her shiver.

"Not in this life," she fires back, chin tipped up.

We split, each heading to our rooms.

And just before my door closes, I call out down the hall: "Good night, Fi-Fi."

Her gasp echoes, followed by a muttered curse.

I can't help but laugh.

Chapter 10
Seraphina

Wherever I go, Killian goes.

He's never minded. Never complained. Some places I know he'd rather be anywhere else—but he always loves gym day.

I've got my standing spin class, and I never miss it. Most of the women are moms, hustling in after dropping their kids off at the gym's daycare. They chatter as they set up their bikes—about husbands who don't pull their weight, or who makes the best weeknight Crock-Pot meals. I chew my piece of minty gum, always enjoy listening, even if I never join in.

Once, a woman asked what I did for a living.

"Sales," I said.

She'd nodded, assuming pharmaceutical sales. I didn't correct her.

Somehow I didn't think, "No, I sell my pussy, actually. And I'm quite popular because I squirt and suck dick like a champ." That wouldn't have gone over well. So I kept my mouth shut.

The only reason Killian didn't come into class with me today is because he scoped the list and saw it was all women. He loves the gym. Spin class, on the other hand, not so much.

Looking right, I can see him in the weights section. He's watching me, but not watching me—eyes flicking to the door, to the room, always scanning. If anyone headed this way, he'd be on their heels before they even stepped inside.

The music thumps, the instructor shouts through her mic, and a projector beams a route across the curved wall— hills and sharp turns, scenery changing as we sweat in place.

Still, my eyes keep wandering to the other side of the gym. Killian's lifting. Heavy. The kind of weight that makes the other men stop their own sets just to watch. A pair of twenty-something girls pause mid-step as he knocks out a brutal round of pull-ups, shirt stripped off and tossed aside.

And I take advantage of it too. The ripple of his back muscles. The way his shoulders flex and shift with every rise and fall. The kind of body that makes you forget to breathe.

I shouldn't be staring. But I can't stop.

Class ends in a blur of sweat and music. I drop my gum, spent from the hour, into the trash and gulp down water, dabbing at my damp neck with a white gym towel.

I respond to a few nosy texts from my sister—mostly asking if Killian will be my plus-one to Ro's party, if we've fucked yet, and then complaining about Stacy, some woman Daniel works with that my sister hates so naturally I do too.

Sliding my phone back into the thigh pocket on my leggings, I glance toward the weights. I don't see Killian.

Stepping out onto the deck that overlooks the floor below, I find him easily enough. One of the twenty-somethings has cornered him. She sways on her feet, leans in as she laughs at something, her hair flipping over one shoulder like it's rehearsed. And he's smiling.

My teeth grind together. Reckless. Flirting with some rando hunting for a gym boyfriend to film TikToks with while a stalker could be anywhere in this building. He's leaning one arm against the pull-up bar, bicep flexed, body on display like a damn invitation.

I toss my towel into the bin, stride down, and stop at his side. "Ready when you are."

I give the girl a tight-lipped half-smile—just enough to be polite, nowhere near enough to be mistaken for friendly. She doesn't bother to return it. Instead, her eyes trail down my body before she looks back at Killian.

"Sorry, didn't realize you were busy," she says. The hidden implication is obvious—didn't know you were here with someone.

I turn away before I hear his reply. Doesn't matter. He doesn't need to say he's here with me. He isn't. He's just my guard. He can do whatever the hell he wants.

Normally I'd shower and change, but Killian won't let me near the locker-room showers alone, and since that's not happening, sweaty is my only option. I've got a date tonight with a new suitor, so I'll pretty much be spending the rest of the afternoon getting ready.

At the locker bench, I prop one foot up to retie my laces.

"Christ almighty." The words are low, thick, right behind me.

I glance back. Killian's rubbing his jaw, eyes tilted toward the ceiling like there's a vision of the Virgin Mary up there, and she's the only thing keeping him sane.

"You can finish up with your friend," I say evenly. But friend comes out sharper than I intended.

I key in the locker's temporary code, grab my purse, and snap the locker shut.

"Friend?" Killian's voice is full of amusement. "Nah. I'm good."

He falls into step beside me, grin tugging at his mouth. "Got her number, though. I can just call her later."

Oh, fucking perfect.

"Great," I grit out.

He swallows, like it'll hide the smirk he's fighting. It doesn't.

We head toward the exit as a group hustles in, probably late for the next class. Someone bumps my shoulder, my bag slips down to my elbow, and I knock into Killian.

"Jesus," I mutter, fixing my purse. "Sorry."

Outside, his sleek gray sports car waits like a shadow of him—sharp lines, understated, dangerous. He opens my door, like he always does. And I wonder if his little gym crush is watching. Wonder if she notices how natural it looks, the way he steps aside, the way I slip in. Wonder if she thinks he's attached to someone.

Or maybe she doesn't care. She gave him her number, after all. So that must mean he let her know he was single.

I roll my eyes as Killian rounds the car, his big frame

folding into the driver's seat with ease. He tosses a folded piece of paper into the tray near the dash.

Candi, written in bubbly handwriting, a heart dotting the i.

My eyes roll again, sharper this time, before I fix my gaze out the window—ignoring him. Ignoring the fact I can feel his stare on me the whole drive.

The car ride goes quick. Too quick. Manhattan traffic is rarely light, but today it feels like the city is letting us slip right through.

Killian pulls up to the valet and climbs out, already sliding a tip from his pocket for the waiting attendant. I reach down for my purse straps, and my eyes land on it. That little piece of paper. It sits there like a beacon in the tray—Candi's name, the heart dotting the i, taunting me.

My hand hovers midair, paused on the way to my purse.

The other valet hurries up and pops my door, snapping me out of it. I move fast—snatching the paper with one hand and then reaching for my purse straps, hoping if Killian does remember, he won't see me pocket it first.

He rounds the car just as I'm stepping out.

"Feel like grabbing a smoothie on our way up?" I ask casually, trying to redirect him. He usually wants one after the gym, and I'm praying it'll keep his attention anywhere but on the number he left behind.

"You read my mind, woman." He gestures for me to walk ahead of him.

I dip my hand deeper into my purse, pushing the crumpled paper down, but my fingers brush against something that stops me cold. Smooth. Thick. Not supposed to be there.

An envelope.

I pull it out with shaky fingers. White, heavy stock. A stamp pressed into the center—a red-tipped rose.

"Killian," I whisper. The breath rushes out of me, leaving me hollow.

He's at my side instantly, snatching it from my hand, flipping it over, eyes sharp—already in guard mode, scanning the area.

"Anyone give this to you?" His voice is low, lethal.

"No. Of course not."

"You'd tell me."

"I would have told you," I insist.

"Could it have been in there before the gym?"

I shake my head. "No. I got my gum out earlier. I would've seen it."

I stop, mind racing back. "Someone bumped me on the way out. That group coming in—"

He nods, jaw flexing, his thoughts clearly running the same track. His hand clamps lightly at my elbow, steering me firmly toward the lobby. His voice rolls low, brash across my skin like it doesn't belong in a moment like this.

"I'll send for smoothies."

But all I can think about is the envelope in his hand. The fact that my stalker was so close. Close enough to bump me. To slip something into my bag. Close enough he could've done anything.

Anything at all.

Chapter 11

Killian

The fucker's getting bolder.

Every move he makes, he edges closer to her, like he's daring me to snap his neck in front of everyone.

I keep my expression flat, but inside the itch to break him open is alive and well. He thinks he can hover near her, breathe her air, brush her sleeve like it's nothing. Like she didn't belong to me the second I was assigned to guard her.

Not happening.

I slip a hand around her arm, steering her toward the elevators. My thumb rests against the inside of her elbow—not tight, not enough to scare her, but firm enough to remind her she isn't walking alone.

I pull out my phone and Finn answers before the second ring. "We're coming up. Anything today?"

"We're all clear. No one's been by. Mail's light—gave it a once-over myself, dropped it on her counter. That's all."

"Good." My voice is steel. "We'll be up in a minute."

I hang up and thumb out a text to Jaxon:

KILLIAN: Information incoming.

His reply pings back instantly—a salute meme. Typical. Cocky bastard.

The elevator button lights under my knuckle, and only then do I realize I'm still holding onto her. I let go, my hand falling heavy to my side. She rubs the spot like my grip left an ache.

She looks smaller. Not in the way she carries herself— she's never anything less than commanding—but the way her shoulders tuck in, the way her gaze stays glued to the elevator floor. I know what's running through her mind: the what-ifs. The fact that that asshole had been standing right next to her. Too close. Too much risk.

"Hey." My voice cuts through the silence.

She hums, distracted, like she didn't hear me but can't bring herself to say so.

I reach for her chin, gentler this time, turning her face toward mine. Her skin is soft, cool under my fingers. "I won't let anything happen to you."

I hold her eyes, steady, unflinching, because she needs to believe me. Needs to know that whatever monsters circle her world, they'll go through me first.

Her lips part just slightly, and after a beat she nods. She bites her bottom lip, and the motion drags my attention straight to her mouth. Fuck. Dangerous thought. Not mine to have. Not my line to cross.

The elevator dings, doors sliding open, and the moment cracks in half like it never existed.

Down the hall and inside, she stops at the kitchen island and drops her purse with a soft thud. I set the envelope down beside it—the sound sharper, a flat smack against the counter.

"Don't touch it," I warn, already moving.

At the end cabinet I've got a stash—security-guard essentials just in case. I tear it open, pull out a pair of gloves, and snap them on. The latex clings, sealing me into that headspace I know too well: threat assessment, not emotion.

I ease the flap open with my blade and tilt the envelope. A glimpse is all I need for my jaw to lock tight. Photos. Of her.

My chest burns, but I push it down, scanning for residue. Edges clean. No visible powder. I bring it close and sniff, sharp and cautious. Nothing.

"Get me a bag and a swab," I tell Finn, voice clipped.

He's already gloving up, pulling a field-test kit from his pack. Sera—pale but steady—opens a drawer and pulls out a gallon-size Ziploc bag. She holds it up. "This okay?"

"That's good, babe."

The word slips out before I can catch it. It scrapes my throat raw, and I nearly choke on it. I act like nothing happened. So does she. But her cheeks flush, betraying her. Finn doesn't so much as twitch. Professional to the bone.

He rips open a swab. I take it, brush the cotton carefully along the envelope's seams, corners, between the photos. I watch the strip like it's gospel. White. Still white. No reaction.

"I still don't want you to touch them," I tell Sera. She needs to hear it, understand it. "I'll take them out, but you keep your hands clear. We'll still send it off just in case."

Her voice strains thin, like she's holding something back. "Do you think he would try to poison me?"

She blinks fast. Not enough to stop the tears.

Fuck. Every instinct in me screams to close the distance, to wrap her up and make her believe nothing can get through me. But I stay rooted, jaw tight, and hand Finn the envelope instead. He slides it into the bag.

I catch the top photo as I pass it. My gut knots. "He gave this to you while you were out. If he hoped you'd open it, it could've been laced with something—something to make you groggy, sick. Force you to the bathroom. Separate you from me."

Her hand trembles against the counter.

"Not knowing who the prick is means we don't know what he wants," I press. "So we act like he's capable of anything."

Her gaze drifts to the photo in my hand. It's from her date with Elijah a few nights ago—plates midcourse, salads half-eaten. Taken through a window, which means the bastard was across the street, watching.

"The date was last minute, but he still found you. That's the message." I'm talking to Finn, but Sera breathes, almost too soft to hear, "Oh my God."

"That's another clue." I want her to hear the reassurance in my tone. "Somehow he's got access to you. We'll figure out how."

I slip the photos into the bag, peel the gloves off, toss

them in the trash. Seal the bag, hand it to Finn. "Get one of the guys to take it in for testing."

Sera's pale, her posture unsteady. "You should lie down," I suggest.

"No. I don't have time. I need a shower."

Dammit. I was hoping she'd cancel the date. "You could—"

"No." Her chin lifts, stubborn as I've ever seen her. "I'm not letting him scare me into the dark. Into hiding. I'm not giving him that."

I get it. I hate it. But I get it.

She turns toward her bedroom, and I call after her, "Mind if I scan your purse for trackers?"

I already did. First day I found out about the stalker, I swept her entire place—her car, her clothes, her bag too. But I need peace of mind. He could have slipped more than just an envelope in there.

"Have at it," she says, vanishing into her room.

I glance at Finn. "Get extra guys on tonight's date. I want them there early. Put them in uniforms for the restaurant—staff coverage."

He nods. "I'll call the restaurant. Get on it now."

Good man.

I watch the closed bedroom door, my jaw aching. I don't like this. Don't like the stalker getting this close. And I sure as hell don't like her going out on another fucking date.

Chapter 12
Seraphina

The shower is everything.

Worth every obscene dollar I dropped on the custom head system. The water pressure alone could bring a dead woman back to life, and the heat soaks into every tense muscle until my head tips back against the tile.

I should be thinking about tonight. About getting dressed, about keeping my chin high, about pretending I don't have a stalker who could be waiting outside every window.

But my mind strays somewhere else. Someone else.

Killian.

I picture him shirtless, the faint trail of hair running down his chest to that narrow line disappearing beneath his shorts—the one that all but begs me to pull them down, see what he's hiding. Broad shoulders, corded muscle, strength wrapped in restraint. I imagine those shoulders between my thighs, my legs draped over them while he feasts on me like he's starving, the scruff of his trimmed beard only making everything feel more amazing.

My hand drifts, but it's the shower wand I reach for. I switch it to my favorite setting, aim the stream right where I want it. The jet hits, sharp and perfect, and I bite my lip. I think of his fingers, thick and rough, driving into me. Of his cocky fucking mouth closing around my nipple—tugging, teasing, devouring until I break.

The orgasm comes fast, ripping through me before I can stifle the pant that escapes my throat. My free hand slaps against wet tile, steadying me.

And then another thought hits—what if he heard me?

What if Killian thought I was in trouble, kicked the door in, and found me like this? Would he watch? Would he join me?

The image of him standing there, eyes hard and hungry, makes my pulse stutter. My body heats all over again, need sharper this time.

Soap suds cling to my skin, slick and slippery, as I bring the wand back between my thighs. Bracing against the shower wall, I let it push me higher, harder, until the pleasure tears through me again, stronger than the first time. My mouth opens on a silent cry, every nerve burning, every thought painted in steel-gray eyes and the wordless promise behind them.

The shower leaves me flushed and loose-limbed, skin tingling from the heat and... other things.

Now I'm put back together. Hair smooth, makeup flawless, dark-green lingerie hugging me in all the right places. The minidress hanging in my closet matches—emerald silk with a sinful hemline. I'm choosing jewelry—still irritated about the running toilet I forgot to schedule maintenance for—when it hits me.

Fuck.

The phone number.

Candi-with-a-heart. Killian's next potential fuck buddy, folded neatly in my purse. The purse he said he was going to scan.

I cinch my robe tight, heart hammering, and hurry to the door. But when I swing it open, I nearly collide with Killian's fist, raised and ready to knock.

I freeze. Breathless. My cheeks blaze, heat spreading down my neck.

His brows lift slightly, like he notices. Pretends he doesn't.

And God help me—he's changed. All black, suit pants and fitted shirt with the sleeves rolled three-quarters up. Casual, lethal. Those forearms—veins, muscle, strength—make me want to sink my teeth in.

"I scanned your bag." He sets it on the bed like a finished task. "No bugs."

He drifts back to the doorway, shoulder against the frame, ankles crossed—the picture of relaxed control. Except his eyes give him away—already darker, heavier on me than they should be.

"You know, I had a few extra minutes to run back to my car." His tone is lazy. "You know what happened to that piece of paper?" He says it like a question, but it's not. It's a game.

Shit. He saw it. Knows it ended up in my purse.

Fine. If he wants to play, I'll play.

I tilt my head, all innocence. "Nope."

Then I undo the robe and let it slide off my shoulders, tossing it to the bed. Green silk and lace gleams under the light, and Killian's mouth actually parts. His gaze drags down me, slow and shameless, and something tight coils in my belly.

I saunter past him like I'm not on fire, grab my black stilettos, then return—close enough to smell the clean bite of his cologne.

"Find anything out about the pictures?" My voice comes out lower than I mean it to.

His eyes darken, stormy gray, his reply a husky rumble. "We're pulling the gym's security footage and member list. The restaurants, too—cameras and staff."

I slip on one heel, then shift closer, bracing a hand against his forearm to steady myself as I slide into the other. His skin is warm under the thin sleeve, muscle flexing tight when I lean into him. His throat works.

He clears it.

I almost smile, almost ask another question, almost think about pressing my palm lower—just to see if he's hard for me. But Finn's footsteps echo down the hall, breaking the spell.

"Oi, Shaw?"

In an instant Killian moves, one hand searing around my bare waist as he turns me, the other braced over my head as he nudges the door shut. My back hits the wood, breath trapped in my chest. He cages me in, his body heat wrapping around me, mint and something darker on his breath.

Finn's voice carries from the hall. "We've lads in place at the restaurant for tonight. Blended in already."

Killian turns his head slightly to the side, but his eyes stay locked on mine. "Okay."

"What's the matter?" I whisper, pulse thrumming. "Don't want Finn to see me like this?"

His fingers flex against my skin, tightening. His face lowers, impossibly close. "I don't want anyone seeing you like this."

The words drop heavy between us, vibrating through me. His eyes flick from mine to my mouth, lingering, and for a moment I swear he's going to kiss me.

Heat pools low, thighs pressing together. My thoughts from the shower flood back, sharper now, so real it aches.

And then his voice drops, low, steady, stripped of any teasing. "I wasn't going to call her."

The air leaves my lungs. My throat works as I swallow.

"What you do is no business of mine."

His gaze narrows. "Isn't it?"

A knock jolts us both, sharp against the door. I yelp, and Killian's mouth twists into a grin that only makes me wetter.

"Kill?" It's Finn again.

"Be right there," he calls, stepping back. He picks up my robe, holds it out.

Our fingers brush, the touch sparking hot and impossible to ignore as I step away from the door. He pauses at the knob, looking back at me one last time.

"We leave in ten."

His eyes drag down my body again—slow and deliberate, like he's memorizing every detail. As if he wants to see this when he looks at me tonight, wearing the dark-green dress for my date.

Then the door clicks shut, soft and final, leaving me—heart racing, knees weak, and skin burning where his hands just were.

***

Walking into the restaurant, I lean toward Killian, my voice low. "Maintenance will be by later. The toilet won't stop running."

He gives a short nod, presses two fingers to his earpiece. "Finn, you hear that?"

A muffled Irish reply comes through—"Aye, got it."

Then Killian straightens, hand firm at the small of my back as he steers me into the dimly lit dining room.

Daniel Ruiz is already there. My date.

Older. Not old. Silver just starting at his temples—the kind that looks deliberate, like he could've dyed it in that way politicians do: enough to look dignified, not enough to look frail. His posture screams for a camera—one hand resting casually on the table, chin lifted, eyes scanning the room like there's a press corps hiding behind the ficus plants.

When he stands, his smile is the practiced, calculated

kind. Perfect teeth. Perfect angle. He leans in for the obligatory cheek kiss, and I let him, noting how even his cologne feels rehearsed.

"Seraphina." He says my name like it's a campaign slogan. "You look radiant."

I thank him as Killian pulls my chair out, same as he did at the last date. His hand brushes my back as I lower myself, and I let my dress shift just enough that the silk climbs higher on my thigh. When I glance back to murmur a quiet "thank you," I catch him staring—not at my face, but lower. Eyes sharp, unblinking.

A thrill skates down my spine.

Daniel talks. I half listen. His words are slick, polished, designed for an audience. The country needs fresh leadership. I have eyes on me everywhere I go. My opponents can't find a single flaw in my record.

He doesn't see me. Not really. He sees what I could be to him.

A prop.

A perfect wife for photo ops.

Killian has taken up position at the bar in my periphery. He looks like he belongs there—dark suit, sleeves rolled, forearms braced on polished wood. Watching me. Watching him.

So I play.

I let my fingers trail up the stem of my wineglass, slow and idle, like I'm flirting with the crystal itself. Later, when my napkin "slips" to the floor, I lean down to reach it—only Killian gets there first. His eyes flick down my neckline, catching the sheer lace of the bra pushing my breasts together. When I take the napkin back, I make sure our fingers brush. I offer an innocent smile of gratitude.

His return look isn't innocent at all. It's warning. *You're pushing it.*

And it only makes me push harder.

The sharp clink of glass snaps Killian's gaze to the table next to us as a guest fusses with spilled water. Daniel clears his throat, dragging my attention back to him. His eyes are sharp, evaluating. "Would you be comfortable converting to Catholicism?"

I blink, the commotion at the table next to me forgotten as the guest leaves with a wet lap. "Excuse me?"

"For optics." He says it like it's obvious. "My constituents prefer a traditional family unit. It's important they see us aligned on faith."

Us.

Aligned.

Like I'm already standing at his side at some podium while he raises our hands in victory.

He doesn't pause before continuing. "And when we are married…"

When.

My stomach tightens—not with nerves, but irritation. There's something so casually presumptuous in his tone, like the choice is already made for me.

I force a pleasant smile, leaning forward so my leg shifts again, giving just enough of a tease Daniel might think it's for him. But I know who's really watching. Killian's jaw is tight, his forearm flexed against the bar like he's holding himself back.

Good. Let him stew. Let him wonder if Daniel Ruiz will be the one to pull this dress off me and see what's beneath.

The thought shouldn't thrill me. But it does.

When Daniel starts talking about children—our children—I know I've reached my limit. Two of them, he says, with the kind of precision only a man who treats life like a campaign strategy could muster. Cesarean births. Genders chosen in a lab. A boy first, then a girl.

The smile never leaves my face, but my eyes find Killian's. The smallest tilt of my head is all it takes. I want out, and he makes it happen in a minute.

The ride back blurs. Eve's voice fills the car, light and quick as she asks about the date, then launches into updates about new prospects waiting in the wings. I give her just enough to keep her satisfied, letting her words wash over me until she finally signs off, her call ending the moment the elevator opens into the hush of my floor.

One of Killian's new men is stationed at the door, standing straighter when we approach. Finn is off for the night, so I guess this kid drew the short straw.

"Sir," he says, stepping aside. "Maintenance came by. Left about thirty minutes ago."

The words stop me for a fraction of a second. I haven't seen a single alert from my security system—not so much as a buzz on my phone. That's unusual. Unsettling, but it has happened once or twice when the app was buggy.

I slip inside, heels clicking softly across the polished floors, my pulse already tight in my throat. Past the bedroom, toward the bathroom. And that's when I hear it— water. The toilet is still running.

My jaw clenches.

I push the door fully open and flick on the light.

And in the same instant, dread crashes through me like a wave breaking over stone. It isn't the toilet at all. It isn't anything that simple.

What waits inside turns my blood to ice.

Chapter 13
Killian

"**S**era—wait."

Her name leaves me sharper than I meant it to, but I'd rather snap at her than let her walk in blind. I prefer to sweep the place myself before she sets foot inside. The man at her door tonight is new—trained, experienced, good on paper—but he hasn't earned my trust the way Finn has.

She ignores me. Heels clicking, moving down the hall.

Then it happens so quickly.

A sliver of light spills out from her bedroom. A sound follows it—raw, breaking. Terror. My heart nearly stops.

The bang that comes next kicks me into motion.

I'm running, gun already drawn, muscles locked on instinct. I clear the doorway fast—and my eyes take in the scene in a second.

She's on the floor, water slick under her heels where she's slipped. Tears stream down her face as her eyes stay glued, unblinking, to the bathroom mirror.

"Don't look, baby." I holster the weapon and drop to her side, trying to ground her, to drag her focus back to me. She fumbles, slides toward me, reaching. My arms close around her instantly.

My voice is clipped when I press a finger to my earpiece. "Backup. Now. And call Lucian."

Her body shakes against mine, and I don't give her a choice—I gather her up and carry her out of the room, away from that goddamn mirror. She shouldn't have to see it anymore.

Her name.

Seraphina. Sera.

Scrawled across the glass dozens of times in thick strokes of lipstick. Ledger red. The same shade every companion wears.

It's not neat. It's not staged. It's rage, every letter carved in fury. Tubes of lipstick litter the counter and floor like discarded shells after a firefight.

Two of my men rush in, boots heavy, weapons up. Orders snap out of me in a growl before they can even ask.

"Sweep the apartment. And call Jaxon Kane—have him dig into the system and trace where this bastard came from."

My jaw clenches hard enough to ache. The only explanation is maintenance—he used the appointment as his cover. That means he was in her home. In her sanctuary.

And I'll find him for it.

Then I'll break every bone he has for what he's doing to her.

Lucian shows up in thirty minutes, and it takes almost

that long to get her to stop crying. Even now, she's still hiccuping, her eyes distant, glassy, like she's somewhere far away from this room.

I haven't left her side once. I sat her in the cushioned chair in the corner of her bedroom, pulled a blanket around her shoulders. It swallows her whole, but she looks small anyway. Fragile in a way she'd hate me to admit out loud.

Finn appears at my side with a mug of tea, steam curling up from the surface. "Here, lass."

She takes it, fingers trembling around the porcelain. Offers him the faintest, saddest smile—the kind that guts me, because I know it cost her everything just to lift her lips that much. The warmth seems to help. A little.

"Sera," I murmur, low and careful, like I'm trying not to spook a cornered animal. Which is exactly what she is right now.

I already told Lucian what to expect before he got here. She's not going to like this. Doesn't matter. She needs it.

He crouches down beside me, his suit sharp, his presence heavier than anyone else's in the room. Together we draw her out of the fog, dragging her gaze back to us.

"We need to get you somewhere safe tonight," Lucian says, voice even, implacable.

Her eyes flick between us, slow, unfocused. That's when I realize I've been rubbing the side of her thigh, thumb stroking all the way up to the bend of her hip. Christ. I force myself to stop, but I don't move my hand. I can't.

"Sera," I try again.

This time she blinks, focus sharpening. "No." Her voice is raw, thin but stubborn. "I'm not running away."

"It's not running away," I counter immediately. "It's being smart."

She shakes her head, blanket slipping off one shoulder. "I won't."

I stand when she does, and Lucian joins me, the two of us towering over her. She doesn't back down. She never does. Fire licks through her tears, that iron in her spine making itself known.

"It's being smart," I repeat, firmer this time.

"It's giving in." Her chin lifts, defiant.

Lucian's jaw tightens, patience thinning. "If you can't follow basic safety, Seraphina, then I'll pull the plug on this entire suitor arrangement myself." His tone is absolute, final. "House arrest, if that's what it takes."

The fire in her eyes blazes hotter, sparks flying.

"I won't compromise your safety or the team's because you want to make some sort of noble stand." He holds out a black leather weekend bag he brought with him.

For a second, I think she's going to fight us both right here. But after a long moment, her jaw clenches, lips pressed so tight they turn white.

"Fine," she grits out, each letter bitten through her teeth.

She whirls away from us, storming into her closet, bag clutched in her fists. I hear the metallic scrape of a zipper, the rustle of fabric as she drags items into Lucian's bag.

Reluctant. Furious. But agreeing all the same.

Lucian leans in close, his voice low enough only I can hear. "Don't tell her, or anyone, where you're taking her. Not until we get better tech in here to sweep for mics or trackers."

I nod once. Doesn't matter. I already know where I'll take her.

She stuffs clothes into the weekend bag, zips it with sharp, jerky movements, then grabs a smaller one from her shelf and heads toward the bathroom. She hesitates at the doorway, shoulders tight, before steeling herself and stepping inside. It's spotless now, every trace scrubbed away. But I know what she sees isn't clean porcelain or glass—it's the memory of red scrawled across her mirror.

By the time she comes back out, the kitchen's crowded. More Ledger men. Lucian's reinforcements. He doesn't play games when it comes to companion safety—and Seraphina's already been taken from us once. Not again. Not ever again.

Lucian and I split the orders between us, sharp and clipped. "Sweep the building." "Trace maintenance logs." "Pull footage." Finn will stay onsite, overseeing everything. He doesn't need the reminder, but I give it anyway. "Don't let anyone through that door unless it's one of ours."

When she reappears, she's changed—sweatpants and a soft top, white sneakers, her hair pulled into a ponytail. Makeup gone.

And Christ, I love her like this. Bare. Unvarnished. Real.

But it pisses me off too—that this room full of men gets to see her like this, when I want it for myself.

Her eyes flick to Finn. "I thought this was your night off."

He shakes his head, steady. "Wouldn't sleep a wink until I knew your place was secure."

A flicker of light returns to her eyes. Small. Fragile. But enough.

The mood crashes again the moment we exit the elevator and walk into the lobby. Bags in one hand, my other resting at the small of her back, guiding her out. My gaze sweeps every corner as the doors open, scanning the lobby, the valet line, the shadows outside.

Three Ledger men are already stationed, covering angles.

I get her into the passenger seat myself, ignoring the valet's offer to take her bags. I don't let go until everything's inside and the door shuts.

Her sigh fills the cabin when I climb in beside her, the sound deep, weary. Her head falls back against the headrest like she's finally exhaled the weight of the night.

She feels safe with me. Safe enough to let go a little. I keep noticing it. And I like it. Fucking love it. Too much.

Which is exactly the problem.

Because every second I sit here, I'm split in two. Half of me wants to wrap her in armor, lock her away somewhere no one can ever touch her again. The other half wants to tear that soft cotton off her body and bury myself inside her until she forgets anyone else exists.

Both urges are violent in their own way. And I can't give in to either.

The duality drives me insane—because I can't protect her cleanly, and I sure as hell can't fuck her cleanly. And the longer this goes on, the more I'm losing my grip on which one will win.

Chapter 14

Seraphina

The second we walk through the door, I know.

Killian didn't say where we were going, but I can tell it immediately when he unlocks the door and ushers me inside. His place.

The air hits me first. It smells like him—clean, sharp, and threaded with whiskey. It's disarming, like walking into a space I shouldn't be allowed in, private and unguarded in a way he never is.

He carries my bags down the hall toward a room, leaving me standing in the middle of his living space. My eyes roam before I can stop them.

"You collect records?" I ask, a little surprised, noticing the shelves stacked neatly against one wall.

"Eh, I'd warn you against hearing me sing to them though," he calls back. "My Irish tends to come out and it's a bit frightful."

The corner of my mouth lifts before I can stop it. "That Irish coming out a little wouldn't be so bad, huh?"

It's meant to be casual, teasing—but the words come out softer, heavier, like I'm hinting at something else entirely.

He reappears, one brow raised. "I wouldn't wish it on my worst enemy."

I let out a breathy laugh, grateful for the banter, even as heat coils low in my stomach.

He gives me a short tour, his hand brushing along a light switch here, a wall there, as if reminding himself the space belongs to him.

It's beautiful in a way I didn't expect. All rich browns and leathers, dark grays and metal accents. Masculine, sleek, but lived-in.

Either he has an eye for interiors, or he hired someone with one. Either way, I like it. It tells me something about him—that even with the chaos of his work, he cares about the space he comes home to. Even if, from the look of things, he hasn't been home much since he took on guarding me.

The realization tugs at me.

So does the guilt.

I should have told him sooner. About the stalker. About the notes, the roses, the way I'd brushed it all off as if ignoring it would make it go away. Naïve. Stupid. And now —after tonight—I know better.

It's not just me at risk anymore. I see how wrong I was, and the weight of it presses down on me until I can hardly breathe. Someone could get hurt. Maybe even him.

And that thought cuts deeper than I want to admit.

"Hungry?" Killian asks after the tour, his voice rougher than usual.

I shake my head, offering a faint smile. "Not really."

His mouth quirks like he doesn't quite believe me. "Building doesn't have the amenities yours does, but I can make a mean grilled-cheese sandwich in a pinch."

That actually earns a laugh from me, small but real. "I'm okay. Just tired. I think I want to sleep."

He nods once—no argument—and guides me to the room where he dropped my bags. His room.

"Bed is brand-new, actually. Mattress too." He rubs the back of his neck. "Haven't had a night here yet to break it in." He gives me a wink, and my stomach flips, butterflies tangling in my chest at the thoughts that evokes.

He opens the en suite door, gestures toward the towels stacked neatly. "Fresh. Shower if you want."

"Where are you sleeping if I'm in your bed?" I ask, unable to stop the words.

Something flickers across his face at the way I said your bed. Something I can't name but feel all the way down to my toes.

"Out here." He tips his head toward the living room. "Don't argue. It's decided."

I nod, pretending not to notice the stubborn finality in his tone. He leaves, pulling the door shut, the slow close saying more than he realizes.

Alone, I take a moment to look around. A few framed photos rest on a shelf. His mother, I think—the same eyes, the same set to the mouth. But no one else. No girlfriends smiling at his side, no lingering traces of another woman's claim. I didn't expect relief, but it's there all the same.

The bed is huge. Pressing down on it, it's soft, the fluffy

covers cozy. But a detail on the footboard makes me squint —then chuckle.

A ring, bolted to the corner post. I lean over, check the other side. Sure enough, a matching one.

"Killian Shaw," I murmur to the empty room, "what a kinky man you must be."

I unzip my bag and frown. Of course. I didn't pack anything to sleep in.

Feeling ridiculous, I crack the door open and peek out. Killian's at the bar across the room, whiskey in a crystal glass, the amber catching the low light. He looks carved from stone, but softer too, as he lifts the drink to his lips.

"I, um..." My cheeks heat. "Didn't bring anything to sleep in. You wouldn't happen to have a silk pajama set lying around?"

The chuckle that rumbles from him is unexpected, low, and genuine. I like it. I like him like this—lighter.

"Not quite my style, angel," he says, disappearing to his closet for a moment before returning with one of his shirts. He hands it over without comment and turns away, leaving me the room again.

Angel. The word clings, softer than baby had been, heavier somehow. I thought it had only been a slip, but this is very intentional.

It shouldn't mean anything, but my chest gives a traitorous little squeeze all the same.

The cotton is soft when I pull it over my head, brushing against bare skin. It hangs loose, the hem brushing my thighs. The smell of him clings to the fabric—clean, sharp, faint whiskey—and my nipples pebble immediately against the inside. Silk pajama sets may never compare again.

I climb into his bed, switch off the lamp, and sink into the sheets. They smell like him too, and I hug the pillow, inhaling deeply. I stare at the ceiling, telling myself sleep will come easy. That my mind won't stay caught between fear of what waits outside and the warmth of the man who just gave me his shirt.

But my body knows better.

A thud jolts me awake.

Somewhere between staring at the walls and pushing out thoughts of Killian and my stalker, I must have dozed off.

My heart hammers, chest rising too fast, the sheets tangling around my legs as my eyes adjust to the dark. It takes a moment to remember where I am. Not my room. Not my bed. The space smells like whiskey and cedar, and the ceiling above me isn't familiar.

Killian's place.

I whisper his name into the shadows. "Killian?"

No answer.

The silence makes everything worse. I know I heard something. My mind flashes a thousand ways it could go wrong—my stalker finding us, slipping inside, Killian fighting him to the death in the living room.

It's ridiculous. A giant like Killian would make noise if that were happening. A lot of noise.

Unless... unless he left me here. Or worse, invited someone over. Someone who dots her i's with hearts and something very passionate is taking place on the sofa out there. My mouth goes dry at the thought, hot and bitter in my chest.

I glance at the clock. Nearly one in the morning, and curiosity wins.

Sliding out of bed, I pad across the floor, bare feet silent against the rug. I press my ear to the door. Nothing. Not a sound.

Slowly, carefully, I ease it open and nearly gasp out loud.

He's there. Right there. Leaning against the wall outside my door. Asleep.

The thud must have been him shifting. The position looks brutal, like his spine is twisted, his head against the wall, body folded wrong.

I kneel beside him, nudging his shoulder gently. "Killian..." I whisper.

His reaction is instant. Predatory.

Before I can blink, I'm flat on my back, his body caging mine, his hand around my throat.

"Killian—" it's supposed to be a cry of recognition, but it slips out as more of a plea. "It's me."

His eyes open, blinking fast, the tension in his face slowly easing. His grip loosens. His other hand presses at my hip, where his shirt has ridden up. My stomach, my panties —bare beneath him.

"I just didn't want you to sleep on the floor," I manage, breathless.

"Seraphina." My name leaves him like a prayer, a whisper that melts every inch of me.

My heart pounds so hard I know he can feel it. My thighs part without thought, and at the same moment his hips shift—just barely—grinding into me. The smallest taste, but enough to drench me instantly. My body knows. My body wants.

My hands drift over his warm skin, feeling the tension in his shoulder muscles. I tilt my hips against him, subtle, and his breath drags in like I burned him.

The hand at my hip slides higher—slow, deliberate—searing a path up my body. The grip at my throat adjusts, his thumb caressing the length of my jaw.

"Seraphina," he rasps. "We can't do this."

He doesn't mean it. I know he doesn't mean it. Because his hips roll into me again, firmer this time, and I can feel him thickening against me.

"What are we doing?" I whisper, rocking with him, my legs snaking around him.

His hand travels up, around my rib cage, the pace glacial, torturous. I arch into the touch, silently begging for his palm on my breast, his mouth on my skin.

"We can't cross this line." The words sound like pain, like every syllable scrapes his throat raw. His body contradicts him with every subtle press, every almost-thrust that tests and teases the edge.

"I can't keep you safe like this." The whisper ghosts over my lips, so close I can taste his breath.

A tiny shift from me and my bottom lip brushes his. Not a kiss. Barely a touch. But enough.

Reality slams back into him.

He tears himself away in an instant, moving off me as fast as he pinned me. My body aches with the loss, skin burning, heart hammering against emptiness where his weight had been.

And I can't help but wonder—if I hadn't moved, if I hadn't brushed his mouth—what would've happened?

His voice is gravel, low and rough as he grabs my hand and pulls me up. "Let's get you back to bed."

The words shouldn't make me shiver, but they do. My pulse stutters in my throat. "Will you... stay in here with me?"

For a moment I think he won't answer, but then he nods once. A sharp, clipped gesture. Maybe because he doesn't trust his voice either.

I climb into the bed, sheets cool against my bare skin. He doesn't follow. Instead, he takes the chair in the corner— dark leather, the one that creaks softly under his weight. He sits wide-legged, forearms resting on the arms of the chair, eyes locked on me like a predator who doesn't chase because he knows his prey isn't going anywhere.

My breath catches when I see what he's wearing. Not the suit. Not the crisp white shirt and tie. Just gray sweats, slung low on his hips, and nothing else. Bare chest, shoulders broad and cut, every muscle flexing with the tension he carries like armor. A dark tattoo covers one pec.

He's beautiful in a way that makes my mouth dry, dangerous in a way that makes me ache.

I lie on my side, hand under my cheek, top leg bent, trying to breathe evenly. My heart pounds anyway, traitorous and loud. My body hums with memory—how close he was earlier, how his heat pressed against me, how I wanted him even with the lies whispered from his lips.

My gaze drifts down, and I see his cock straining against the fabric. Thick. Hard. The outline obscene in the dim light. My lips part. My thighs press together instinctively.

I can't help myself. I slide my hand down, between my legs. My finger brushes my clit through the damp cotton of my panties, and my eyes flutter shut. A spark. A tease. My hips twitch.

"What are you doing, Seraphina?"

My eyes snap open. His voice is rough, deeper than usual, threaded with something dangerous. He hasn't moved. He's just watching me—watching me like the devil watches his favorite sinner set herself on fire.

Heat licks up my neck, but I don't stop. I slip my hand beneath the elastic, find the slick heat between my lips. My finger slides through it, slow, then circles my clit. A broken whimper escapes, high and needy.

"Christ," Killian curses, his jaw tight. He knows. He knows exactly what I'm doing.

"I'm not crossing a line," I whisper, breathless. "You're not touching me. I am."

His nostrils flare. His hand drops to his lap. He rubs up his shaft through the sweats, slow and deliberate. My pussy clenches so hard it aches.

"Show me." His command cracks the air like a whip.

I roll onto my back, shove the covers down, spreading my legs to his gaze. "You want to see my wet pussy in your bed?" A grumble escapes him at my teasing. "Knowing you can't touch me." I spread my legs wider, arching into my touch, wishing it were him.

"Careful, little killer." The warning only makes me wetter.

My panties cling to me, wet and transparent in the dim light. My fingers tug the elastic aside, and I touch myself—open, glistening, swollen.

He growls low in his chest, the sound vibrating through me. "Good girl. Don't hide from me."

I rub tight circles over my clit, hips rocking into my hand. My eyes lock on him, hungry for his reaction.

"Not when you're playing with your tight little cunt in my bed." His patience snaps. He frees his cock, fist wrapping around the thick length. "Making my sheets smell like your sweet pussy."

My breath catches at the sight of him—veins bulging, the head swollen and pierced with silver that glints in the light. The barbell runs clean through the crown, obscene and gorgeous. My mouth waters. My cunt clenches. I want it inside me so badly it almost hurts.

"You're staring." His grin is devilish, teeth sharp in the shadows. He strokes himself slow, the metal flashing with every pass of his fist.

"Well," my voice is full of breath, "you've given me a lot to stare at."

He chuckles, deep.

"You want it, don't you? Want this cock splitting you open, that ring dragging over your clit until you come so hard you forget your own name?"

"Fuck. Yes." The word rips out of me on a moan. I circle

faster, wetter, the obscene squelch filling the quiet room. "Oh, Killian..."

"Keep going," he orders, pumping his cock, fist twisting at the head. Precum leaks over his hand, catching the light. "I want to watch you fall apart for me."

"I wouldn't stop... even if you asked me to." My thighs tremble, knees open. My clit throbs against my fingers, every nerve raw. My breath stutters as the orgasm claws up fast, relentless.

"That's it, angel," he rasps, stroking harder. "Rub that pretty little clit. Come for me. Show me how sweet your pussy gets when she's desperate for cock."

I cry out, back arching, climax crashing over me like fire. My cunt pulses around nothing, begging to be filled.

"That's it, little killer... make yourself come for me." Killian groans—guttural, wrecked—pumping himself faster. "Fuck—look at me."

My gaze locks on his just as his cock jerks, cum striping his abs, dripping down his stomach. He curses again, teeth clenched, his dick twitching with every spill.

The room reeks of sex. Hot. Raw. Forbidden.

He snatches a handkerchief from the dresser beside him, wipes himself off with rough efficiency. His chest still heaves, muscles flexing as if he's fighting the urge to cross the room.

I drag my fingers through my wetness one last time and lift them to my mouth. Slowly, deliberately, I suck them clean. My tongue circles each finger before pulling them free with a wet pop.

Killian curses under his breath, fist tightening in the cloth.

I smirk, wicked and smug, settling back into the pillows. "Good night, Killian."

His jaw flexes, but he doesn't answer. He just watches me like I've become his newest obsession.

Chapter 15
Killian

Fuck.

What did I do?

I crossed a line that can't be uncrossed. The one rule drilled into my head from the start—never get involved. Keep it clean, keep it professional. I'm her body-guard, nothing more.

Except last night, I sat there in the dark and watched my mark—my mark—pleasure herself in my bed. Her knees spread, her pretty little moans muffled in my sheets, while I sat across the room like a sick bastard, fisting my cock until I came harder than I have in years.

I should've looked away. Should've walked out, slammed the door, done anything but stay and watch. But I didn't. I stayed. I wanted every fucking second burned into me.

Now it's morning and I'm punishing myself the only way I know how. Sweat pours down my back as I crank out pushups on the floor, then pullups, then free weights—

anything to chase away the image of her mouth falling open when her fingers slid over her clit.

She's still asleep. Still tangled up in my sheets, in my bed. Innocent as sin after ruining me with the sound of her coming.

And all I can think about is sliding in behind her, one arm wrapped tight around her waist, my hand between her thighs to see just how wet she gets when she teases me. I want to feel it—her heat, her slick, her back arching when I tug that long blond hair and bury myself inside her.

Fuck.

Several doors open at once.

My bedroom door creaks and my heart drops.

This is what I've been dreading. What the hell am I supposed to do when I see her? Pretend nothing happened? Apologize for it? Or just haul her onto the kitchen counter, spread her wide, and eat her cunt for breakfast like I've been craving since last night?

Before I can decide, the front door bursts open too. A whirlwind of bags and brown hair breezes past Finn.

Eve. Of course.

She's balancing enough takeout containers to feed the entire security team.

Finn shoots me an apologetic look over her shoulder.

"We bring stalker updates and French toast!" Eve declares like it's just another Saturday morning.

I wipe the sweat from my face with the hem of my tank, the fabric damp against my skin. My pulse is still kicking hard when movement at the bedroom door catches me.

She steps out.

Fresh from my bed, hair a little messy, eyes flicking over me before she can stop herself. Her gaze stalls low—on my stomach, on the sweat still dripping down it—then snaps away like she wasn't just looking.

But the pink climbing her cheeks tells a different story.

My mouth curves into a half grin before I tip my water bottle back for a long drink.

Yeah. Definitely should've spread that pussy open for breakfast.

Eve's already tearing into the bags, chattering about croissants and syrup while she lines up enough food to feed a platoon. I move to the counter, grab a couple of mugs, and pour out coffee. I tip one toward Seraphina, raising my brows in question.

"Coffee?"

She nods, a little too quick. Like she needs it. I know she does—she has coffee every morning, the same way, the same flavor, along with a cold glass of pineapple juice. Had a few of her favorites delivered with the groceries this morning, along with a few other things she hasn't noticed yet.

We can't go back to her place for another night or two, not until the team finishes upgrading her security. So she's here. In my space. In my bed. Driving me fucking insane.

I turn to Finn. "What'd you find?"

He sets down his fork, wiping his mouth. "The restaurant, first. Photos were taken across the street. Lad named Elijah, wasn't it?" His accent is thicker when he's serious. "Several cameras in the area, but none caught anyone hangin' about. The buildin' across the way—no surveillance at all, so that was nothin' but a dead end."

Sera dishes a plate, then hands it to me without looking, just as I'm passing her the coffee. Our fingers brush. A small, accidental thing. Except it's not small at all—it's lightning in my veins, quick and dangerous.

Finn clears his throat, carrying on. "The gym, though. Bit of a lead there. Cameras caught someone slippin' the envelope into your purse."

My head snaps his way and I feel Sera shift her eyes to me, then back at Finn.

"It wasn't who you'd expect," he goes on. "Just some woman. Regular at the gym. We tracked her down—she says a man asked her to do it. Told her it was an anniversary game with his fiancée. She thought it was romantic."

Eve scoffs. Sera swallows too hard, a gulp that stalls in her throat. Her fork clatters against the plate. She looks like she's seen her phantom again.

"Did he have..." Her voice cracks.

Finn's gaze flicks between us. He nods once, solemn. "Aye. One brown eye. One blue."

I clear my throat. "What about the penthouse? Cameras catch anything there?"

Finn shakes his head, mouth tight. "Nothin'. Jaxon'll have to explain it better, but the lad was wearin' some sort o' device. Strong one. Knocked out every feed he walked past, so we've no good shot of him."

My stomach knots. I stroke my chin, smoothing the coarse hair of my short beard in one direction.

"But Jaxon's on it," Finn adds quickly. "Says he should be able to trace it soon enough. They're rare, aye? Unique. Now that he knows to look, he'll be watchin'."

I know that look on Finn's face. He's holding something back.

"What else?" My voice drops, flat.

He takes a breath, heavy. "The stalker was at the restaurant. When you met Daniel Ruiz. Jaxon checked their cameras. Same device—a scrambler—showed up. Means he was sittin' right there—likely at the table next to you."

Seraphina's chest rises too fast, heaving. She stares down at her plate like it's spoiled, the food suddenly rotten in front of her.

"The spilled glass," she whispers, eyes lifting to mine.

I don't need her to explain. I'm already there.

She'd been teasing me that night, sliding her leg against mine, playing with her wineglass like it was my cock she wanted wrapped between her lips. And I let her distract me.

Until a glass shattered right next to us and broke the moment. It was him.

Watching. Pissed. Right there.

Fuck.

I should've been watching the guests. Should've been working. Not imagining her tits in my hands.

My head tips back, eyes on the ceiling as my hands plant on my hips. A rough huff tears out of me, sharp with frustration.

This is exactly why I can't get wrapped up in her. Can't let her into my head. Because that prick got right next to her and could've done anything. If he meant to kill her, she'd already be gone.

I glance at her, jaw tight. I know this is going to start a fight, but fuck it.

"We need to stop the suitor dates."

The flicker of fear in her face burns away in an instant, replaced by pure fire.

"Excuse me?" she snaps.

"You heard me." I fold my arms across my chest. "It's too dangerous. The bastard is getting closer every time. You keep parading around on these dates, you're just handin' him opportunities."

Her chin lifts, eyes flashing. "I'm not canceling my life because some psychopath wants to rattle me. You think hiding me away is the answer?"

"It's keeping you alive," I bite back.

Her hands slam down on the counter. "It's my choice. My contracts. My future. You don't get to decide for me."

"Like hell I don't," I growl, stepping in close, heat sparking between us. "Not when your choices put you in the crosshairs."

Her lips part like she's about to let me have it, but Eve's voice slices through the air.

"You two fucking?"

"What?" Sera shrieks, spinning toward her.

"No," I say flatly at the same time.

"No one would care. I'm just asking." She pushes more.

"Strictly professional." Not even I believe the lie I'm telling.

We're not very convincing, apparently. Eve leans back against the counter, smirking like the devil herself. She lifts her mug, eyebrow cocked, sipping slow while some plan clearly takes root in that wicked mind of hers.

"Well, too bad," Eve chirps, not even pretending to be fazed. "But nothing we can't fix. And I know just the thing..."

She pulls a tablet from her bag, fingers flying across the screen until she spins it around.

Barrett Hall. The pro football player they talked about that first day they sifted through prospects.

"Team calls him Bear," she says, smug. "Led them to the Super Bowl last year. They swept it because of him."

I don't need to read more. I already hate the bastard.

He's about my height, about my build. Even the same brown hair. Except he's a prick—I can tell just by the smirk in his profile photo. A playboy because pussy falls into his lap, not because he knows what to do with it. He wouldn't give a shit about Seraphina. She'd be another trophy on his shelf, right next to that goddamn Super Bowl ring.

"Surely football dick will still be around in a few weeks when this stalker settles down," I mutter.

"Weeks?" Seraphina's voice cuts sharp.

Eve grins. "He's free tonight."

"No." My answer is instant.

"Set it up," Sera tells her.

"This is fucking stupid, and you know it," I snap.

"Calm down," Eve sing-songs. "I can get somewhere exclusive. Members-only, high rollers. Stalker boy can't get in everywhere, surely."

I don't like this. Not one bit. I don't know who the bastard is, where to find him, how to kill him—and meanwhile, she wants to keep prancing around like she's vetting homecoming dates...

"Eve's right," Sera says, defiant. "We can go somewhere

private. Jaxon can watch for the scrambler. If he's around, you guys can... do what you do."

I stare at her. Long enough she shifts against it. I want to shake her until she sees reason. I want to kiss her so hard she forgets every fucking suitor on that list. Kick Finn and Eve out, throw her on the counter, and show her why she doesn't need to look at anyone else.

But I don't. I can't get involved, because even through her teasing last night, she's the one set on finding a final contract to spend the rest of her life with.

So instead, I grind out, "If I smell anything, we're leaving."

"Of course." She meets my eyes, unflinching.

"This stalker escalates again, and this is over," I add. "Dates are done."

"Captain Killjoy," Eve mutters.

"I'm serious."

Eve just smirks. "Trust us—we know."

I roll my eyes as Seraphina leans toward her. "Set it up."

They sweep up the remnants of breakfast while Finn and I clear the table. Then the girls disappear into my room so Sera can change, leaving me pacing my own kitchen like a caged fucking animal.

Finn pours himself another coffee, like the man's got it hooked into his veins twenty-four-seven.

He leans back against the counter, mug in hand. "I know, you don't like it, but maybe it's good she's goin' out. Might draw this prick out, force him to move. If she stays locked in the penthouse, he could just wait her out. Five years, Kill. He's already proven he'll wait."

It pisses me off. "Then we use a decoy. Someone else to lure him out without putting her in the crosshairs."

Finn shakes his head, patient as always. "That's just puttin' someone else on the line. You know it. This—" he nods toward the closed door of my bedroom, "—this is the best we've got. Bring her out, show her off, pull him from the shadows."

A pause stretches. From behind the door, I catch the sound of Sera and Eve giggling, muffled but bright. It twists something sharp in my chest.

I rub my eyes, jaw aching. "I'll think of something else. Some other plan."

Finn's quiet a beat, then says carefully, "I know you've stayed away from the family... but—"

"No." My answer is instant, hard.

He studies me, but I see the uncle in him, not the soldier. He walked away from the Irish too. Got out a little after I did. He knows why I left, why I won't go back.

"You don't have to talk to your brother," Finn says anyway, soft but steady. "But you could pull on a few old strings. Some of the boys are only still there 'cause they can't get out. But if it came down to it—between you and him—"

"That's enough." My voice is low, dangerous.

He doesn't. "They'd choose you, Kill. And you know it."

I give him a long, hard look. My gut twists with the ghosts I've tried to bury—memories of blood on my hands, the crime family I was born into, the one my brother runs now because I walked away from the throne.

"No." My tone is harsh. Final.

"No Irish."

Chapter 16

The dress fits like a second skin. Black, asymmetrical hem, the slit running high enough to tease with every step. Against my tan and blonde hair, it's a warning flare—look here, want this, never touch.

Tonight's venue is members-only. Premier access, exclusive drinks, whispered promises in velvet booths. The Ledger's name opens doors everywhere.

In the limo, Killian explained Finn's point to draw the stalker out. To force him to move. Maybe if you go somewhere he can't follow, he'll get sloppy. Desperation makes mistakes.

It serves my purposes of finding this final contract without Killian's constant pushing.

But he never once looked at me while he said it. His eyes stayed on the window, the city lights flashing against his sharp cheekbones, his jaw tight.

I pretended not to think about his cock. The piercing at

its tip. The guttural sound he made when he came last night, watching me writhe in his bed. The way my orgasm ripped through me, knowing he was part of it. Knowing it was forbidden.

Finn rode in the back of the limo on our way to the date. He's been with us all day. Which meant neither of us dared mention last night. But I caught the glances Killian thought I wouldn't—the flash of his eyes, the grind of his jaw every time Eve mentioned the word dates.

The limo slows, pulling to the curb. Killian gets out first—tall and broad, dark against the street lamps. I expect his hand next, that steady pull that always grounds me.

But it isn't his hand that reaches for me.

It's Barrett Hall's.

"Stunning," he says, voice warm but uncertain, as though he doesn't know how to breathe in my presence. His eyes sweep over me with something that looks more like awe than arrogance. Not the cocky playboy Killian muttered about on the way here.

"What a pleasure it is to meet you, Mr. Hall."

I smile and take his offered hand, sliding easily into the crook of his arm. His bicep flexes beneath my palm—solid—and for a fleeting second it could be Killian's arm under my touch.

His rumble is deep. "Please. Barrett." He raises an eyebrow, taking my hand and placing a kiss on my knuckles.

Barrett smells like spice and clean soap. He nods at the security waiting by the door, and they wave us in without hesitation.

Behind us, Finn—and a very stern-looking Killian —follow.

Inside, the bass hums low. Velvet shadows, gold light dripping from chandeliers. Barrett leans in, tells me again how beautiful I look, his hand warm at the small of my back.

Behind him, a sound cuts through—the long exhale of a man losing patience.

I glance past Barrett's shoulder to Killian with a tight smile. "I'll know where to find you if I need you."

Then I let the pro-football golden boy lead me deeper into the club, into a private booth in the VIP section. I sit, cross my legs slowly, the slit in my dress spilling open just enough to tempt.

But all I feel is the weight of his stare across the room.

Leaning against the bar like a storm bottled in flesh. His thundercloud eyes locked on me, jaw hard, body coiled.

My Irish giant.

Watching.

Waiting.

Barrett is... nice.

Not what I expected at all. He's talkative, but not the kind of man who fills the silence with his own accomplishments. He tells me about his nieces—adorable little girls near the same age as my niece and nephew. His face softens when he talks about them, about teaching them to throw a football in the backyard.

He has a big family. Eldest of seven. Mom and Dad still married, still together, still in love. He laughs when he says they drive him crazy sometimes, but there's pride in it. Warmth.

And when I ask what he's looking for, he doesn't dodge. Doesn't throw out some playboy line about having fun while he's young. He says it straight: "The perfect someone to make a life with."

He makes subtle moves as we talk. A brush of his hand against mine when he reaches for his drink. A lean a little closer when the bass drowns out our voices. Eventually, he turns fully toward me, his palm finding my thigh. He bends close, his lips brushing my ear as he speaks over the music.

And I let myself lean into him.

The hand on my thigh slides a little higher. His voice is low, deep, threaded with genuine attention. But that's not what has every nerve in my body sparking.

It isn't Barrett.

It's not even Killian anymore.

It's her.

The gym girl. The one who dots her i's with hearts.

She's here. At the bar. And she's walking straight toward my bodyguard.

Candi's long brown hair swishes as she struts up to Killian, bright red mini clinging like shrink-wrap. His eyes are locked on mine—mine—until she cuts between us, trailing her hand along his chest like she owns him.

She must have said something, all teeth and eyelashes, because his mouth quirks. And then—God help me—he looks right at me. Holds my gaze before turning back to her.

Like he's making sure I'm watching.

My stomach twists. Barrett doesn't notice, too busy telling me about some prank his teammates pulled last season. All I hear is the pounding of the bass and the blood in my ears as Killian signals and the bartender slides a drink across to Candi.

She toys with the straw between her lips, slow and deliberate, like it's an invitation for Killian to stuff her mouth with his cock.

He turns toward her, elbow propped against the bar, his posture lazy, dangerous. But his eyes—his eyes keep flicking back to me.

Barrett leans in, warm breath brushing my ear. "Dance with me?"

I nod before I can think better of it. Anything to move, to distract myself. His hand finds mine—steady, polite— guiding me to the floor.

Killian doesn't move. He just keeps up his little performance with Candi.

The music swallows us, pulsing lights flashing. Barrett isn't a good dancer, but I don't need him to be. I just need him to not be Killian.

He steps behind me, hands settling at my hips, his mouth close enough to skim my neck. It's enough to sell the scene. Enough to make it look like I'm his.

But I'm not looking at him.

I'm looking at Killian.

He's still at the bar, still watching me even as Candi flirts like she's auditioning for Pornhub. He plays with the ends of her hair, twisting a strand between his fingers like he's fixing it. Then he drops it, dismissive.

She giggles. Throws her head. Rubs his arm.

My pulse spikes. I turn in Barrett's arms, loop mine around his neck, force myself to look at him instead. His hands glide to my back, then lower. Not quite cupping my ass, but close. He whispers a compliment—something about how beautiful I am—but it's background noise.

Because in the mirrored walls of the club, I can still see Killian.

Candi is still there.

Then he pulls out his phone. Smiles down at the screen.

My chest tightens.

She leans into him, hand on his forearm, whispering into his ear. He's punching something in—her number? Her fucking number?

Asshole. He told me he wasn't going to call her. And it's stupid, so stupid, but the jealousy tastes bitter in my throat. I've been teasing him, taunting him, dangling what he says he can't have... but I don't like being on the other side of it.

I'm not supposed to be on the other side of it.

I'm the one looking for a husband. My final contract before I quit the Ledger and have a life of my own. Someone to give me a child or two. A comfortable life I've saved for.

Candi makes a show of kissing his cheek, her hand sliding slow down his arm before she saunters away, hips swinging, throwing a look over her shoulder that screams follow me to the bathroom and bend me over the fucking counter.

Killian doesn't move. Doesn't chase her.

But his head turns, eyes tracking her, a smirk tugging at his mouth that says, maybe I will.

Finn appears at Killian's side. I can't tell if he's delivering a message or if Killian is. Their mouths move low, tight. Finn nods, and then Killian pats his arm once before walking off—straight in the same direction Candi just disappeared.

Finn's hand goes to his earpiece. Within a minute, two Ledger guards are planted at the bar like little watchdogs.

Heat scorches my chest. He just… left me. Dumped me to security detail while he went for a quick fuck in a club bathroom?

Fuck him.

One song passes.

Barrett pulls two glasses of water from a passing tray for us, and my eyes scan the doorways as I sip through the straw.

He takes our glasses, giving them to another waiter, and pulls me back into him.

I press my ass against Barrett, grinding deliberately until I feel the hard ridge of his erection. My gaze cuts between us, a pointed callout without a single word. He grins like the devil himself.

"How far is your place from here?" I ask.

His smile spreads, slow and sinful. "About fifteen minutes."

His hands roam, bolder now, grabbing a cheek and pulling me flush against him.

"Want to get out of here?"

"With you?" He takes my chin between his fingers, tilting my face up, his eyes dark. "Anywhere."

Then his mouth is on mine—warm, open, teasing with tongue until I accept it. He goes deeper, hungrier, arms wrapping around me as he devours every inch of my mouth like he's starving.

But it's just... nice. It's not fire and brimstone. There is no tension making me feel like I'll suffocate without him.

But still, this is what I'm looking for, right? Nice. Comfort. Something steady. And Barrett is steady. He could be a good choice.

"Let's go," I whisper against his lips.

He doesn't hesitate. Just takes my hand and leads me out.

The guards fall in step immediately, and one clears his throat. "Miss Wylde—?"

"I know." I cut him off, sharp. "Get the car and follow behind us."

Barrett's car is already rolling up to valet, sleek and gleaming under the lights. He opens the door, helping me inside like the perfect gentleman.

The guards look dumbfounded, frozen for half a beat. But they'll follow. They'll call it in.

They'll tell a certain Irishman that I left.

And I know he's going to be livid.

Chapter 17

A woman like Candi? She's a fucking joke for a man like me.

She thinks she wants it hard. Thinks she knows rough. She doesn't. What she really wants is some guy who eats her out for a few minutes, tugs her hair a little while he fucks her, then pats her on the ass and tells her she's wild.

A man like me? I'd run through her in seconds and feel nothing. Like starving for days and settling for crumbs. Doesn't touch the hunger. Doesn't satisfy a damn thing.

But Seraphina doesn't need to know that.

What she does need to know—what I'd be lying if I said I didn't enjoy—is the fire in her eyes when Candi came up to me. The way her jaw tightened, her smile faltered imagining what she wanted with me. To know why I hadn't texted her yet. Why I wasn't back at the gym. When I'd make time for her.

Then my phone buzzed.

A text from Finn, the stubborn bastard. Always watching too close.

> FINN: Stop trying to make your mark jealous. I've got someone out here to talk to you.

It made me laugh. Finn would never say shit like that out loud where anyone could hear. Professional to the end. But he knows me in a way no one else does. Knows the blood I come from. Knows what I am, and what I've walked away from.

And he was right. It was worth it just to watch Seraphina practically combust across the room. She probably thinks Candi slipped me her number again. She was trying to—batting lashes, leaning in, playing with her straw like it was practice for her throat.

I brushed her off. Told her I was on assignment. No personal matters during assignments. That line alone damn near made her squirm, eyes lighting up at the idea I might actually be interested.

She touched my arm on the way out, lingering like she thought she'd left a mark. But I saw her friends waiting just past the doorway. She wasn't hunting me—she was hunting an ego stroke.

No matter.

Because Seraphina showed her cards tonight.

And they're jealous as fuck.

Finn leans in close, his mouth almost to my ear, Irish brogue rough against the bass pounding through the club.

"There's a lass from back home," he says. "Owes me a

favor. Still got a foot in both worlds. She can pull strings that might be useful."

I cut him a look. "I already told you no. I'm not draggin' the Irish into this."

"You're a stubborn bastard, Kill," he fires back, steady as stone. "You always were. But you don't have to go runnin' back to your brother. This isn't that. This is a woman who knows people, knows things we can't touch. And if it helps keep Seraphina breathin'—"

I grind my jaw. He knows exactly where to stick the knife.

Finn's eyes don't flinch. "You can hate me for sayin' it, but you're not thinkin' clear when it comes to her. Let someone else play a part."

I blow out a slow breath. "Fine. A few minutes. That's all." I jab a finger toward the dance floor where she's wrapped around Barrett fucking Hall. "Get a few of our boys in here. Eyes on her every second. I don't want dick-wad making a single move I don't know about."

Finn nods once. "Done."

I don't look back. Can't. If I turn around and see her playing seductress for some pro cock-wipe, I'll end up storming that floor and breaking Barrett's fucking hand for touching her.

So I keep walking. Toward the exit. Toward the dark. Away from the very thing I can't admit I want.

I recognize Nora from half a block away.

An old friend of my mother's—the kind she could lean on when the family name turned everything else toxic. I haven't seen her in years. And if memory serves, she was more than "close" to Finn a time or two. The way her eyes find him right away tells me I'm right.

Finn thanks her for coming, kisses her cheek. Supposed to be friendly, but the way his hand lingers on her arm says otherwise.

"Thanks for coming, Nor."

"Good to see you, Killian." I can see the age around her eyes from the woman I remember, but the intensity is no less present. She'll cut you down just as quick as she'll invite you to sit at her table.

"He tell you what this is about?" I nod to Finn, but Nora shakes her head.

So I give her the rundown. The stalker. The five years. The photos. The near misses. How every time we try to pin him, he slips. Best theory we've got is a former client—or some asshole who wanted in the system and got shut out.

Nora shakes her head, slow. "You're lookin' too high, Killian. Look lower. More common. He's stayed invisible this long because he isn't anyone you'd normally look at."

That sticks. My teeth grind as I turn it over.

"And what sort of things are you into these days that you think you can help?" I ask.

Her mouth curves, sharp and knowing. "Because I still know the gutters you and Finn crawled out of. I've got ears in kitchens, janitors in buildings, doormen who see more than they should. The ones nobody notices. The ones nobody asks. You think this bastard's a ghost, but ghosts leave footprints—and the overlooked are the ones who see them first."

She leans in a little. "Let me stir that pot. Get word out in the circles that don't make it onto your security feeds. Somebody's seen him. They just don't know what they were lookin' at."

I study her, weighing it. Jaxon can scrape every feed in the city. But Nora? Nora's the kind who can slip through the cracks and make the nobodies talk.

And she's right—if this stalker hides in plain sight, it's the people no one sees who'll find him.

I'm nodding before I've even made the decision. Already know I'm going to agree. I pull my phone out. "I'll drop you what we've got so far."

Nora slips hers from her pocket, but my screen stays stubbornly blank. No service down here. I roll my eyes.

"Here," she says, taking my phone straight out of my hand and plugging her number in.

I take it back, tuck it away. "I'll send it in a few. Would've liked this done yesterday."

She chuckles—warm but edged. "Finn explained your... need for urgency."

The way she says it makes my head snap toward him. Like he gave her more than he should've. He just shrugs, innocent as a saint.

Nora lays a hand on my arm before she goes. "Say hi to your mother for me, Killian. Tell her she doesn't need to be a stranger anymore."

I nod once because I don't trust my voice.

Her eyes linger on Finn, longer than they should. "Good to hear from you, Finn."

"Thanks, Nora," he says, softer than I've heard him in years.

She turns the corner and disappears.

I don't wait a beat before I turn on him.

He lifts a hand. "Don't start with me, boy." No heat in it.

"You and Nora?" I push, half-grinning.

He shakes his head. "Nothin'. Silly summer affair when we were younger."

We're walking back toward the mouth of the alley when I mutter, "Maybe think about givin' her a call one day when you're off work."

Finn smirks, but before he can answer my phone buzzes. Jaxon's tag flashes on the screen—file incoming. I swipe it open and it's a video.

From Seraphina's phone.

My jaw tightens as I realize Jaxon intercepted it, rerouted it to me before it ever touched her screen.

Grainy footage. Inside the club, and I know instantly it's from the stalker. But it isn't her the lens is on.

It's me.

The bastard zooms in, closer and closer, until it's clear: I'm standing across the room, eyes locked on her. Watching her every move.

My chest goes tight. This isn't just about catching her anymore. This is a message. A warning. I'm the obstacle. I'm the threat.

"Finn," I growl, shoving the phone toward him. "He's in the club."

But before Finn can respond, pounding feet slap the pavement.

My hand goes straight to the handle of my knife—always my first instinct before the gun.

It's one of ours. One of the men who's supposed to be with Seraphina.

"Why the fuck are you out here?" I bark, grabbing him by his collar.

He's bent, breath ragged. "Neither of you answered your phones."

My stomach drops. "What happened?"

"Seraphina left—"

The world stills. "What?"

"With her date. She left in his car. Told us to follow behind. We couldn't reach you, so the second man's tailin' her now. I came to find you."

Everything in me goes cold. Then hot.

She left. With him.

I bite down on the fury threatening to tear me apart and step in close enough the guard flinches. "You don't run to me," I snarl. "You don't leave her. You stop the fucking car. Throw yourself under it if you have to. Put a bullet in the bastard's skull if he doesn't stop driving. He can't take her anywhere if his brains are on the pavement, can he?"

He goes pale, but I don't ease up.

We break out of the alley, my phone vibrating as soon as the signal returns. I pull up the Ledger app, her tracker blazing bright.

This isn't jealousy. It's not want. Not the ache burning through my veins every time I think about her. This is duty. The job. That's the story I'll keep telling myself as I move, tracker searing into my palm like a brand.

Because one way or another, Seraphina's coming back with me.

And when she does, I'll make damn sure she understands—bad girls who don't listen learn fast. The only safe place for her is right where I fucking put her.

Chapter 18
Seraphina

Barrett's penthouse is nice. Cold. The kind of space decorated by some designer his mother probably picked out. Tasteful, elegant... but lacking any trace of him.

I step out onto the wide, curved balcony and let the city greet me. The skyline glitters under the night sky, a million lights battling the glow of the moon. Beautiful. Distant. Untouchable.

My hands glide over the smooth railing. I jut my hip, feeling the cool steel beneath my palms.

Barrett comes up behind me, tall flute of champagne in hand. "For you," he says.

"Thank you." I take it, the bubbles crisp against my lips. His body crowds mine—not demanding, but present. His callused hands skim down my arms, and he breathes me in.

He doesn't push. Doesn't assume. "I don't expect anything from tonight except a chance to get to know you," he murmurs.

"So, get to know me," I answer, my voice softer than I intend. If only he realized I'm already known—watched, studied, touched by a man who pretends he doesn't want me.

Barrett shifts my hair over my shoulder, lips pressing warm against the side of my neck. My eyes slip closed. My head tilts back, rests against him.

For a heartbeat, it's Killian's mouth I feel. Killian's rough hands on me.

Barrett's hands explore—respectful but sensual—sliding over curves like he's savoring the chance to touch. I pretend it's Killian. His tall, thick form pressing me forward into the railing. His lips, his heat, his weight.

His hand traces up my bare thigh, sliding beneath the hem of my dress. He exhales when he finds the silk of my panties, when his fingers brush the wetness there.

A groan vibrates against my ear. He thinks it's for him.

"You feel incredible," he whispers, mouth trailing fire along my neck.

I moan, low. "Do I?" Not for you. For him.

His other hand cups my breast, thumb teasing the hard peak through my dress. Below, he rubs slow circles over my pussy through the thin silk before dipping beneath the band. A thick finger slides between my lips, gathering my wetness before circling back to my clit.

"You're already so wet," he rasps. "For me?"

"Yes," I lie, wrapping a hand around his neck. For him.

He chuckles against my skin, lips brushing my jaw. "I want to take my time with you."

"You should," I whisper, tilting my head to give him

more access. Because he won't. Killian would ruin me fast and filthy—because he couldn't stand anyone else having me.

Barrett's finger moves in tighter circles, drawing another moan from me.

"God, you're perfect," he says. "Every man in that club wanted you, and you came with me."

I bite my lip, eyes squeezing shut.

"Lucky you." But unlucky me. Because the only man I wanted is probably tearing the city apart looking for me.

My mind betrays me, conjuring the thick weight of Killian's pierced cock, the way I'd lick around it, taste him, drive him mad until he finally gave in and fucked me deep.

Here, in Barrett's arms, I pretend. Pretend this is what it feels like to give in to Killian. To stop fighting. To let go the way he refuses.

But the pleasure doesn't build. It stalls, stutters. Because it isn't Killian.

It isn't tension and heat and stubborn will pushing against every breath I take. It isn't the man who makes me want to break rules I didn't know I had.

I rock my hips, trying to chase it anyway, trying to wring something out of Barrett's touch. But the climax doesn't want to give itself over. Not to him.

"You're unreal, you know that?" Barrett murmurs against my neck, his finger circling slow. "Any man would kill for this."

One already might.

Before I can answer, before I can tell him another lie, pounding rattles the other side of his door.

Barrett curses, pulling his hand from between my thighs.

I smile. Because I know exactly who that is.

I tug my dress down, smooth my hair, and lean against the patio door like I've been there all night. Sip champagne while Barrett stomps through his perfect, personality-free penthouse and yanks the door open.

The thunderstorm that is Killian eases into the room. He doesn't explode. He never does. He's a slow detonation, building the anticipation until all you can do is wait for the boom.

His eyes find me in an instant. Not the black of my dress. Not the champagne in my hand. Me. His gaze latches onto me like gravity itself dragged him forward.

Barrett steps in, trying to plant himself as a wall. "What the fuck's your problem?"

Killian doesn't need to answer. Doesn't need to push. He is the push, the weight, the darkness that nothing stands against. Barrett might be built like him—tall and solid—but he doesn't have that heaviness. That inevitability. Killian would thunder past him without a thought.

"We have an issue," Killian says, voice low, carved from stone. "Date's over."

Barrett bristles, unwilling to let another man walk into his penthouse and take over. His jaw tightens. "What, you think you own her?"

He doesn't own me. Barrett Hall sure as fuck doesn't. But Killian—

Killian looks at me like he knows better. Like he can see

every inch Barrett's touched, every spot his lips lingered, and he's cataloging them. Marking them.

I set down my champagne and saunter toward Barrett. My smile is sweet, deliberate. "Thank you. I had a lovely night."

He half-blocks Killian, defiant to the end, and takes my chin between two fingers. Tilts my head up. "I'll call you," he whispers before pressing a tender kiss to my lips.

No tongue. Barely there. But enough. Enough to nearly shatter the fragile hold Killian's got on himself. His hand flexes into a fist, dangerously close to the knife at his side, and I keep my eyes locked on him the entire time. Smiling, wicked, daring.

"Let's go," he growls. Low, lethal, sending a shiver down my spine.

I step past Barrett with a flirty, "See you around."

Killian falls into step behind me. Following me into the hall like the storm he is. The elevator attendant waits, holding the door. We step inside.

It's like walking with a hurricane at my back, pretending it isn't about to tear me apart.

The doors close. Tension builds with each floor, pressing tighter, hotter, until the lobby's lights flood through the crack of the opening doors.

I head for the exit, chin high. But his grip clamps around my upper arm—firm, commanding, unyielding—and wrenches me to the right.

"Killian—" I exclaim under my breath.

He says nothing.

The ladies' room door slams against the wall as he

shoves me inside. Two women at the mirror startle, lipstick tubes clattering.

"Out."

One word. Barked, brutal. They scatter, heels urgently tapping out their retreat, leaving me alone with the tempest I dared to poke.

Chapter 19
Killian

The door slams shut behind us, echoing off the tile. The air is thick—perfume and powder from the women who just fled—but all I smell is her.

She tries to stand tall, chin lifted, like she's in control.

My laugh is sharp, humorless. "You think you're clever, don't you?"

She blinks at me, feigning innocence. "What are you talking about?"

I crowd her back against the counter, planting my hands on either side of her hips. No space. No air. Just me pressing in until she has nowhere left to go.

"You know exactly what the fuck I'm talking about." My voice is low, dangerous, meant for her alone. "Walking out on my men. Letting him put his hands on you. Pretending this was about him."

Her lips curve, the smallest, smug smile. "Wasn't it?"

"Bullshit." I lean in, so close my mouth brushes her ear.

"This wasn't about Hall. This was about me. You wanted me to see it. To feel it."

Her lashes flutter, but her tone stays cool. "You're imagining things."

I tip my head, study her, then pull my phone from my pocket and shove it in her face. The video glows between us —grainy club footage. Not her. Me. The stalker zooming in closer and closer while I watched her across the room.

"That's what you're calling imagination?" I snarl. "He was in the club tonight. Filming me, because he knows I'm the wall between him and you. And you ran off like some teenager rebelling against her parents."

She stiffens, but her chin doesn't drop. Always stubborn —and God if I don't want to fucking break it.

I lean in, mouth ghosting along her jaw, my words a growl against her skin. "Say it, Seraphina. Admit it."

She shakes her head, playing dumb. "I don't know what you want me to say."

Fine. If she won't use her mouth for the truth, I'll make her body speak it for her.

I drag one hand down her side, slow, deliberate. Her breath catches, but she keeps her eyes fixed on mine, defiant. My palm curves over her thigh, thumb pressing the hem of her dress higher until I'm sliding beneath.

She stiffens. "Don't—"

"You don't want me to stop." My voice is quiet, razor-sharp. "You want me to prove you're a liar."

My fingers find her panties, damp silk clinging to her. I press against her, feel the heat. She presses back, a small sound breaking in her throat.

"You're wet," I murmur. "But not for him."

"Yes," she snaps back, chin high. "For him."

I smirk. "Liar."

I push under the band, thick finger sliding through her hot cunt. She ignites instantly, her hips betraying her even as she glares at me.

"Stop pretending," I rasp, circling her clit, working her fast enough to have her panting. "Your body already knows who it's for."

Her hand fists in the front of my shirt—not pulling me closer, not pushing me away. Just holding on like she can't decide which lie to tell.

I play her mercilessly, pressure building tight in her. She moans, sharp, then bites her lip to smother it.

She's close. I feel it in the way she trembles, the way her hips buck for more.

And just before she can fall, I pull back.

Her eyes fly open, blazing. "Killian—"

I smile, slow, cruel. Slide my hand down her thigh like I never touched her. "Not until you admit it."

"Admit what?" Her voice is ragged.

"That you wanted me. That all of this—" my fingers press into her again, teasing, withdrawing "—was never about Hall. It was about getting me to break."

She shakes her head, stubborn, breathless. "No."

I plunge back between her legs, working her hard and fast. Her moans echo in the tiled room, raw and helpless.

And again, just before she tips over, I stop.

She's shaking now, furious, desperate, lips parted like she'll scream.

I lean in, mouth brushing her ear. "You'll say it, angel. Sooner or later. Because I'll keep you right here, begging and dripping, until you do."

I drag my mouth up the column of her throat, tasting sweat and champagne. When I reach the soft place beneath her jaw, I suck hard enough to mark her. I want anyone to see she can't belong to them.

My fingers work her faster, deeper, until she cries out, arching her back, one leg kicking wide to give me more.

"Killian—" she gasps, voice breaking.

Her head tips back, lips parted, eyes wild. "Someone could see," she warns, a desperate whisper.

I grin against her skin. "Let them. Make your peace with God now, angel. Because when I'm done, you'll be screaming my name while you come on my hand."

Her breath stutters, her hips grinding down onto my fingers, and I know she wants it. I can feel her unraveling, feel the truth in the slick heat soaking my hand. My mouth hovers over hers, so close we're breathing the same air.

She teeters, right there at the edge—and she calls it out. "Yes—yes, it's you. I wanted you."

That's all it takes.

I crush my mouth to hers, swallowing her confession. My tongue drives into her, ruthless, claiming, erasing any trace of that bastard Hall she let near her tonight.

She shatters. Loud. Her cries ricochet off the marble walls as her pussy clenches around my fingers like a vise. She grinds against my hand, holding me there, milking every ounce of her release while I keep her pinned to the counter.

"That's it," I rasp against her lips, still working her with relentless precision. "Make a mess on my hand like a good little slut. So wet for me you can't fucking lie anymore."

Her nails dig into my shoulders. She sobs out another moan, thighs trembling.

"Not him," I snarl, curling my fingers deep, rubbing her clit mercilessly. "Never him. Only me. Say it."

Her voice is broken, wrecked. "Yes, you."

And Christ, I fucking love it. Love the sound of it. Love the way her body bows under me, surrendering while she spills over my hand again and again, until she can barely stand.

Her cries fade, and before she can catch her breath, I spin her around. Her palms smack the counter, catching her weight. Lust still burns in those deep blue eyes, her chest heaving, skin flushed.

I'm quick—too quick for her to protest. I shove her dress higher, drag my knife free, hook it under the band of her panties. One sharp pull and the silk gives, the sound of tearing fabric echoing in the tiled room. I tug them from between her legs, damp and ruined, before sliding the blade away.

Her panties are soaked. My fist tightens around them, and I lift them to my face. Breathe her in.

Fucking heaven.

I slide them into the inside pocket of my jacket like I've claimed a prize, then grip the firm globes of her ass.

"Such a bad girl," I murmur, kneading her cheeks. Pulling them apart, appreciating her tight asshole, waxed and smooth, begging to be filled. "Running from me."

Her mouth opens, ready to argue—so I pull my hand back and bring it down hard. The sharp crack fills the room.

She gasps, eyes flying wide, arousal sparking hotter through the surprise.

I massage her again, rough, filling my palms with her. Watching her face in the mirror. "When are you going to learn, angel? The only safe place for you... is with me."

Another smack. Her body jerks, but the sound that leaves her throat isn't pain—it's a whimper, hungry and desperate.

I reach around, finding her clit, throbbing and slick. She cries out as I spank her again, my fingers circling ruthlessly.

"Tell me what you want," I growl against her ear.

"You," she gasps, pressing back into me.

Another smack. "Be specific. Use your words."

Her voice fractures. "I want your cock. I want it deep. Hard. Until I can't breathe."

"That's my good girl." I pinch her clit between two fingers, precise and punishing. She rises to her toes, body bowing, mouth open in a cry that shatters into moans as she comes again—harder this time, wrecked, surrendering everything to me.

When she collapses against the counter, I turn her back to face me. Her dress is still hiked high. One of my hands grips her reddened ass, squeezing until she flinches, the heat of my strikes burning beneath my palm.

The other stays between her legs, her cum running down my palm, dripping down her thighs.

Oh, fuck. She's a juicy little killer. And I want every drop of her pleasure to belong to me.

"You're going to go to the limo," I tell her, voice steady, leaving no room for doubt. "You're going to sit like a good girl. No panties. Soaking the seat for me while I take you home. And if you behave, I'll eat that sweet pussy of yours all night."

Her lips part, trembling—ready to answer—but I don't let her.

I grab her chin and crash my mouth to hers first, taking what I want. The kiss is brutal, consuming, my tongue forcing past her lips and claiming every sound she tries to make.

When I finally tear my mouth from hers, I tighten my grip on her ass until she flinches. My voice is a growl against her swollen lips.

"Say it."

"Yes," she whispers, wrecked. "I'll be good."

The corner of my mouth curves slow, dangerous. Like she just signed her soul over to the devil.

I lift my fingers—wet with her—and slide them into my mouth. Suck them clean with a low moan. "Mmm. Not bad." I tease her.

Her eyes flash, anger sparking through the haze of pleasure, but I don't let it grow. I open the bathroom door, ushering her out with a hand on her back as she hurries to pull her dress down.

She climbs into the limo first. I follow. Then Finn. Then the guard who came running earlier. The other sits in the front with Felix.

I lean back, watching her knees clamp together,

knowing why. Freshly fucked on my hand, ass burning from my strikes, her panties still warm in my pocket.

She thinks she played her little game tonight. Thinks Barrett Hall meant something.

But when we get home, I'm going to make damn sure she forgets every touch but mine.

Every single one.

Chapter 20
Seraphina

That bastard.

I squirm the entire way back to his apartment. Longest thirty minutes of my life.

Killian sits there, acting indifferent, while my destroyed panties sit in his pocket, one scarred eyebrow cocked high in hidden amusement. While his men ride in silence around me, none of them knowing his fingers still smell of me—my pussy, my pleasure.

I've never come so hard from being fingered. Ever.

But it's not just that leaving me shaken.

It's what I discovered in that bathroom when he kissed me.

His dick piercing isn't the only one he has.

His tongue is pierced too.

I never noticed it before. Never saw him play with it, never caught the flash of metal. It must be discreet. Hidden. But I felt it—cool and hard against the heat of his tongue as he shoved it into my mouth, claiming me.

The thought of that bar sliding over my clit while he licks me open makes me wet all over again.

His promise—to lick my pussy until I scream.

Now it has new life. A new edge.

Walking from the limo to the door of his building feels like walking to my execution—and I'm going willingly. The doorman nods as they wave us through. The elevator ride is short, quiet. Finn and one guard ride up with us. Another stays behind in the lobby.

It's too calm. Too normal. And I'm a live wire, buzzing with anticipation and dread.

Because as a Ledger companion, I know my role. I'm hired to fulfill fantasies. The pleasure belongs to the client, not me. That's the deal.

But Killian isn't promising me duty. He isn't promising me a job well done.

He's promising something else.

Something only for me.

At his floor, the guard stationed at his door nods, then slips off for the night. Finn lingers long enough to give Killian a quick update, then takes his leave too.

All is quiet. No action. No threats.

Just me and him.

Killian unlocks the door and ushers me inside.

And when it shuts behind us with a heavy click, my stomach drops.

Because now I'm trapped.

Alone with the beast I riled up.

The second the door shuts, he's on me.

My back hits the wood with a thud, his mouth slamming

onto mine. His kiss is rough, devouring, swallowing my squeal. I know the guard still stationed in the hall can hear every gasp, every scrape of my heels on the floor.

I don't care.

Killian rips at my dress, fist curling at my chest until the fabric tears down the middle. I gasp into his mouth as he peels it off me, leaving me in nothing but my heels and a black, strapless bra.

"Killian—"

His knife is out in a flash, gleaming in the low light. The cold tip slides between my breasts, slipping under the satin. A single upward slice, and the bra parts like paper, falling away.

"Jesus," I gasp, heart pounding.

"Quiet," he growls, lowering his mouth to my breasts. His tongue is hot, his teeth sharper. He sucks hard, nips at the soft flesh until I arch into him with a cry.

Then he bites—just enough to pinch, to sting, to claim.

"Oh God—"

He lifts me like I weigh nothing, my legs wrapping around his waist. His mouth is back on mine, his teeth tugging at my bottom lip.

"I'm not makin' it to the bed," he mutters against my lips.

"Don't care," I breathe.

He half carries, half staggers us down the hall, but stops short, pinning me against the wall. His mouth claims me again—brutal and hungry—leaving my lips swollen and wet.

Then he drops me to my feet.

Before I can steady myself, he kneels, dragging kisses down my stomach. His teeth scrape my hip, making me moan out loud.

"Killian..."

"Spread for me." His voice is a command, dark and low.

He hooks my thigh over his shoulder, pressing his mouth into my pussy like he owns it.

The first sweep of his tongue has me crying out, clutching his hair. The cool scrape of the piercing over my clit makes me see stars.

"Fuck—yes," I moan, rocking against him. His scruffy beard feels amazing between my thighs, just like I'd imagined a hundred times.

His tongue is merciless—curling, flicking, plunging deep. He isn't eating me out because it's expected. He's devouring me because he wants to. Because he craves it. Because he wants me writhing on his mouth until I break.

This man loves to eat pussy.

"Killian, I can't—"

"You can," he growls against me, and sucks harder.

I come hard, a scream tearing from me. But he doesn't stop. Doesn't slow.

He shifts, hooking my other leg over his shoulder.

Then he rises. Stands to his full height with me in his arms, my back pinned to the wall, my pussy spread wide for his mouth.

"Hold the doorframe," he orders, his voice rough.

My hands fly up, clutching the wood above me as he buries his face between my thighs, sucking me like he's starving. The pressure is unbearable, exquisite—his tongue piercing dragging relentless patterns until I'm sobbing out his name.

"Say my name," he rasps, teeth scraping me. "Say the name of the man you really wanted tonight."

"Killian!"

He groans against me, tightening his grip, forcing me to ride his face as he devours me. My body bows, trembling, pleasure tearing me apart as my scream echoes through the apartment.

Only when I'm trembling, sobbing through another orgasm does he lower me carefully. My legs hook back around his waist on instinct, clinging to him.

His strength is terrifying. Intoxicating.

My body is wrecked, limp in his hold, but my eyes are locked on him—on his mouth, on the line of my release glistening down his chin and throat.

I lift a hand, cup his face, and lean in. My tongue drags up his jaw, lapping at the salty-slick line of cum he coaxed from me. His breath rumbles low, rough, as I chase the trail higher, licking him clean.

Before I can stop myself, I press my mouth to his, tongue plunging deep. The taste of me is everywhere, flooding between us, dizzying.

His growl vibrates against my lips as he kicks the bedroom door open, never breaking the kiss. The frame shudders from the impact, then the door slams shut behind us, the sound echoing like a gunshot.

He tears his mouth from mine just long enough to rasp, "You think you've come enough tonight?" His smirk is wicked, hungry. "I'm just fuckin' getting started."

Killian sets me on the edge of his bed, his massive frame dropping to his knees in front of me. In a single motion, he rips his shirt over his head—muscles flexing, skin glistening. His belt hits the floor, followed by the heavy clatter of his knife.

Then he reaches for me.

My heels slide off one by one under his rough hands, and before I can catch my breath he's spreading my thighs wide, dragging me open.

"Feet on my shoulders," he orders.

I obey, trembling, heels digging into the hard muscle.

"Now watch."

His head dips, mouth sealing over me, tongue plunging deep while his piercing scrapes across my clit. I grip his hair, knuckles white, forcing myself to keep my eyes open like he commanded. His gaze flashes up through thick lashes, locking with mine even as his mouth devours me.

"Killian—fuck—"

He slides two fingers inside me—thick and ruthless—thrusting hard while he sucks on my clit. The wet sounds echo in the room—obscene, delicious. I hear them as clearly as I feel them—his hand pounding into me while his mouth wrecks me.

Pleasure tears through me, raw and brutal. I come hard, screaming his name, thighs clamping around his head as I drip down his fingers. He doesn't stop until I'm gasping, undone, trembling against the sheets.

When he finally pulls back, his lips glisten with me, his chin wet, his fingers still pumping slow inside my pussy.

"You taste better than sin," he growls, dragging his thumb over my swollen clit one last time.

I can't think. Can't breathe. The only thought left in me is that I want him inside me—now.

But first... "I want a taste."

I push up, licking my lips, grinning wickedly. "Stand up," I murmur.

His brows lift, but he obeys. He rises, towering over me, and unzips.

My breath catches.

His cock is long. Thick. Hard veins running down the shaft, the gleam of a piercing through the crown. I wrap my hand around him, stroking slow, savoring the heavy weight. Then I lean forward, licking a long strip up his length before sucking the head into my mouth.

"Oh, fuck," he grunts, head falling back.

I swirl my tongue around the metal bar, tugging at it, pulling moans out of him as I take him deeper, hollowing my cheeks. He hits the back of my throat, and I stay there, gagless, holding his gaze as I swallow around him.

When I pull off with a wet pop, his eyes are black, feral. His thumb drags across my bottom lip, smearing spit.

"You know why I'm the most coveted companion?" I whisper, voice wrecked.

The way his jaw ticks says he already knows.

"Because I come like this—" I press two fingers between my thighs, moaning as I plunge inside myself, my release dripping down my hand. His nostrils flare; his cock jerks in my grip.

"And because..." I lick my lips, stroking him slow with

the hand that was just in my pussy, coating him in my release. "There isn't a dick I can't take without gagging."

I look up at him—daring, wicked. "So fuck my mouth, Killian. See if you're big enough to find my limit."

He grips the side of my head, cock sliding heavy over my tongue. I open wide, letting him thrust deeper. My throat stretches, burns, until his balls slap against my chin.

He groans, low and guttural. "Fuck—no one's ever taken me all the way before. No one could."

The words vibrate through me, my eyes watering as I accommodate his size. His growl rumbles above me—dark and primal—and it makes my pussy clench hard around nothing.

"Deep breath," he rasps. "Now."

I inhale through my nose, and he pushes back into my mouth, filling me until I can't breathe. His cock drills straight down my throat, his piercing dragging along my tongue as he groans.

"Christ, angel. You're swallowing me whole."

I gulp around him, throat working, the sound obscene. His hand fists in my hair, holding me steady as he fucks my mouth, using me like I'm made for it.

"Take it," he snarls. "Take every inch of me."

He thrusts harder, pushing me to the limit of my held breath until I slide off, spit running down my chin, dripping from his cock as I suck in a deep rush of air. The sight of him glistening with my saliva makes my thighs press together, desperate for relief.

He smirks, wiping the mess across my lips with his thumb. "Filthy girl."

Before I can answer, he tears open a condom and rolls it down his thick length. My body aches—ready—but he's not done teasing.

He presses me back against the bed, spreading me wide. His thumb circles my swollen clit until I cry out, writhing beneath him.

"You're already dripping for me," he mutters, voice low and hungry. "So fucking wet, I could slide in raw."

"Killian, please—"

"Not yet." He toys with me, rubbing slow until I'm panting. Then, finally, he presses the head of his cock against me and pushes forward—slow and relentless.

"Oh my God—"

I can feel every inch stretching me, filling me. My body is so small compared to his, but I take him. Perfectly.

His eyes never leave my face as he sinks deeper, watching every flicker of pleasure and pain. "Look at you," he growls. "So tight. Taking me like you were made for my cock."

"Fuck," I moan, clutching at his shoulders. "You're too big—"

"Too big, and you're still begging for more. Say it. Say you love it."

"I do. I love it," I cry, arching as he bottoms out, buried to the hilt.

"Good girl."

He pulls back slow, then slams into me—hard enough to rattle the bed. I scream his name, nails clawing down his back.

He fucks me mercilessly, driving deep, pounding until

the headboard knocks against the wall. His mouth is every-where—my neck, my lips, sucking my nipples raw as he thrusts.

"You feel that?" he grits out, his pace brutal. "That's my cock splitting you open. No one else has ever filled you like this."

"Killian—yes—don't stop—"

"I'm not stoppin' until you come all over me. Until you squeeze me so hard I can't breathe."

His fingers work my clit again, and the pressure deto-nates. I come screaming, shaking beneath him, my pussy clamping down around his thick length.

He curses, driving into me harder. "That's it, angel. Milk my cock. Make me give it to you."

He pounds once, twice more—then groans, long and low, spilling into the condom as his body trembles above me, slowing his thrusts until he finally pulls free.

On his knees between my legs, he strips the condom off, ties it tight, and tosses it aside. His eyes drop to my pussy—swollen, wet, still fluttering from the aftershocks—and his lips curl into something wicked.

"Christ, look at that sweet cunt. Dripping like she's beggin' for more. You think I'm finished? No, angel. I'm gonna fuck you 'til this mattress is soaked through, 'til you're cryin' and beggin' and there's nothin' left in you to give."

He tears open another condom, sliding it down his still-thick cock, never breaking eye contact.

"By the time the sun comes up, you won't remember your own name—only the way I fucked you all night long."

Then he leans forward, pressing my thighs wide again, and buries his face between my legs. His tongue drags through the mess he left behind, licking me clean with slow, deliberate strokes.

"Gotta clean up the first mess, angel," he growls against my pussy. "Before I make the next one."

And with the way he's devouring me, I know he means it.

Chapter 21
Seraphina

"Seraphina..."

The sound of my name drifts through the dark, pulling me forward. I'm running, bare feet slapping against the ground, lungs tearing with every ragged gasp, but the shadows stretch and shift until I can't tell where I am—only that something is behind me, and I have to keep moving.

Out of the corner of my eye, movement catches—a swirl of fabric, the twirl of a gown as skirts fan out, the deep dip of a woman's body into her partner's arms. The darkness reshapes itself, and suddenly I'm not running anymore. I'm in the center of a grand dance floor.

The opera house.

Masked faces whirl around me in endless circles, their movements graceful, their waltz elegant and precise, but the music that drives them feels wrong—distorted and hollow, like a broken record scraping against the silence.

I search the sea of dancers, my chest aching with

urgency, hunting for him—my stalker. Every spin and dip hides him, but I swear I see him just beyond the crowd, standing perfectly still in the shadows. My heart leaps, but when I lunge forward the figure dissolves into darkness. Another shape rises in its place, broader, taller—Killian, maybe—his storm-gray eyes catching the light for the briefest moment before he too vanishes, swallowed whole.

The press of dancers grows heavier, suffocating, until another face shimmers into view. My twin. Stasia. Her eyes stream with tears; her lips form a scream I cannot hear as the dancers orbit around her, pulling her in and out of the light. One moment she is there; the next she disappears into shadow, always just out of reach.

"Stasia!" I shout, pushing through, desperate to catch her hand, but my heavy dress weighs me down like lead.

I reach, fingers grasping at the air, but when I finally make contact it is only with darkness—cold and slick—slipping through my grip.

I trip on the layers of skirts and the floor drops away.

I crash hard onto tile, the impact knocking the breath from my lungs. The world is no longer the gilded opera house but a sterile, airless chamber, heavy with despair, the weight of it pressing against my chest until I can hardly breathe.

A sudden flash cuts across the black. White light burns my vision, strobing like static—jagged and disorienting.

"Seraphina!" Killian's voice thunders in the distance— close enough to hear but far too far to reach me. I try to push up, but my arms won't move—my hands feel pinned to the floor, fused to the cold tile.

Another flash bursts through the dark.

And then I see him.

He is seated in the shadows, his figure indistinct except for the eyes. One burns blue and vivid, glowing like a shard of ice, while the other is dark and lifeless. He watches me with a smile that doesn't belong to the living.

In his hands rests a single white rose.

It should be pure, but the petals are dipped in red—each one dripping with blood that trails down the stem and stains his fingers, falling in steady drops onto the floor.

Terror grips me, choking off my breath.

"Seraphina—wake up."

The voice changes, grounding me, pulling me free. I jolt upright with a gasp, eyes flying open.

Killian is there, sitting at the edge of the bed, his hand heavy on my arm, his storm-gray gaze fixed on me. His chest rises and falls with calm steadiness, but his eyes betray his concern.

"Angel," he says, softer now, rough with something that feels too much like care. "It's me. You're safe."

But my pulse won't slow, and the bloody rose is still etched into the back of my eyelids—a vision I can't shake no matter how tightly Killian's hand holds me to this moment.

"Do you want to talk about it?" Killian's voice is low, careful, like he already knows my answer.

I shake my head, my throat tight. "No."

He doesn't press. He just shifts, pulling back the covers and climbing in beside me—his bed, the one where he claimed every inch of me until the late hours of the night. My body is still sore in all the right places, stiff from his relentless pace, but my heart hasn't stopped hammering since I woke.

"Tell me about something," I whisper, the words fragile, broken.

Without hesitation he drags me into his chest. I sprawl across the hard planes of his body, one arm banded around him, the other tracing feather-light touches up and down his arm. The gentleness is so at odds with him it almost undoes me.

He's quiet for a moment, then his deep voice fills the silence. "I like to make things. With my hands. Wood. Iron. Glass."

I blink, my cheek pressed to his chest, listening to the steady thump of his heart.

"I rent a shop not far from here," he continues, his tone a little gruffer now, like he's not used to sharing this. "Some of the furniture in my place—I built it. Those chairs in the living room, the midcentury ones. Took me weeks to get the angles right." He pauses. "Cutting boards are popular too. My mother puts in requests around Christmas—says her friends won't stop asking for them."

The image steadies me—Killian, not with a gun or knife in his hands, but with wood shavings on his shirt, his focus bent on something solid and harmless.

My breathing slows. He notices. His arm tightens around me; his lips brush the side of my head. "It's okay to be upset, Angel."

My throat burns. I want to resist, but the words tumble out anyway. "It was so real. The dream." My voice cracks. "I was on a cold floor... and there was a man sitting in the dark. He had a rose."

I swallow hard. "The petals were white, but the tips... they were dipped in blood."

His body stiffens beneath me, but his hand never stops moving along my arm—steady and grounding.

He doesn't think it's necessarily a bad thing—my dream. Maybe it isn't just fear. Maybe it's memory: pieces of the first encounter with him, the moment he fixated. If I keep poking at it, maybe I'll gather enough fragments to remember who he is, where our paths first crossed, and what he really wants with me.

The thought makes my stomach drop. Chills race down my arms.

Killian's mouth dips lower, kissing a trail over my chest until my nipples pebble beneath his tongue. My back arches, ready to lose myself in him again, but his phone vibrates twice on the nightstand. He groans against my skin.

"That'll be Finn."

He rolls over, grabs the phone, thumb sliding across the screen. I can see the messages when he opens them, clear as day. He makes no effort to hide them. Relief floods me when there's no Candi—no girl with a heart by her name. Just a small circle of people.

His mother. Finn. Lucian.

And Angel.

The name catches me, pins me. He could've saved it for someone else. But deep in my bones, I know it's me.

I throw my leg over his thigh, needing his focus back on

me. His eyes flare dark and molten in an instant. He grabs my chin and crushes his mouth to mine. Even his softest kisses ignite me like kindling, but this one burns hotter, sharper.

"Do you have to go?" I whisper against his lips.

"Yes," he murmurs back, just as quietly. Neither of us wants to break this bubble—because the second he opens that door, he goes back to being my bodyguard, and I go back to being hunted.

His palm strokes down my back, heavy and warm. "Are you sore?"

"Yes." I smile when he growls. "But it feels good."

"Good," he mutters, taking my mouth with more command, biting my lip as he pulls back. "That means I did my job and fucked you properly."

He gets up, stretching, then heads into the bathroom. The tap runs, water rushing into the deep tub. His cock hangs thick and heavy, hard even now, and I can't stop staring. It must be the length of my forearm—a monster between his legs—and I can hardly believe I had the whole thing down my throat last night. My throat aches at the memory, but heat pools low in my belly anyway.

He catches me. Of course he does. He seems to catch everything I do.

"Stop looking at my cock like you want to suck it." His voice is amused, edged with that dark tease.

"But I do," I answer, shameless.

"Fuck, Angel…little killer is what you are." His brogue slips through, just enough to make me shiver. His smile sharpens, wicked. "Then get over here."

He strolls back to the bed, jeans hanging open, no

underwear—his cock free and heavy against the deep V of his hips. A runway straight to sin.

"Crawl over here and tell your bestie goodbye."

The devil's grin curves his lips, and I obey. The covers slide off as I move, back arched, tongue out, mouth open in invitation. He guides his cock between my lips, and I hollow my cheeks, sucking hard as he curses under his breath.

When I pop off, I press a kiss to the cool metal of his piercing, smirking up at him. "Will I be seeing you later?"

His thumb hooks under my chin, tilting my head until his storm-gray eyes pin me in place. "Take a bath. Eat what you want. But—"

"I won't leave," I cut in.

His smirk deepens, approval rumbling in his chest. "Good girl." He tucks himself back into his jeans, zipping them up. "When I get back, I'll take you to your penthouse."

A weight lifts from my shoulders. "Really?"

He pulls on a black tee and a black leather jacket and—fuck—if he doesn't look good.

"Security upgrades are done. No more keeping you prisoner." His mouth quirks, but there's something behind it—like he'd rather keep me locked in here, in his bed, for just a little longer.

"Take a bath. Eat some breakfast. Be good."

The command lingers after he walks away, heat pooling low as I realize I want nothing more than to obey.

Chapter 22
Killian

Seraphina's body is burned behind my eyelids every time I blink: the arch of her spine, her head thrown back, the sound of her voice breaking as she moaned my name. The way her fingers teased herself raw, soaking me every time she shattered.

I made her come until she was trembling, until she drenched me, until my bed was ruined in her pleasure and my cock refused to work anymore.

And still, it doesn't feel like enough.

But I've got to push that back—lock it down. Especially where Finn and I are headed.

Irish territory.

We've passed through before—you can't walk two blocks in this city without brushing up against their grip— but this is different. This is the heart, the epicenter: where the leaders live and breathe the business, where the enterprise spreads out like veins of poison, and where my brother sits like a king on a throne.

The kind of place I swore I'd never set foot in again.

Nora meets us in the back of a narrow bar, tucked away where the noise won't travel. She doesn't waste time, ushering in a skinny kid who looks like he hasn't slept since birth, his apron still damp from dishwater.

"Go on, then," Nora says, giving him a push forward.

He wrings his hands, glancing between me and Finn like he's about to be gutted.

Finn softens his voice just enough. "Nothin' will happen to you, lad. Just tell us what you saw."

The boy swallows, eyes darting between the three of us. "I don't want trouble with Cormac," he blurts, voice cracking. "If he finds out I talked to you—"

I cut him off, my tone low and final. "My brother won't hear a word of this. He's not part of it. This isn't an Irish problem."

The relief on his face is faint but enough to keep him talking.

The kid swallows before he cuts into it. "It was during the trainin' last night. Ledger crew of servers bein' trained for the Masquerade. Nothin' unusual there—they were expected. But...there was one man with them. A late add-on. His name wasn't on the roster."

My jaw tightens. "And no one questioned it?"

The kid shakes his head quickly. "He acted like he belonged. Just sat there in the back, quiet as anything. Didn't talk, didn't move much, just watched."

"Watched who?" I snap.

The boy's eyes dart up, then drop back to the floor. "Not the girls. That's the odd part. He didn't so much as look at them. Just sat there, watchin' the other servers until it was time to go out on the floor."

My jaw tightens. "And?"

"He never picked up a tray. Not once. I noticed because the rest of us were runnin' like dogs all night, sweatin' to keep up. But him? He just sat out on the floor a bit, hat pulled low, phone out like he was recordin' somethin'. Then he was gone. Didn't see him again the rest of the night."

Finn leans forward, his tone low but firm. "Anything else stick out?"

The kid hesitates, then nods. "Aye. His eyes. One brown, one blue. He looked right at me before he left." The boy shudders. "Creeped me out somethin' fierce."

Finn and I lock eyes, and it's all we need: no words. It was him. The kid saw his face—clear as day. Until now, the only person who's ever laid eyes on the bastard was Seraphina, and she doesn't remember enough to point him out.

I lean in. "Think you could sit with someone, go through a description? Help us sketch him out?"

The boy nods quickly. "Aye. But I've gotta be back at the club by eight. Next trainin' shift."

That grates. "Why're you workin' for Lucian? Cormac finally easin' up on the Italians?"

The kid scoffs, shaking his head. "You know he'll never do tha'. I got myself in a way, and Lucian helped me out. Said I could work it off. Club's out of Irish territory, so Cormac hasn't out—"

"Yet," Nora says.

I think a minute, then nod. Some of this heat is my fault

—my fault and Lucian's. I know my brother will carry the grudge for years. The Irish will keep coming for the Italians until they are satisfied they've paid in blood.

This kid doesn't need to be wrapped up in that.

Had I not killed my cousin—pushed my brother onto the Irish throne early—things wouldn't be like this.

"If you get in a way again, you come to me first."

The boy swallows, nodding. "Aye. I will."

"Good lad." Finn ruffles his hair. "Let us go out the back first, then give us a few minutes before ya head out."

Finn and I turn to leave, but the kid calls after me. "Oy, Kill…schools were better when you were here, y'know. Fuckin' all the teachers an' such."

Finn barks a laugh so loud it rattles the glasses behind the bar.

Nora cuffs the kid upside the head. "Watch your feckin' mouth or I'll tell yer mother what you're up to."

He rubs the spot, grinning like a devil. "It's true, though. Things were better when Kill was here. Just…don't tell Cormac I said so."

Finn and I slip out the back, the air sharp as knives, my mind turning over what the boy gave us: one brown eye, one blue. A ghost who doesn't carry trays, doesn't belong, leaves no trace but a camera feed.

Finn mutters low as we cut down the alley. "Could be one of the Italians. Could be some rogue client who thinks he's owed. Could be—"

"Could be anyone," I finish, jaw tight. "That's the problem. He's hidin' in plain sight. And if he was bold enough to walk into a Ledger trainin', he's—"

Before I can finish, two black cars screech to a stop, boxing us in. Doors open, men spill out, and the weight in my gut tells me who it is before he even steps into the light.

Cormac.

My brother.

He doesn't rush. He strolls, hands in his pockets, his men fanned wide. His smirk is the same one he wore at sixteen when he cut his first throat—when he realized he liked it.

"Well, well," he drawls, Irish lilt sharp as a blade. "Look what crawled back onto Irish soil. Didn't think we'd see the O'Malley family's shame in this part of town. Sorry, it's Shaw now, right?"

My brother looks just like me: a few inches shorter, not as thick. Where I have a short beard, he's clean shaven. It somehow makes him look more sadistic and vulnerable at the same time.

I don't move. "I'm not here for you, Cormac."

"You're not supposed to be here at all." His smirk curdles. "Lucian's dog, sniffin' round territory that doesn't belong to him."

My hand twitches toward my knife, but I don't pull. I don't need to. My silence is enough, and Finn's steady at my side—a shadow with teeth.

Then the bar door bangs open, and the kid steps out. He freezes the second he sees the cars, the guns. He should have waited longer before leaving.

"Shit," I mutter under my breath and shift, blocking him from Cormac's view. "He's not part of this. Just a kid leaving his job."

Cormac tilts his head, eyes narrowing. His men twitch, hungry for an excuse.

"Let him walk," I say, voice low but hard.

For a beat, the air hums, sharp with the weight of choice. Then Cormac chuckles—mean and humorless. "Still got that soft spot for kids, do you? Thought I beat that out of you years ago."

The kid pats my shoulder twice and slips away, bolting down the alley while I keep my eyes locked on my brother.

Cormac circles me, slow, like he's sizing up prey. He's younger, but his eyes are old with rot.

"What are you here for?" he asks.

"None of your business," I say flatly.

His smirk widens. "And what if I make it my business?"

I square up, my voice a razor's edge. "Then it'll be the last decision you make, little brother."

The chuckle that leaves him is humorless. His men tense, hands twitching like they're waiting for a signal.

Cormac lifts his hand, shapes his fingers into a gun, and closes one eye like he's sighting down a barrel. He clicks his tongue, mimics a recoil, aiming straight at my head.

"Mind your days, Kill. You've a debt to repay. A big one. Killing our own cousin is going to cost you," he spits on the ground, "and your Italian handler."

I take one step closer, close enough that he has to tilt his chin up to meet my eyes. "Funny thing about debts, little brother—they only matter if I let you live long enough to collect."

I hold my brother's stare a moment longer than appropriate so he will be sure to feel the weight of those words.

"Enjoy sitting at the head of the table, Cormac, and remember—you're only sitting there because I walked away." I take a measured step back and Finn does too.

His gaze flicks down, landing on my thigh. A dark chuckle rolls out of him. "Still carryin' it, eh?" His chin jerks toward the strap. "The knife our father gifted us."

My hand brushes the hilt—casual, deliberate. "Yeah. Difference is, I know how to use mine."

His men stiffen, hands twitching at their jackets, but Cormac only smiles wider—sharp and thin.

I'm done here.

We turn; Finn slides into the driver's seat as I drop into the passenger. The engine roars, and as we pull away I catch my brother in the sideview mirror.

Cormac stands in the street, hands loose at his sides, that wolf's grin carved into his face—watching. And I know if I were to come back, he would still be waiting.

There's nothing like being back home.

Killian picked me up before lunch and drove me straight here, to the sanctuary of my penthouse. The second the door closed behind us, I let out a long, grounding breath and wandered down the hall. My bedroom felt like a waiting embrace, and I didn't resist. I collapsed backward onto the bed, limbs sprawled, eyes closing for just a second as I sank into the moment.

I didn't even hear him follow, but then—

A low chuckle rumbles from the doorway, deep enough to vibrate straight through me. "My apartment really that bad?" His leather jacket is slung over one shoulder as he leans against the frame.

I push up onto my elbows with a smile. "No."

If anything, his apartment now carries some very fond memories. My smile lingers as I stand and make my way toward him, hips swaying in a way I don't bother disguising. His eyes track me like a predator—slow, deliberate, hungry.

I tilt my chin up when I reach him, craning my neck to meet his stare.

But my expression sobers before I can stop it.

"Killian—what are we doing?"

Heat flickers in his gaze, the kind that makes my pulse jump.

"Who says we have to be doing anything?"

The words land sharp. I know what he means. The sex. He's drawing a line in the sand before I can, telling me not to expect more than what's already happened. Maybe because he's the one escorting me to dates as I hunt for a husband to contract. Maybe because Killian doesn't do anything else but fuck.

It should be the right thing. Keeping it casual. No complications.

The actual right thing would be to fire him—to assign a new bodyguard and stop thinking about his tongue, his pierced cock, the way his control shatters when he lets go. But it's too late for that. I've had a taste. And now I know what it's like when Killian unravels me.

"So…just sex, then?" My voice is soft, but my throat is tight. "It doesn't have to mean anything?"

His arm snakes around my waist, pulling me flush against the hard wall of his chest.

"It doesn't have to mean anything," he murmurs, voice rough enough to scrape—and it sounds like a lie. Or maybe that's just what I want it to sound like.

The heat of him is instant, searing through my clothes, leaving me unsteady.

"We'll walk away when I find a suitor?" I whisper, as

though saying it out loud makes it easier. "No complications?"

I swear I feel his fingers flex against my hip at that, his jaw hardening like he's grinding the words between his teeth.

"None," he says finally.

His mouth claims mine before I can think better of it—hot, wet, consuming. His tongue slides against mine, demanding, and I moan helplessly into the kiss.

Then a sharp vibration rattles between us.

I jolt with a startled yelp, realizing it's his phone pressed between our bodies. He grins against my mouth, amused at my reaction, before pulling the device from his pocket.

The screen lights up: Jaxon Kane.

Killian swipes his thumb across the screen, bringing the phone to his ear.

"Shaw."

A long, exaggerated smooch noise echoes through the speaker.

"Sorry to break up make-out time."

Killian's face hardens, all sharp lines and fury. His grip on my hip tightens until I feel the bruise forming. "If you're watching her cameras right now, I'll put a bullet through your eyes myself."

I gape, heat rushing up my neck.

My mouth works soundlessly before I manage to get out, "Excuse me? I did not sign up to be some goddamn reality show on display."

Jaxon's laugh filters through, dry and careless. "Relax, princess. I'm not a perv. Just making sure the new system is actually doing its job since you two finally made it back."

I roll my eyes, looking around, trying to spot where the cameras are.

"And don't worry, I'll keep your little forbidden affair between us girls."

My phone buzzes with a text from Stasia—a reminder about Aurora's birthday party. The gifts I bought arrived, wrapped beautifully, and Ro instantly started shaking them.

The normalcy in all this chaos makes me smile.

Killian, however, doesn't smile. His jaw flexes once, twice. "What do you want, Jaxon?"

"Grumpy! Sheesh." There's a lot of typing. "The kid gave me a composite of your stalker. I'm running it through every facial-recognition system I can bend to my will. But it's gonna take time—a day, maybe two."

Killian lowers the phone and pins me with that searing stare. "You want to see it?"

Every instinct screams no. To hide. Pretend none of this exists. But that's not an option anymore. My throat bobs as I nod, making my way out of my room and toward the kitchen. "Yeah. I need to."

Following me, Killian lifts the phone back to his ear. "Send it."

"Already did," Jaxon says, and then his voice is muffled like he's eating something. "There's more. No scrambler last night, so I got him on the cameras. Not his face, though. He knew he would be recorded—kept his head down, hat pulled low. But...I caught some warped reflections when he moved through the kitchen. I'll see what I can do with them and add them to the composite."

No scrambler.

My stomach knots, icy realization washing through me. "Maybe he didn't have time to prep. He wasn't ready for last night."

"Bingo," Jaxon says, mouth even more full of food than before.

"Just what I was thinking," Killian adds.

There's a knock at my door, and the guard opens it, letting Eve in with Finn trailing behind her. She raises her eyebrows in greeting.

Jaxon mumbles, "Mmm, so good." He's literally licking his fingers clean on the other end of the line. Like—Christ almighty—I'm running for my life and he's chowing down on something.

"What the fuck are you eating?" Killian bites out, like it's been bothering him too.

"The world's best fucking chocolate chip cookies. Freshly baked by my future wife." He kisses someone on the other end. Eve makes a big show of rolling her eyes.

"Okay, I need to go smear melted chocolate on someone and then lick it off."

"Fucking Christ, Jax," Eve blurts out. "Could've died happy never hearing that."

"Hey," he bites back—their friendly banter always entertaining. "I had to hear about your fucking nipple piercings. I will never be the same."

Someone laughs, and the phone muffles again. "Gotta go." The call ends, and we fill Eve in on the news. A peek at

Killian's phone and I smirk. He's looking at chocolate chip–cookie recipes.

He catches me, and I bump his shoulder with mine.

"Cookies sounding good?" I ask, already heading to the cabinet to pull the ingredients. I have a recipe memorized because Stasia and I make them all the time for the kids.

"I'm always ready to eat."

His voice is deeper, and I blush at the double meaning—which he totally intended. If Eve caught it, she doesn't let on.

"What was different about last night? Why hadn't he been ready?" I ask, my voice cracking as I measure out flour and brown sugar while my heated skin cools.

"Hmm." Eve taps a long red nail on her lip. "Nothing out of the usual." She sits at one of the barstools as I begin scooping cookies onto baking pans. Killian steals a chocolate morsel from the edge of the bowl, and I smack his hand.

"I looked up a few places, made a few calls, and sent the details to Barrett."

Killian bristles at the mention of last night's date.

"Why didn't you send it through the Ledger app?" Killian asks. That's right: all the suitors are already Ledger clients. They have their own profiles, and all scheduling goes through the app.

"I was on the go, okay! Elena called and needed me to taste-test some cheesecake. It was an emergency." Elena is Eve's best friend and former Ledger companion—retired, snagged her billionaire, and now runs an up-and-coming cheesecakery. I can't imagine a tasting being an emergency.

I think on it a moment. "So, you didn't put it into the

app yet? That's it, then." My voice is hopeful, but I don't know what this will do to help us. "When did you submit the location to the app?"

"About thirty minutes before you were scheduled to arrive."

"It has to be someone accessing the app." Killian's fingers fly across his phone, sharp and precise, like every keystroke is a weapon. "Sent it to Jaxon. We'll see if he can work this into his facial scan and find out who accessed the app around that time last night," he mutters, no-nonsense.

The next knock at my door isn't one guard but a flood. Ledger security files in—a dark wave of suits and weapons —and suddenly my penthouse feels less like a home and more like a fortress. There's a low hum of conversation that falls nearly silent when I pull the first pan of cookies out of the oven. Instantly every pair of eyes in the kitchen swivels toward me like bloodthirsty wolves.

I realize too late—I should've doubled the batch. Maybe tripled.

They're gone in seconds—hands darting in, voices gruff but amused, like men at war suddenly reduced to a pack of overgrown kids.

Killian's voice cuts low from the corner, where he's talking with Finn at the edge of the kitchen. His jacket finds itself hung on one of the chair backs. I glance up just in time to see him turn, only to find the pans already picked clean.

The drop of his shoulders and the look on his face nearly make me laugh. Adorable, even. Except he's trying very hard to cover the disappointment—jaw flexing, eyes narrowing —like he's just been robbed at knifepoint.

He clears his throat. "Jaxon said no major app usage last night, aside from a few clients that don't match the profile and the janitors changing shifts."

Finn claps his hands, calling the team to the living room to show off the latest security upgrades. Killian follows, still glaring daggers at one of the guys who has the audacity to be chewing the last cookie.

I can't help the smirk tugging at my mouth as I reach for the flour again, setting to work on another batch.

"Men," Eve mutters, swirling her wine and rolling her eyes. "Nothing but big babies."

The second batch is finished right as the briefing winds down. The men shuffle through the kitchen like a parade of giants, each one snagging a cookie or two in salute before disappearing out the door.

A few linger—Finn among them—and of course he's the one to swipe the very last cookie from the tray.

Right on time, Killian strides back in. His eyes drop to the island, scanning the tray for what's left. Crumbs. Chocolate smudges. Nothing more.

His hand twitches near the handle of his knife.

Finn lifts the cookie halfway to his mouth, then freezes. "You really gonna stab me over a cookie, Shaw?"

Killian's voice is flat, edged with that lethal calm. "I was thinkin' about it."

A laugh bursts out of me before I can stop it. "Thank goodness we don't need to do that."

I turn, grab the smaller pan cooling behind me, and slide it across the island right in front of him. "Just for you, big man."

I pat his solid chest twice, my fingertips tingling even through his shirt. His mouth curves, slow and dangerous, but it's a smirk all the same as he looks down at his private stash of cookies.

I slip past him, heading down the hall to meet with Eve in my bedroom, and from behind me I hear the low ripple of snickers and a very distinct, very shushed "ooooh."

Killian's quiet warning follows, dark and amused. "You can still get stabbed."

Finn doesn't miss a beat. "Wish I got my own pan of cookies made special just for me."

"I'm sure Nora can help you with that."

Inside my room with Eve, I can't stop smiling while we hatch a plan to try and catch a stalker.

Chapter 24
Killian

We're probably not going to get lucky twice in a row, but we'll try.

The girls planned another suitor date, keeping things as normal as possible. No sudden changes, no tipoffs to make the bastard stalker think we're closing in.

Still, I'll admit it—there's a sting knowing she's going out again. Another man, another pointless dinner. I tell myself it's for the job, for the purpose of luring the stalker out into the open. That sooner or later she'll change her mind about this final-contract business.

Because despite what I told her in that doorway—despite what she thinks—I've got no intention of letting this remain casual. It's not just sex. Not for me.

It's a claiming.

Taking what's belonged to me for a long damn time now.

A year at least. Fuck—longer, if I'm honest. Since the

first day I laid eyes on her when I joined the Ledger. She was just leaving the hospital then—done with long nights and the steady drip of blood and death. She and her twin had been nurses for a few years, but the Ledger won out in the end. The money, the security…was too good. And maybe she already knew she wasn't built to watch people die anymore.

Now she sits across from men who'll never deserve her, while I stand at her shoulder pretending I'm not one breath away from tearing their throats out.

Tonight's date is at the movies—Jaxon's idea because of the cameras that monitor the audience. Creepy as hell when you think about it—rows of faces staring blankly into the dark. But creepy works for us.

Tonight goes one of two ways.

The stalker shows with his scrambler again, and Jaxon traces the signal. We find him. End of story.

Or he leaves the scrambler at home again, and the cameras catch him. Jaxon's got his facial-recognition system primed, ready to scan every seat in that theater.

Either way, we'll get him tonight.

Finn rides up front with Felix—old man's been driving for the Ledger longer than I've been alive, or close enough. Reliable as stone.

I'm in the back with Sera. She's wound tight, nervous in the way she won't quite settle against the seat.

She holds a breath, then releases it, like she's letting go of a thought with it. She seems to change her mind, because she blurts, "I'd like to go to my niece's birthday party—"

I nod, already knowing. "I'm workin' it out."

She nods at that, relieved, and looks at her lap.

"I'll make sure you get there, angel."

She smiles—more genuine now—but it's laced with anxiety about tonight, and I remember: she hasn't looked at the rendering of the stalker yet.

"You want to see that picture Jaxon sent over?" I ask, voice low. "Might help."

She hesitates, then nods. I hand her my phone, the composite already pulled up.

She studies it. Long. Silent. Her eyes narrow just a fraction, like she's digging through old memories, trying to see if this face ever brushed against hers. After a minute she exhales and shakes her head, giving the phone back.

"Maybe it'll jog somethin' later," I tell her.

"Maybe."

I watch her. She turns her head toward the window, picking at her nail. She feels my stare and, after a moment, her gaze comes back to mine. A second passes. Then her expression shifts—less nerves, more...something else.

Intrigued.

My eyes drop to her mouth—pink gloss catching the low light, her full bottom lip begging. I can already feel her lips around my cock, wet heat swallowing me whole.

She runs her tongue across her bottom lip. Fuck.

"You seem nervous," I say, my voice heavier than it should be. My cock's thickening in my slacks, no chance of hiding it now.

"Maybe I am," she breathes.

My gaze doesn't move. "You want a distraction, little killer?"

Her grin is pure sin—like a siren calling me straight to the rocks.

"Maybe I do."

She slips off the seat, onto her knees on the limo floor, and crawls toward me. The hem of her miniskirt rides up, baring more of her thighs. If I were behind her, I know I'd see the soft mound of her pussy outlined in panties. I wonder what color she put on for me tonight. Wonder if she's already wet.

She kneels between my spread legs, hands gliding up my thighs, slow and teasing.

"I could use something to take my mind off things, big man."

Then her palm presses against the length of my cock. It throbs at her touch, straining against the fabric.

After every way I fucked her last night, she's still starving for more.

What a perfect fucking angel she is for a bastard like me.

"Take my cock out."

She does it without a word. No rush—traffic's thick tonight, plenty of time. She unzips my pants, and I lift my hips just enough to help her drag them down. She reaches under the band of my boxers and frees me—cock and balls heavy in her hands.

Her eyes lock on them like they're the key to the universe.

Pre-cum beads at the tip, and still she just looks—hunger written in every line of her face.

"Fuck, angel," I rasp, my hand sliding into her hair. "I could come just from you lookin' at my dick like that."

Her fingers curl around the base of my length—warm and sure—and she leans forward to lick across the head. Her tongue flicks over the piercing, making me hiss through my teeth when she gives it a little tug. That ring has never felt like this before—not until her mouth.

"Open for me, baby," I murmur, hands on each side of her head. "Let me see you take it."

She parts her lips and slides down over me—slow and steady—until the wet heat of her throat seals tight around the piercing and the thickest part of my cock. No struggle. No gag. Just her swallowing me whole like she was fuckin' designed for it.

Christ.

I look down and almost lose it—her lips stretched wide, gloss smeared across the corners, spit slicking my shaft. My cock disappears into her throat like it belongs there.

"Fuck, angel," I groan, tightening my grip in her hair. "You take every inch like you've been waitin' your whole life for this dick."

Her eyes flick up to mine—wicked—confirming it without a word. And then she moans, the sound vibrating around my cock, rattling all the way through my spine.

"Shit."

She pulls back slow, lips dragging over every ridge, tongue teasing the piercing as she retreats, leaving my shaft glistening with spit. Then she swallows me again, all the way down, her nose brushing my stomach as she hums like it's nothing. Like she can do this all fuckin' night.

"Oh my God, baby," I groan, my head falling back for a second before I drag my gaze down to watch. "You feel how the head's rubbin' against the roof of your mouth? How soft your throat is when you take me all the way down?"

Her throat flexes around me, swallowing me deeper, and I can't hold back the low moan that rumbles out of me.

"Good girl," I murmur—calm but filthy—fingers flexing in her hair. "So fuckin' good. Takin' me like you've trained that perfect mouth for this. Like you wanted to choke on me long before you ever got on your knees."

Her eyes glisten as she looks up, lips stretched wide, spit rolling down her chin.

"Look at you," I rasp, thrusting just enough for her to feel the weight of me against her tongue. "Makin' a mess all over yourself just to please me. My messy little killer. My cock-drunk angel."

I moan again when she slides back and down, her tongue flicking the piercing—sending shocks straight through my spine. My thighs tense. My balls draw tight.

"Fuck. You're so perfect like this. On your knees. Throat wide open. You were built to take this cock, weren't you?"

Her hum around me is the only answer I need.

"Slow down—yeah, right there. Suck just the head, let your tongue work the piercing."

I can't stop watching. Can't look anywhere else but down at my cock sliding in and out of her perfect mouth. The sight's enough to tear me apart.

"Good girl," I rasp, thrusting gently up into her, watching her throat flex around me. "My perfect little killer. Look at you—you're droolin' all over yourself—pathetic little thing—and I've never seen anything more perfect."

She pulls back with a wet pop, only to lick down the

length of me, tongue swirling over my balls, tracing the piercing again like she wants me feral. Then her mouth is back on me, hungry now, bobbing faster, her hand twisting where her lips don't reach, spit running freely down her wrist.

"Pulse around me—fuck, yes—squeeze my cock with that throat." She's workin' me to the best fuckin' blowjob I've ever had in my life, and I don't want it to end. But just the thought of spilling into her mouth is making my tip leak in anticipation.

"Fuck, baby. So good." I hold her hair back, obsessed with watching her as I thrust with her movements. "Faster now. Make it sloppy. I want to hear how desperate you are for it."

She moans, her thighs tensing like this is gettin' her off.

But my little killer is going to get so many good rewards tonight after her date.

"Keep lookin' up at me while you choke on it. Let me see those pretty eyes while I fuck your throat."

Those deep-blue oceans open and pierce me, locking me to the pull of her gravity. My thighs tense, my stomach tight, the orgasm building hard and fast.

"No one else gets this, baby. No one else could handle this cock but you, hm?"

She hums like she's answerin' me, and it vibrates along my shaft. I dip my head back, closing my eyes to just feel her before I look at her again—so close to coming.

"You thirsty for my cum, whore?" I stroke her jaw, and her eyes roll back in her head. "Yeah, you are. Because you're my good girl."

She whimpers this time.

"I don't want you to swallow it," I growl, possessive, every word jagged as I fist her hair. "Don't waste a drop. You hold my cum in your mouth for me, angel. I want to see it on your tongue."

Her hum wraps around my cock like a fist, and I can't hold it back anymore. My balls draw tight, my thighs lock, and I empty myself into her mouth.

"Fuck—fuck, angel," I groan, head tipping back, the muscles in my stomach clenching as I spill. The piercing drags against her tongue with every pulse—sharper, dirtier—wringing more out of me than I thought I had, and she takes it all, lips sealed, careful not to let a single drop escape.

It's almost too much—her throat flexing, her tongue still teasing as she holds me deep. I twitch inside her, every nerve lit up, every thought burned away except mine.

When the last pulse fades, she slides off me slow—lips glistening, eyes heavy and shining like sin.

"Open," I rasp.

She parts her lips, tilting her head back so I can see it—my cum pooled on her tongue, thick and white against the pink.

"Fuckin' beautiful," I whisper, swiping my thumb across her wet lip before sliding it inside.

"Not a drop," I remind her.

Her lips seal around my thumb, sucking it clean as I pull free. The sight alone makes my cock twitch again, already aching to get hard for her all over.

My hand shifts to her throat—not enough to cut off her air, but enough that I feel her pulse jump beneath my palm.

"Swallow."

Her throat works around the command, muscles tightening under my grip. I feel her gulp it all down—every last drop sliding past my hand.

"Good girl," I breathe, voice rough with satisfaction. "My good fuckin' girl."

Chapter 25

Seraphina

I've never almost come from giving a blowjob. Not without touching myself.

But with Killian—his cock in my mouth, his filthy words, the way I made him feel—I almost did.

God, I wanted to so badly.

He doesn't even wipe himself off. Just slips his cock, still hard and slick from my mouth, back into his pants and zips them. A tug of his shirt, a shift of his shoulders, and within seconds he looks like nothing happened. Untouchable. Controlled. While I'm a mess on my knees, panting, my lips swollen, my thighs pressed tight together because I'm dripping for him.

"Come here, baby." His voice is low—a command more than an invitation.

I'm half pulled, half climbing onto his lap. The moment I straddle him, his hands clamp to my hips, grinding me down against his cock beneath his slacks.

"You felt so fucking good," he growls, claiming my mouth in a kiss that's all tongue and teeth and possession.

The friction nearly undoes me. I could come so fast if he let me move how I want. I know how wet I am—I know I'm about to ruin his pants. And he knows it too.

"You want to keep being my good girl tonight? On your date?"

I nod, breathless.

"While you pretend you want these fucks you're courting?" His tone sharpens with anger, and the sound makes me gush harder, heat flooding between my legs.

"Yes," I pant against his mouth.

"You want me to make you come so hard you'll think about it the rest of your life?"

"Please, Killian."

I'm desperate now, grinding slow because he won't let me go faster, won't let me hump him the way I need. His grip is iron, controlling every roll of my hips, every brush of my clit against his cock. He's killing me with restraint.

The limo turns, slowing as it pulls into the movie theater lot.

"When you're on your date tonight," he murmurs, nipping my lip—slipping into that Irish brogue that undoes me. "I want you to kiss him."

I freeze. "Kiss him?"

"Kiss him, baby." His gray eyes are darker now, storms I can't escape. "Kiss him and let him taste my cum on your tongue."

A broken whimper tears out of me at the thought—how dirty, how wicked it is.

"Let him get a taste of what he'll never have." His hips grind harder, a slow press that makes my clit throb, and I know—he's going to leave me on this high. He's not giving me the release I want.

"Let him taste what belongs to me."

He rests his forehead against mine, his voice softer but no less dangerous. "Will you do that for me, angel?"

The car slows to the curb. My heart pounds. My pussy clenches. And I nod. "Yes."

His mouth curves into a wicked smirk as he stops my hips dead. The sudden loss of friction makes me ache, my clit pulsing, my body begging.

His gaze drops between my legs, a finger lifting my skirt just enough to give him a view of what's beneath. My pale-pink panties are soaked, nearly transparent with how wet I am. The groan that rumbles out of him is raw, reverent.

"Gorgeous," he whispers—just like he did when he was looking at his cum in my mouth.

He slides a finger beneath the damp fabric, stroking between the lips of my cunt. When his nail flicks my clit, I jolt, crying out as a surge of an orgasm threatens to crash— only to fizzle when he pulls away.

My entire body trembles, desperate, needy.

He slips the finger into his mouth, sucking it clean with a satisfied hum.

"Let's go."

The limo door opens, and the humid night air hits me as I step out—aching and damp—Killian's words echoing in my skull. Kiss him. Let him taste what belongs to me.

My date waits outside the theater, bouquet in hand. I'm just able to apply a fresh swipe of pink gloss to my lips—still tingling from Killian's dick—when he smiles politely. Says my name with the kind of reverence men use when they think they're winning something. He doesn't matter in tonight's game. I thank him, take the flowers, and slip my arm through his.

Inside, he orders us drinks—some overpriced sparkling cocktail that tastes like syrup—and we sit in the dim glow of the lobby bar. He talks: about work, about stocks, about whatever the hell he thinks will impress me. I smile when I need to, nod at the right times, my hands folded neatly in my lap.

But every so often, my eyes wander. To him.

To Killian.

Standing at the edge of the crowd like a shadow come to life. His gaze sweeps the theater, cataloging every face, every movement—the watchful guard. And then—he looks at me.

It's like being struck. My breath stalls, my pulse leaps, and his promises are there, swimming in his eyes. Mine. Good girl. Kiss him with my cum still on your tongue.

By the time we file into the theater, the previews are about to start. My date guides me to our seats, his hand lingering a second too long at my waist.

The lights dim. The room hushes. The first trailers roll.

He leans in close, whispering a comment against my ear. His arm brushes mine, testing—casual but deliberate. I nod, smile politely, though my mind is elsewhere—tracking every subtle shift in the dark. Killian's outline a few rows back against the wall, posture coiled, eyes fixed. Not on the screen. Not on anyone else. Me. Always me.

Halfway through the film, a couple kisses on the screen. Sweet. Predictable. A cue.

My date has been trying to figure out the right time to break the touch barrier, so it's the perfect opportunity to do it for him.

I turn my head, touch my date's jaw with my fingers, guiding him to face me. My lips brush his first—soft, grazing—before I open for him. His tongue meets mine, eager, greedy.

But my eyes are on Killian.

He's watching. And when our gazes lock, I slide my tongue into my date's mouth, and I nearly come undone. Killian's irises are so blown they look black, pupils swallowing the steel gray I know so well. His mouth curves, slow and feral, into a smirk that makes heat pulse low in my belly.

Approval. Possession. Pleased with me.

And I realize why. Because he said they'd know I belonged to him. And by kissing my date—just like Killian wanted, the taste of his cock lingering—I've made that true. I'm saying I do belong to him.

The movie winds down, some sweeping finale I barely register. I'm too aware of myself, of my shadow watching over me. For the millionth time tonight, I peek back at Killian.

He's standing attentive now, one hand pressed to his ear. Communicating with Finn, Jaxon, or one of the other guards, no doubt. Business as usual.

But it strikes me that his plan worked almost too well—

he distracted me so completely I almost forgot why we were here in the first place.

The stalker.

A shiver runs through me. Is he here? Watching? Sitting somewhere in this dark theater, eyes pinned to me?

As if he hears my thought, Killian's gaze cuts to mine. He gives his head a slow shake, deliberate. No. He didn't show.

Relief crashes into me, loosening my chest. But disappointment lingers too—sharp and unwelcome. I want this over. I want him caught. I want to move on.

The lights rise, and people stand, gathering jackets and empty popcorn tubs. My date turns toward me, lips parting like he's about to ask if I'd like to grab a bite to eat, but he doesn't get the chance.

Killian is suddenly there, looming, every inch the professional bodyguard. "It's time for her to go." His voice is calm, clipped. Business.

But when his eyes slice to mine, there's nothing professional about it. They're feral, wild, still echoing with the promises he made in the back of the limo.

He leads me through the crowd without hesitation, a hand at my back that burns through my dress, steering me down a side hallway and out a service door. We spill into the cool night air of an alley, the scent of damp asphalt rising around us.

And then he's on me.

My back slams against the wall, his body pinning mine, his mouth devouring me. All command, no patience—his kiss demanding everything I have left to give. His weight presses me harder into the bricks, his cock thick and unrelenting against my belly through his slacks.

The world shrinks to nothing but him—his taste, his heat, his promise finally snapping its leash.

His thigh wedges between mine, hard muscle pressing up against me, and I can't stop myself—I grind down on it. Desperate. Starving.

A growl rumbles from his chest. His mouth drags to my ear, voice a dark snarl. "Such a fucking slut. You'll use anything to come, won't you?"

"Yes," I whine, hips rolling against him shamelessly. "Yes."

I don't even see him move, but suddenly his knife is in his hand, the glint of steel catching the alley's dim light. My heart stutters, heat flooding me. He slices through my panties with a quick flick, the fabric giving way like nothing. He tucks the ruined lace into his pocket—souvenirs, just like before.

The flat of the hilt brushes my bare slit, and I gasp, thighs trembling.

"Look at you," he murmurs, dragging the handle against my clit in slow circles. "So wet, angel, I could fuck you with this handle, couldn't I?"

"Please," I pant, clutching at his shoulders.

"Quiet." His gray eyes cut to mine, razor-sharp. "The car's right there. Guards just on the other side of this wall. You want them to hear you fall apart on my knife?"

The shame, the danger, makes my pussy clench harder.

He strokes the hilt over my clit—steady, relentless. My hips buck, chasing it, my nails digging into his chest through his shirt. I bite my lip, fighting the moans building in my throat.

"Come for me," he whispers, calm and brutal. "Be my good girl and come quiet."

The orgasm tears through me, my body trembling as I smother the sounds against his chest—my clit pulsing against the cool, unforgiving handle. My release soaks him, slicking my thighs, wetting the weapon still pressing against me.

Before I can catch my breath, he shifts the knife, pressing the hilt to my entrance. My eyes fly wide.

"Killian—"

"You can take it," he rasps, propping his booted foot on a ledge so he can sling my leg over his thigh. He spreads my pussy lips with his fingers and watches as he wets the weapon with my juices, then carefully slides the handle inside me, stretching me open with a filthy squelch. "So fucking wet...Christ, you were made for this."

The intrusion is obscene, raw. My body clamps down around it, every nerve ending on fire. He pumps it in and out, fucking me with his weapon, the steel handle coated in my slick.

"Shhh." He clamps his palm over my mouth, eyes burning into mine. "Stay quiet while I ruin you."

I sob against his hand as the second orgasm slams into me—harsher, wilder than the first.

"You're safe with me, baby." My release gushes, dripping down his hand, down my thighs, soaking the alley floor. He works the knife, never letting the blade come close to me. "As long as I'm by your side, I'll never let you get hurt."

He keeps me pinned there, trembling—still stuffed full of his knife—until the aftershocks leave me weak. He gives me a gentle kiss against my temple, such a contrast to what we just did.

Then he slides the knife free, sucks the handle clean, and wipes the slick hilt across my ruined panties before securing both like trophies.

He doesn't give me time to recover. He straightens, grabs my hand, and leads me out of the alley like nothing happened. My legs shake as we approach the waiting car. The guards take to their doors without a word.

Killian opens mine, and when I bend to climb inside, he smacks my bare pussy—sharp and sudden. I yelp, jerking forward, heat blooming across my ass and cunt.

"Good fucking girl," he murmurs behind me, voice dark silk.

Chapter 26
Killian

The sky seems bluer today than I've ever noticed before. Maybe it's because it matches the eyes of a certain angel I can't stop looking at.

"I'll take some of these plates in, and then I need to jump in the shower," Seraphina says, rising from the table on her wide patio. Sunlight cuts over her, gold across her hair.

Lucian showed up this morning with breakfast, wanting to catch up on the stalker developments and check on Sera for himself.

"I got it, lass." Finn's already on his feet, shooing her toward the penthouse before she can lift a finger.

She chuckles, eyes darting to mine for a split second before she turns away.

A thousand words could've been passed in that look. She could've been saying anything.

I know damn well what I'd like her to say.

When I drag my gaze back to the table, Lucian's staring straight at me—espresso cup frozen halfway to his mouth.

"What?" I ask.

His mouth twitches in knowing amusement. "You fucking kidding me. What? You know what."

"It's not what you think it is."

"It's exactly what I think it is," he cuts in, voice flat as steel. "Don't lie. It's been this way for a while now."

I rub my hands down my face, scratching at my beard. Christ. He's not wrong, and that makes it worse.

"You're a fucking idiot," Lucian says, settling back in his chair, eyes cutting into me. "Love's not something men like us usually get. When an angel falls into your lap, you don't shove her away—you hold on."

The words scrape at me, remembering she said something similar in the conference room, the morning she presented this plan for a husband. It's like broken glass in my chest, because I realize she thinks no one would be able to see past her being an escort—how she earned her living. That she can only get what she wants with a contract because she's not worth more.

"I've been tryin' ta tell him," Finn returns, shaking his head.

I snort. "That's rich. Bit of a hypocrite, don't you think? Or do we not speak the name Nora anymore?"

"Exactly my point. I wasted years watching from a distance when I could've had a good woman by my side. Time I'll never get back. Don't make the same mistake."

I look between them, jaw set, every instinct fighting what they're saying. But fuck if it doesn't burrow under my skin.

Lucian tips his head, calm again, like the storm already

passed. "The only rules you're breaking are the ones you've made for yourself, Kill."

Before I can answer, his phone buzzes. He checks the screen, mutters a curse, and answers. His tone sharpens fast—business, not pleasure.

Finn leans toward me while Lucian's distracted. "Last night...why you think the stalker didn't show? You think he figured our plan?"

Lucian ends the call, pocketing his phone with a grim look. "I think I know why. Barrett Hall's demanding a new car. Says his was nearly destroyed. Spray-painted all down the side: 'Ledger whore.' Windows smashed. Tires slashed to shit."

So that's it. He wasn't at the theater because he was busy destroying the car of Sera's last date.

I huff out a dark laugh—no sympathy in me. "Should've torched it for good measure."

Lucian leans back, a smirk tugging at the corner of his mouth. "Careful, brother. You're in deep. Deep enough you're even siding with her stalker—attacking her dates for him."

I bark out a laugh. "Not siding with the bastard. But if Barrett Hall's penthouse happened to go up in smoke, I wouldn't shed a tear. The Irish are quite good with explosives, after all."

I tip my coffee cup at him, and he tips his in return. An amused look passes between us. He knows all too well.

He spent a long night at my side once, wiring a building under construction to blow—along with a parking deck packed with luxury cars owned by crooked politicians.

"Who's blowing up penthouses?" Eve's voice cuts through. She strolls in like she owns the place, immediately plucking a pastry off the tray. Finn's already pouring her a cup of coffee, attentive as ever.

"Unfortunately, no one," I answer dryly.

Sera returns then, hair wrapped in a towel, the scent of soap clinging to her. Since Eve's stolen her seat, she takes the one next to me. Too close. Or maybe not close enough. Neither of us makes a move to shift.

Lucian's tone turns flat. "Your stalker trashed Hall's car last night."

Her mouth falls open, eyes snapping to me. I try to school my expression, but the ghost of a smirk slips free.

She tsks, elbowing me with a whispered, "Behave."

If only she knew what that word does to me.

We both remember the night I came to get her from Barrett Hall's penthouse—the way she pushed, the way I pushed right back until she came apart on my hand, pink-cheeked and gasping in that bathroom. My cock throbs just thinking about it.

Across the table, Eve watches too closely, lips curling when her gaze locks with mine. Mischief lights her stare. "Well, if the stalker didn't show, seems another date is in order."

"No," Sera and I snap at the same time.

Eve grins like a cat that's cornered two birds.

Sera shakes her head. "It doesn't matter if I'm on dates or going to the gym. He tries to get to me. Suitors aren't important anymore."

My heart stutters, then races.

She doesn't elaborate, but I want her to. Christ, I want her to—to say she's abandoning this final-contract nonsense altogether.

But a darker thought gnaws at me: maybe she only means to postpone it until the stalker's dealt with. Maybe I'm just a good fuck—not the man she sees standing at her side for the rest of her life.

The idea cuts deep. Deeper than I want to admit. And I swallow it down like poison.

"We've got a plan for your niece's party." Sera worries about endangering her family, but I've thought of that.

"Finn'll take one of the girls out—blonde, close enough to pass for you from a distance. He'll make sure eyes follow the decoy. Meanwhile, you and I slip out clean. We'll be in Stamford before they've even cut the cake."

She bites her lip, still unsure.

"You can trust us, angel." My voice comes out rougher than I mean it to. "I'm sending two plainclothes guards ahead tonight. They'll blend in, keep an eye on the place. Stay through the party, leave the morning after. No one's laying a hand on your family."

Her shoulders loosen just enough to tell me she believes me. Then she gives me that small, grateful smile that always hits like a punch to the chest.

"Thank you," she says, slipping her hand over mine. She holds it there longer than she should, squeezes once before letting go. Clears her throat and looks away, like the pink rising in her cheeks might give her away.

I drag in a slow breath, because every instinct in me wants to pull her hand back and never let it go.

Eve's been locked in on Sera and me—sharp eyes cutting between every look we've let slip. I know she's putting together what Lucian already has.

Lucian's half distracted, grinning down at his phone in a way that says it's his woman on the other end. Eve catches it too and rolls her eyes. "I'm getting out of here before I lose my appetite for the rest of the day."

Sera pouts faintly. "I wanted a workout buddy."

"You stay, Eve. I'm headed out anyway." I push to my feet, asking Finn, "You can handle point today?"

He nods without hesitation.

"You're leaving?" Sera's disappointment flashes— maybe I'm imagining it. Maybe I'm not. God, I hope not.

"Just some errands. A few hours. Tops." I lean down, bracing my hands on the arms of her chair, forcing her gaze to mine. "You'll stay in the building until I get back?"

She nods, but there's heat in her eyes she doesn't hide fast enough—a silent longing, gone as soon as it shows. Still, it wrecks me.

And there goes my cock, twitching like it has a mind of its own. At this rate, I'll die with a permanent hard-on thanks to this woman.

Finn follows me to the front door. "What errands?"

"The kid called," I mutter. "Think he's into somethin' he's not saying."

Finn's jaw works. "Things are worse for folks than they let on. Cormac's got his boot on everyone's neck. They're scared."

I pin him with a look. "And what exactly do you expect me to do about it?"

His stare lingers, heavy. "You know there's a lot you could do. Might be the only one who can."

I stare off for a moment, weighing too many thoughts I don't want to voice, then decide not to push. "You give Nora a call yet?" I ask, tone coy, knowing Finn's long kept that particular desire tucked away.

He smirks like the devil with a secret. "Might have."

Kicks his feet, shoves his hands in his pockets. "Takin' her out day after tomorrow."

A grin tugs at me—sharp but genuine. "Good man." I clap him on the shoulder.

Then I blow out a sharp breath and yank the door open. "Irish problems aren't mine anymore."

Finn's voice follows me into the hall, low and steady. "You might not get to keep tellin' yourself those lies forever."

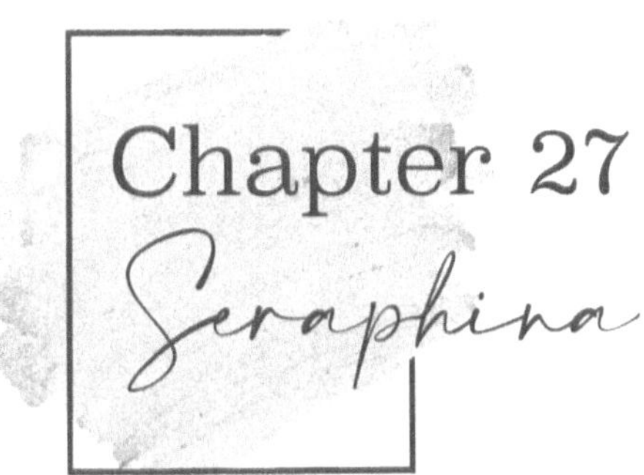

It's been more than a few hours, and normally I'd start to think something was wrong. But Killian's texted me a few times—checking in, letting me know where he is. I appreciate it more than I'll admit out loud: the reassurance, the breadcrumbs he leaves, each one closer and closer to his return.

The last ping was a picture of a little bakery I love, with a question: The pistachio macarons still your current obsession?

The way he notices makes me smile.

> SERAPHINA: I wouldn't say no to a lavender one also

I text back.

When he doesn't reply right away, I add:

> SERAPHINA: If you want to get back into the penthouse, I demand payment in macarons.

I hesitate, then bite my lip, fingers flying faster than my brain: I'll take a slutty selfie in substitute.

I send it before I can erase it. My stomach flips. I know exactly what I'm doing—flirting with him. I also know I shouldn't. I'm the one who started this whole suitor mess, after all.

But when I told them the suitors didn't matter anymore, I meant it. Not just because of the stalker.

Because my Irish giant has crowded every corner of my mind. There's no room left for anyone else.

A new bubble pops up on my screen.

KILLIAN: Are you objectifying me?

SERAPHINA: Hell yes

I type back, grinning like an idiot.

SERAPHINA: Show me something, big man.

My cheeks burn even though I'm alone in the penthouse. Finn's stationed quietly outside the door for another hour until the night guard comes to relieve him, but it still feels like someone might see what I just sent.

A minute later, my phone pings.

Killian in a bathroom. Looks like the bakery. A mirror selfie—and my mouth goes dry.

His shirt is caught between his teeth, baring a torso that looks carved from marble. Abs, chest—all of it on blatant display. One hand holds the bakery bag, the other his phone. He's angled, flexing. Sexy.

SERAPHINA: Very nice, Mr. Shaw

I type, biting my lip so hard it hurts.

Another pic arrives. This one makes me chuckle—he's clearly propped his phone up, stripped his shirt off completely, and caught himself flexing from behind. Broad shoulders, back roped in muscle, arms pulled tight.

Another buzz. This time he's facing the mirror, arm pressed low against his side, biceps swelling, abs tight, torso curved just so.

Fuck. He's a beautiful specimen of a man. And he's showing off...just for me.

A new text follows:

KILLIAN: Someone walked in and caught
me. I may be banned for life.

I laugh out loud, clutching the phone to my chest.

SERAPHINA: Three pictures? I tease. One
was acceptable.

He fires back instantly, cocky as ever:

KILLIAN: Just making sure there's no
competition.

I roll my eyes, still smiling like a fool.
Then another ping.

KILLIAN: Show me something, Miss Wylde.

My cheeks heat. I've done enough boudoir shoots to

know how to hit the angles, but this feels different. This feels personal. For him.

I'm already stretched out on the rug in front of the fire, the faux fur soft against my skin. So I shift, arching my back just right, making sure my ass pops, toes pointed. A pose that could imply the POV of him standing over me, looking down the line of my body. Imagining me on my knees, pleasing him.

I snap the picture before I can talk myself out of it and hit send.

A beat later, my phone buzzes with his reply. Just one word.

KILLIAN: Fuck.

Then:

KILLIAN: Running by my apartment to grab something. Be back soon.

Instantly, my pulse quickens. Waiting has never felt this unbearable.

To keep myself occupied, I make one of my favorite cocktails—a pussy-friendly one. Grey Goose vodka, cranberry juice, and pineapple juice, shaken and poured into a martini glass. Tart, sweet, and smooth. The cranberry helps fight against UTIs; the pineapple helps my sweet pussy's pH levels.

Things a good companion makes sure to take care of.

I curl up by the fire—not for the heat but for the cozy aesthetic.

Earlier, Eve and I talked about making a timeline, piecing together the events that triggered the stalking. She thought it might help. So I grab a pad of paper and a pen and start taking a trip down memory lane, noting every strange thing, every date, every text. It's exhausting, and I've probably been at it an hour when the door finally opens.

I know those boots. That walk. Killian.

I've shifted to my favorite chair, legs tucked under me, when he rounds the corner—two brown bags in hand. One from the bakery, one plain. He must've stopped home to change, because somehow he looks even more unfairly attractive than he did this morning, in all black.

"Your payment, ma'am." He sets the bakery bag in my lap, deadpan but with a glint in his eyes.

I grin like an idiot, and he likes it. I can tell.

The plain bag he drops in the chair across the room. Then he checks his gun before storing it in the drawer of my coffee table. His knife comes off his belt next, set within reach on the table. Every movement only adds to the dark, dangerous sexiness that clings to him like a second skin.

He drops onto my wide couch, one foot on the floor, head resting against the arm so he's facing me.

I've already fished out a pistachio macaron, taken a bite. Peeking inside the bag, I find more—different colors, different flavors. "Thank you, Mr. Shaw," I tease, standing and walking toward him with the second half of the macaron between my fingers.

For once, I don't guard myself. I just climb onto the couch, hike one leg over, and straddle him.

His hands find my hips immediately, squeezing, running up my sides and back down again.

"You like macarons?" I ask, voice huskier than I intend.

I lean down, kissing him—just a brush of tongue.

He answers against my mouth. "Don't. But tasting them off you? Might come to love them."

I smile and kiss him again.

"Hungry?" he murmurs.

"Starving. If I don't have some hot pasta soon, I may die."

He chuckles, handing me his phone, already open to the Caviar Black app. "We can't have that."

Still straddling him, I make my selections while his hands stay on me. He rubs, massages, traces idle circles as I scroll, never once taking his eyes off me. By the time I finish and set the phone aside, I'm flushed and fidgeting in his lap.

He cups my ass and pulls me closer, kissing me deep and slow, his tongue warm against mine.

"I'll have you know," he growls softly, "I walked around half of Manhattan with a raging hard-on because of you."

I throw my head back, laughing. "I'll take that as a compliment."

"Please do."

He sits up, pressing kisses along my chest, breathing in my perfume like it's oxygen. Then he stalls, a flicker of something uncharacteristically bashful crossing his face. "I got something." He hesitates. "For you."

My smile softens. His hand grips my hip like a warning to hold steady as he leans forward, dragging the plain brown bag into his lap.

"It's not much," he mutters. "Just something. You don't have to keep it."

I cup his face, thumb brushing against the scruff of his jaw. "Thank you," I whisper, lips grazing his.

I pull the item out, blinking at first, not sure what it is.

"It's for your light," he says.

And then I get it. My breath catches. A sun-catcher—but not the tiny kind for a window. This is for the whole room— and I can imagine it saturating the space in beautiful, fractured colors and prisms of light.

My expression must give me away, because his lights up to match mine.

"Will you put it up?" I ask, barely more than a breath.

He nods, trying to play it cool, but I can tell he's nervous —and God, I like it.

It doesn't take long. When he flips the switch, I gasp.

Rose and yellow reflections scatter across every surface, my entire room bathed in shifting color. Like living inside one of my sun-catchers.

"It's the most beautiful thing I've ever seen," I say, spinning toward him, heart swelling.

He watches me, and the softness in his eyes nearly unravels me. I hug his neck, kiss him hard. "Thank you. It's the most thoughtful gift anyone's ever given me."

"You made it yourself, didn't you?"

He shrugs, murmuring, "Been working on it here and there. It's okay if you don't want it up."

Before he can finish, I jump into his arms, wrapping my legs around his waist.

"I love it," I whisper fiercely. "I want to keep it here forever."

My heart lurches as the words slip free, because what I really want...is to keep him here forever, too.

***

Dinner arrives, and with music soft in the background, we eat and talk like any normal couple. Except we're not. At least we're saying we're not.

He asks about my family, and I'm honest. I'm not ashamed of what I chose for my life. But I know they are, and it makes me sad. They mostly tell people I'm still a nurse, working shifts alongside my sister. The lie is easier for them to swallow than the truth.

So I ask him a question back. Why the Ledger? Why choose to guard escorts?

He doesn't hesitate, doesn't flinch like it's something shameful. His mother was a sex worker. His father married her, had him and his brother, but people never let her forget what she did for a living—like it was a stain on her, like she should hang her head in shame. That never sat well with him.

The words sink into me, heavier than I expect. Love is not in the cards for some of us. That's what I told him. What I believed. Yet the way he speaks about his mother—with respect, with pride, with love—undoes that certainty thread by thread. Maybe it isn't the work that makes someone undeserving. Maybe it was only me convincing myself it did.

"What happened to her?" I whisper.

His voice goes quieter, lower. "She walked away. Had to. Left me and my brother. Our father raised us." His jaw flexes hard. "He wasn't a kind man. Crossed a line I could never follow him across. So I left too. Took my mum's name. And here I am."

I swallow. "What did he do?"

This time he hesitates. His eyes flick away like the truth is too heavy to set between us, but then it comes anyway. "He burned down a church with his enemy inside." His throat works, and I know there's more.

The words fall like lead. "Children's choir inside too. Called them collateral damage."

I gasp, hand flying to my mouth.

"I tried to stop him," Killian says, voice rough as gravel. "Tried to get them out. He fought me. Gave me this scar." His finger brushes the line above his brow. "Held me back. Made me watch."

Tears sting my eyes before I can stop them.

"My father was a big man," he says quietly. "So I became bigger. To make sure no one could ever stop me again. Not when people needed saving."

I stare at him, my heart breaking and swelling all at once. For the man who tried to save them. Who's carried that fire in his chest ever since.

And in that moment, I know—I will only see the shadows around him as proof of his strength. His heart. His refusal to be anything like the man who made him.

A man who will protect those around him—but deserves to be protected too.

Chapter 28
Seraphina

I wake in my bed, every inch of my body remembering where Killian touched me last night. My thighs ache, my lips are swollen, my skin still tingles.

Beside me, he sighs deep in his sleep, chest rising slow and steady. We'd gone to bed wrapped around each other, skin to skin, no barriers between us. And now, we wake the same way.

We'd talked until the hours blurred—about childhoods and rebellions, first kisses, first heartbreaks. Everything about my twin sister. And he didn't hold back telling me about his brother, Cormac—the image of their father.

We'd talked like people who didn't want the night to end, who didn't want to stop learning each other.

But when we did touch—when we couldn't hold off any longer—the sex wasn't just sex. It was more. Deeper. Reverent. Especially that last time, when the box of condoms ran empty. He'd been ready to stop, but I hadn't let him. I wanted him raw—to feel him, all of him. And when I asked, something snapped. He became an animal, a devil brought to earth, worshipping only me.

I rub my hand over his chest now, sliding down his abs, loving the hard cut of muscle. My leg is still thrown across him, and even in sleep he's hardening under my touch.

It makes me wet—knowing how easily he responds. Maybe that's just him. Or maybe it's what I do to him. Either way, I'm soaked.

My hand sneaks under the covers, wraps around him, and strokes his length until he's thick and hard in my grip. I watch his face—careful, slow—not wanting to wake him just yet.

When I can't hold back any longer, I ease myself over him. I grip him at the base, rub the head of his cock against my entrance until he's slick with me. My body clenches with need as I finally push down, sliding him inside me inch by inch.

A low moan rumbles from his chest. His mouth falls open, breath spilling out as I start to move—slow, steady. My eyes drink him in.

He stirs, exhales harder, and when I take him to the hilt, his eyes snap open. Heat sears through me at the way he looks at me—like I'm his entire fucking world.

His hands clamp on my hips, possessive, demanding.

"Christ, angel," he rasps, voice rough from sleep. "You're riding me in my sleep now? You that desperate for my cock?"

"Yes," I whisper, shameless, rocking harder. "I couldn't wait. I needed you."

His grip tightens, dragging me down harder on him. "Filthy little thing. Taking me raw again...soaking me already." He pinches both my nipples until I gasp. "Show me how bad you want it. Touch yourself."

My hand slides between us, rubbing tight circles against my clit, each thrust sending sparks through me.

"That's it," he growls, eyes locked on mine. "Look at you. Riding me, playing with your pussy. You gonna come for me, angel?"

"Y-yes," I gasp, thighs trembling.

"Do it. Let me feel you. Let me feel that pretty cunt clench around me when you come."

I cry out, hips bucking, his thumb taking over as he rubs my clit harder, faster. My whole body locks tight, then shatters, pulsing around him.

"Fuck, that's it—take it. Take all of it." His voice breaks rough, his thrusts meeting mine, deep and relentless. "Gonna fill you up, angel. You'll feel me all day."

"God, yes," I beg, still grinding through my orgasm. "I want it, Killian. I want you."

He slams me down once more, groaning as he comes, spilling into me. His arms lock me to him, mouth crushing mine in a bruising kiss as he fucks me through the last waves.

When it's over, I collapse against his chest—panting, trembling—his heartbeat thunder beneath my cheek.

And even with his cum leaking down my thighs, even with my body wrecked from him, all I can think is: I don't ever want to wake up without this. Without him.

The plan comes together at Jaxon's. His fiancée, Cassidy, greets me with a hug—warm and genuine—before I see who my stand-in is: Sylvia, a Ledger companion about my size, long blonde hair falling down her back. A friend. She slips into my clothes without hesitation, ready to play the part.

"Thanks for doing this, V," I nearly whisper, hugging her as Finn and two guards flank her, heading for the waiting limo.

"Don't make me regret letting you take my car," Jaxon mutters, pressing a set of keys into Killian's palm.

A matte-silver McLaren gleams inside Jaxon's private garage, and Killian grins like the devil himself as he opens my door. "Ready, angel? Better hang on."

The city blurs behind us as he races us out, weaving through traffic with reckless precision. I should be nervous, but instead I feel...free.

Killian keeps a pace like hell is chasing after us, and we're pulling into my sister's in record time.

The second I step into the yard, the birthday girl comes barreling toward me. My niece launches herself into my arms with all the force a sugar-high seven-year-old can muster. I spin her once, laughing, her little tiara sliding crooked across her head.

Then she spots Killian. "Killian!" she squeals, as if he's been part of the family forever.

He crouches, catching her hug like he's done it a hundred times, and the sight makes my chest ache in ways I don't want to name.

Oliver's next—my nephew, ever the serious one. Killian ruffles his hair in greeting, and Oliver doesn't miss a beat before launching into an enthusiastic lecture on everything he's learned about the praying mantis. Killian listens, nodding solemnly, as if my nephew has just handed him classified intel.

Inside, the party is in full swing. Kids scream and chase each other, icing flies, balloons pop. Adults cluster in little pockets—moms gossiping near the kitchen island, uncles crowding the grill outside.

Eventually, the crowd ebbs into the backyard, and my sister finally slips away from her hosting duties to collapse into the chair beside me. For the first time all day, there's quiet between us.

I hand her my bottle of amber beer. She gulps it greedily, not even pausing to wipe her mouth.

She tilts her chin, pointing across the yard. "That's Stacy." She says the name like it's coated in something sour. "Self-proclaimed Daniel's 'work wife.' Even after he's told her to knock it the hell off."

I follow her gaze to the woman in question—laughing too loud, leaning too close to my brother-in-law.

"She doesn't just ignore boundaries," Stasia continues, rolling her eyes. "It's like she's trying to push him into an affair."

My sister looks back at me, eyes sharp with mischief. "She doesn't know I keep that dick well satisfied and on lockdown."

I choke on a laugh. "Not very girls' girl of her."

"Certainly not."

My sister's eyes track him across the yard—Killian, who just glanced my way again, giving me a small nod. There's the faintest tug of a smirk at his mouth, like he knows exactly what he's doing to me.

I feel Stasia's stare burning into me.

"Don't start," I mutter, dragging from my bottle.

"I like him for you," she says simply. "And I know you like him."

I groan, tipping my head back.

"Maybe more than like him?" she presses.

I don't bother lying. Not to her. "A lot more than like him."

Her smile softens. She slides her arm around my shoulders and leans her head against mine.

"Yeah, that's more than obvious. He feels the same way about you."

My heart stutters. "Yeah?"

She huffs a laugh. "Don't be naïve. Anyone can see it. He's crazy about you, sis."

Before I can answer, Aurora yells out, "Cake!" from across the yard. Stasia groans, but I push up from my chair. "I'll get it."

Killian follows me inside, that shadow at my back. "Need a hand?"

"If you're offering."

I'm setting the cake on the counter, arranging candles, when the back door creaks open again. Stacy breezes in, a too-bright smile plastered on her face. She goes straight to the fridge for a lemon water before turning with sugary sweetness.

"Oh, that cake looks delish," she gushes as I press candles into the frosting. "Daniel loves frosting, you know—make sure he gets a great piece."

I freeze, staring at her. She smiles like we're girlfriends sharing a harmless secret.

"You know, if you just want to cut a piece now, I'll take it to him."

Like it's normal. Like it's acceptable to carve into a kid's birthday cake before the candles are even lit just so she can hand-feed her little crush.

The audacity.

I turn slow, hand reaching next to me without even needing to look. My fingers land on cold steel—Killian's knife—and I draw it in one fluid motion. He doesn't flinch.

"Let me tell you something, Stacy." My voice drops, sharp enough to cut without the blade. "You seem shit at respecting boundaries, and Stasia has to behave and play *Desperate Housewives*, but I don't. So I'll make this crystal clear for you. Leave Daniel alone. Stop being a pathetic little pick-me. Show my sister—his wife—the respect she deserves. Otherwise..." I tilt the knife, smiling razor-sharp. "I'll cut off your tits and shove them down your throat."

Her face drains. "How dare—"

"Try me." I stab the knife into the cutting block, hard enough it stands upright. Then I turn back to the cake, calm as ever, adjusting a candle.

Stacy makes a strangled sound and storms out with a huff.

Behind me, Killian growls low. His heat presses into my

back, his hands gripping my hips. His mouth dips to my neck.

"I'm so fucking hard right now."

I smile, and his hand slips beneath the hem of my dress, finding my panties. He growls again when his finger slides between my legs and comes away wet.

At the same time, he pulls his knife free from the block.

The cold tip grazes my sternum through the fabric of my dress, making me shiver. Slowly, tenderly, he drags it upward, the flat edge gliding over one nipple, then the other, until they're pebbled hard beneath the thin material. A taunt. A promise. A seduction from the blade he knows better than his own hand.

I gasp, arching against him.

"At the birthday party?" I whisper, breathless.

"Are you ever satisfied, little killer?" he rasps, pressing the blunt edge of the knife in just enough to remind me of its presence. "Have I not been fucking you well enough?"

I look back at him, catching his mouth in a hungry kiss. His tongue tangles with mine as the blade teases higher, then lowers, while his free hand strokes me beneath my dress.

"I'm satisfied every time you touch me," I whisper against his lips. "I just can't get enough."

He holds my stare, and I hold his, heat crackling between us—

The door bursts open. Kids flood in, shrieking with laughter. In an instant, the knife is gone, slipped back into its sheath; his hand pulls from between my legs. Killian steps aside like nothing happened at all.

I take a shaky breath, trying to look composed, the kitchen suddenly too small.

He leans down, voice low in my ear. "I can't get enough either, little killer."

He presses a kiss to my cheek, a promise wrapped in heat.

"And I don't want to."

Chapter 29

Being with Seraphina feels easy. Natural. Like I've been meant to sit beside her all along. Watching her with her family, hearing her laugh spill into the night, I catch myself thinking about things I don't usually let myself think about.

Like how my mother would love her.

She'd take one look at Sera—all fire and sharp edges, with a heart she tries to hide—and she'd adore her. The thought's dangerous, but it settles in me anyway, curling somewhere deep where I keep things I don't want to lose.

The night's winding down, most of the guests long gone, and it's just us now—Sera, her sister, Daniel, and me. Plus the two plainclothes I arranged. She hadn't even realized who they were until I pointed them out earlier, and the shock on her face had been worth it. Good men. They blended in exactly like they should.

We're gathered around a fire pit in the backyard, the soft crackle of flame carrying over the quiet. The plainclothes at the front of the house. Daniel's got a beer in hand, leaning back easy, and the girls are off on one of their stories, laughing so hard they can't finish a sentence.

"This one patient," Stasia starts, wheezing through her laughter. "Didn't realize we were twins. Total dickhead. So—"

Sera chimes in, grinning wide. "So we didn't tell him. Everyone on the floor played along."

I lean forward, elbows on my knees, smirking at the way their laughter feeds off each other.

"He'd see me one shift," Stasia says, "then Sera the next —and every time he'd swear something was off. Different shoes. Different lipstick. Hair pinned one day, loose the next."

"And we just played dumb," Sera finishes, eyes bright with mischief. "Let him drive himself crazy trying to prove we weren't the same person."

They collapse into laughter again, heads tipping together like it's the oldest joke in the book. Daniel shakes his head, grinning despite himself.

And me? I just sit there, taking it in. The glow of the fire, the sound of their laughter, the way Sera's eyes catch the light. It feels like family. It feels like home.

All day, I've watched Daniel with Stasia. The little touches, the way his hand finds her waist, the way she leans into him like it's the most natural thing in the world. And I've envied him for it.

Because I've wanted the same with Seraphina. Wanted to hold her hand, rest my palm on the small of her back, pull her against me just to feel her there.

But I didn't.

Because this thing between us—it's barreling toward a place we've been pretending not to see. And we're both getting to the point we don't care anymore.

Me? I'm already there.

She's been sitting beside me on the wicker loveseat, her thigh brushing mine every so often, and every brush has been torture. So when Daniel gets up to fetch Stasia another beer, he bends and kisses her before stepping away.

That's it for me.

I look at Seraphina. She's wearing the happiest, easiest smile I've ever seen, and she's looking right at me.

"Fuck it."

I pull her flush against me, tilt her chin up, and kiss her like I've wanted to all damn day. My arm locks around her waist, holding her close, and my stomach drops when she kisses me back—her hand slipping onto my thigh, fingers curling on my knee as she leans into me.

Daniel passes behind me, patting my shoulder once on his way to the cooler. "About time."

Stasia's grinning too, her smile full of approval as she looks at her sister—at us. And that does something to me. Cuts deep, because I know how much Sera and her sister love each other. That bond? I'll never have it with my own brother. Cormac and I are too far gone, on opposite continents even when we stand in the same room.

Daniel returns, settling back into his chair, beer in hand. He points at Sera. "So, tell us. Hardest patient you ever had. Which one made you finally get out of there?"

Sera takes a deep breath. "Oh, gosh." She chews her lip,

thinking. "Not sure if it was one in particular or just the buildup, but...one of our last nights in the ER together was brutal."

Stasia nods. "Yeah. That one was rough."

I glance between them. "What happened?"

Sera's voice softens. "Drunk driver accident. Couple in the car, and they brought all three in. The woman was in the worst shape. Stasia's team took her first, but it was going bad. They called me in too. There was so much blood..." She shakes her head, eyes distant. "Seeing what the collision did to her body was awful. But what made it worse was...she looked like us. Blonde. About our age."

Her voice cracks, just a little. "I was doing chest compressions while they tried to save her, and all I could see was Stasia. Couldn't stop picturing it. Couldn't do it anymore after that."

The group falls quiet. Even the fire seems to hush, just the crackle of wood filling the silence.

Then Sera lifts her chin, smirking faintly. "So I decided becoming a full-time whore would be better."

The tension snaps like a string, and everyone bursts out laughing.

I throw my head back, laughing with them, but my arm stays locked tight around her, keeping her close.

***

It's late when we leave, the McLaren humming under my hands as I ease us onto the dark stretch back toward the city. I'm not racing this time. I keep it steady, giving her the quiet she needs after tonight. I also don't want this day to end.

That story she told—about the crash, about the girl who looked like her sister—I could see how it dragged her back into the blood and the memories.

But now she's watching me. Not haunted anymore. Not just that.

Her fingers drift to my hand on the gearshift, tracing lazy circles across my knuckles. She doesn't say a word, just looks at me with those eyes—hot, heavy, full of need. Fuck-me eyes.

"You want to know what I was thinking about the last time you drove me home from my sister's?"

Her thighs clench, squeezing together as she shifts in her seat. She's wetter by the second. I know it—can damn near smell it—because I've seen this look before. "How badly I wanted to come over there and bounce on your cock."

That's all I need to know.

"Take your panties off," I order, voice sharp in the quiet.

Her breath hitches, but she obeys, sliding them down her legs and tossing them aside.

I whip the car onto a lonely shoulder, engine still purring low, and pull my cock free, thick and aching. My gaze cuts to hers. "Climb on, angel."

She straddles me quick, the cramped cockpit forcing her close—closer than I can breathe. The second she sinks down onto me, I groan.

"Fuck, yes." My head falls back, eyes squeezing shut at the way her heat takes me in.

But this time, I don't steer it.

She palms my chest, pushes me back into the seat. Her fingers slip under the hem of my shirt. "Take this off," she demands, voice husky.

I peel it over my head and toss it aside.

Her hands are on me instantly, exploring every line of muscle, nails grazing my abs. She pinches one nipple, hard enough I suck in a breath, and a dark chuckle spills from me.

"Christ, angel."

She leans in, mouth hot on my neck, sucking until I know she'll leave a mark. Her hips roll slow, deep, using me for every ounce of pleasure she wants.

"Ride me," I rasp, my hands gripping her ass but not guiding—just holding on. "Take what you need."

She kisses my jaw, then my mouth, grinding harder, moaning into me. Her nails dig into my shoulders as she bounces in the tight space, her pace rough, greedy.

"Take this cock any way you want, baby, because it's yours."

I can't stop the groans tearing out of me. I don't want to. Watching her take control—watching her use me—has me strung tight, ready to snap.

"You own every fucking inch of me."

I yank the thin straps of her sundress down her arms, tugging her tits free of her bra. My mouth is on them in an instant—sucking, biting, devouring. She moans loud, nails scraping through my hair as she rides me harder. Her ass slams down against me and the car horn beeps every time she bounces on my cock. She braces behind her and flicks on the windshield wipers, which move as fast as her pace.

She shudders, head dropping back, and I can feel her

clenching around me, dragging me closer to the edge with her.

"Fuck, Sera," I growl, pulling her back to me, devouring her mouth as I spill deep inside her.

For a long minute, we don't move—just cling to each other, breathless, sweaty, wrecked in the best way.

Her forehead rests against mine, her body trembling in my lap.

And all I can think is—this is it. This is exactly what I want for the rest of my life. Nights like this. Days ending with Seraphina in my arms.

Chapter 30

Seraphina

Yesterday was perfect.

At Aurora's birthday party, I hardly thought of my stalker at all. And the few times I did, Killian seemed to know before the thought even finished forming. He was always right there, his heavy presence chasing it away. One look. One touch. Enough to make me forget the shadows.

We showered together when we got home, steam curling around us, hands roaming like we couldn't get enough. It feels reckless, teenage almost—like falling in love for the first time. Except this time, it's real. It's him.

We can't stop kissing, can't stop touching, and it feels so fucking good.

I've been rehearsing what I want to say. That I don't want suitors anymore. That I don't want to pretend this is temporary. I want him. Officially. Permanently. And I'm almost certain he wants it too.

He keeps giving me that look, like he's about to say

something heavy and then pulls it back, like he thinks I'm not ready to hear it.

He dresses first, tugging his shirt down over the lines of his stomach, and offers, "I'll call down. Get us breakfast from the restaurant in the building."

Twenty minutes later, there's a knock at the door. One of the guards wheels the cart inside, nodding at me before stepping back into the hall.

I'm starving, and curiosity has me eager to see what Killian ordered. My hands make quick work of the first silver dome.

At first, I can't tell what I'm looking at.

The mound beneath the cloche doesn't make sense— pale, stringy, soft-looking. But it only takes a second for my brain to catch up. For my stomach to drop.

It's hair. Blonde hair. And a lot of it.

My scream rips free, high and raw, as I jerk my hands back. The dome clatters from my fingers, crashing to the floor. Tufts of cut hair spill out, sliding across the white tiles like dead things.

"Jesus Christ," I whisper, backing away.

Killian's faster. He yanks me behind him, shoving me against the counter with his body as a shield. His hand fists at his side, the other already reaching for his phone.

The plate underneath comes into view as the hair shifts. The word carved in red, smeared thick across the porcelain.

LIAR.

My stomach heaves. My knees go weak.

Killian's already moving, voice sharp as steel. "Inside.

Now!" he barks, and the guard at the door rushes in, scanning the room for threats.

Killian's dialing even as he pushes me farther back, putting the guard between us and the cart. His voice is clipped, lethal. "Get someone to sweep the kitchen and service corridors. Find out who intercepted the order."

I press a trembling hand to my mouth, heart slamming against my ribs so hard I think it might burst. Hair. It's her hair. Sylvia's. Oh my God—

Killian curses viciously and stabs at his phone again, barking into the line. "Lucian—do you have eyes on Sylvia?"

I hold my breath, every nerve stretched to breaking, until I hear the faint rumble of Lucian's voice bleeding through. Killian's shoulders loosen a fraction, though his eyes stay hard. Relief ripples through me, but it's thin, fragile—a thread ready to snap.

"She's safe?" Killian demands. His chest heaves. "Good. Keep her that way. I'm sending over a picture." He flips the call to speaker, his thumb already moving fast on the screen.

The silence in the room hums with tension, broken only by my uneven breathing.

Killian's jaw clenches, muscles tight. "Keep someone glued to her until I say otherwise. He spotted the decoy yesterday." His gaze flicks down to the floor, to the hair that still curls like straw around the plate. "And this is his message."

The plate's red scrawl burns into my vision—LIAR.

It sears through me, the word twisting in my head until it feels branded there. My throat closes, bile threatening. My hands shake so badly I have to press them against the counter to stay upright.

I can't stop staring at it. Can't stop imagining scissors, a knife, someone's hands in Sylvia's hair while she sat helpless.

And the thought that it could've been me—should've been me—makes the room tilt sideways.

Killian's hand finds mine, strong and unyielding. "Angel. Look at me. Not at that." His voice is a command, rough and low.

I tear my eyes from the plate, dragging them up to him. His steel-gray stare pins me, steadies me.

But nothing will erase the word from my mind. Nothing will stop the echo of it, painted in red.

Liar.

Killian's hand tightens on mine, voice steady even though I can hear the fury vibrating under it. "It's not real, angel. Sylvia's fine. This is just meant to scare you."

Tears spill hot down my cheeks, but they're not born of fear. Anger sears through me, raw and sharp. My stomach clenches, my fists shake.

It pisses me off.

I swipe at my face hard, glaring at the mess on the floor. "This needs to end. I'm done." My voice cracks but doesn't waver. "I'm quitting the Ledger."

I turn, heading back to my room, ignoring the guard who hovers near the door. Behind me, Killian snaps, "Clean this up," the words a barked order that makes even me flinch.

I toss my robe aside, tugging on jeans and a top with

quick, jerky motions. Killian's in the doorway, watching every move like I'm a frightened animal.

"And where are we going?" His tone is clipped, steel.

"To the Ledger," I say, zipping my jeans with a hard yank. "I want my things, so I don't have to go back there again."

He steps in, towering, hands on his hips. "This won't end if you quit your job."

"I know," I bite out, meeting his eyes. "But I won't drag this into the Ledger. I won't compromise the other Companions. Whatever ploys you all want to try to lure him out—I'll be the one to do it. Me."

For a beat, silence hangs, heavy as stone, and I think he's going to fight me on it. His jaw ticks, his eyes hard, but then he nods once, sharp and firm.

"All right." He pulls his phone out, dialing. "Get the car ready."

The Ledger feels different tonight. Quieter. The halls aren't buzzing the way they usually are, because most of the Companions are out on weekend contracts. The weekends are always busiest—dinners, galas, getaways. Everyone but me.

After Lucian reassures me Sylvia's fine, I split off from Killian, heading for my private dressing room. Senior Companions like me and Eve get our own spaces—our wardrobes, our things, a room where we can shut the door and breathe before a contract. We all use the Ledger's salon and services, sure, but these rooms are... ours.

I feel like I haven't been here in forever.

The door hisses open, the automatic lights flicker on, and my breath lodges in my throat.

"Oh my God."

I slap a hand over my mouth as the door clicks shut behind me.

My room is destroyed.

Red paint screams across the walls: LEDGER BITCH. WHORE.

My gowns—Ledger red—are shredded, hanging off splintered hangers like bodies in a gallows. Drawers over-turned, contents scattered, my shoes upended, the air sharp with chemical paint and the metallic tang of something that feels like blood but isn't.

And then I see pictures. Everywhere.

Me. Pinned to every wall. My eyes crossed out in thick black X's.

A tremor runs through me, my hands curling into fists. My pulse slams so hard I can hear it in my ears.

"No," I choke out. "No."

I whirl, my arm sweeping across the wall, sending the pictures raining down like dead leaves. I claw some off with both hands, ripping them, tearing them until shreds litter the already-trashed floor. My breaths come harsh, ragged, fury blistering through my veins hotter than fear.

"This ends. Do you hear me?" I scream at the empty room, at whoever's listening, at whoever's lurking. "This fucking ends!"

I stomp toward the door, chest heaving, when something catches my eye.

A picture.

It's taped dead center on the inside of the door.

My knees nearly buckle.

It's me and Killian. In the car, after last night's party.

"How the fuck—"

It's taken when we pulled off onto the shoulder. When I was fucking him. My head thrown back, his mouth on my breast. Someone was right fucking there.

How the fuck could someone have been there?

"Killian!" My voice cracks like glass.

Chapter 31

A scream rips through the hall, sharp enough to spear my chest.

"Seraphina!" I'm already moving, storming out of Lucian's office, frantic, my heart pounding with every step.

She bursts from her dressing room at the same time, eyes wide, breath heaving. Relief and concern collide so hard inside me I nearly stumble.

We collide in the middle of the corridor. My hand catches hers, and I hold tight.

"Angel, what—"

She shoves something into my palm. A picture.

I glance down, and my insides catch fire.

It's us. Her straddling me in the McLaren, dress bunched around her waist, my hands locked on her hips. Feral, intimate. Someone was there. How?

The edges of my vision go red.

"Drone," I grit out, every muscle coiled like a tripwire. "Had to be a fucking drone."

We're still moving, rushing toward the noise ahead.

The atrium opens up before us, the sound of gasps and murmurs echoing through the vast space. My stomach drops.

Red paint drips in thick, slow rivulets down one wall. Over it, in black spray paint, two words scream out:

TIME'S UP.

The floor is littered with photographs—me and Seraphina. Some are still falling, fluttering like snow from the upper levels of the atrium, tossed down for all to see.

Her face and mine. Our bodies—sprawled open for the world to pick apart.

Around us, Companions, staff, guards—all crowd the railings above, staring down in stunned silence. Lucian's at the far side of the ground floor, his expression thunderous, already barking orders into his phone.

But the truth is a blade in my gut.

The Ledger has been breached.

And the message is clear—nowhere is safe for her.

I don't waste a second and whistle once, sharp. Finn knows the call and his eyes snap right to me. "Get her out. Straight to the penthouse."

Beside me, Seraphina stiffens. "No."

"Angel—"

"I said no." She rips her hand from mine, her eyes blazing even as her breath shakes. "You can't just send me away—"

I turn on her, chest heaving, fury and fear boiling over.

Both my hands come up, cupping her face, forcing her eyes to mine. I kiss her hard, desperate, swallowing her protest before she can finish it.

When I pull back, my forehead rests against hers, my voice raw. "You're not safe here, baby. He could be in the building right now. Do you hear me? I need you safe so I can hunt him down."

Her lips tremble against mine. I see the fight in her eyes, see her want to argue again. But after a long beat, she exhales, shoulders slumping just enough.

"I don't like it," she whispers.

"I don't either," I tell her, my thumb brushing her cheek. "But I can't protect you and chase him at the same time. Please, angel. Let me breathe knowing you're out of his reach."

She nods once, sharp, her throat working. And I finally exhale, a tense, shallow relief.

"Finn." My voice cracks across the atrium. My second is already moving, snapping commands at the guards. They close in around her, ushering her toward the side entrance. My chest clenches when she disappears from view, but I shove it down. She's safe. That's all that matters.

Lucian steps to my side, his expression carved from granite. Together, we herd the Companions, staff, and on-duty guards into the main conference room. Faces pale, whispers sharp, everyone looking for answers they've never been given.

I plant my hands on the table, scanning every one of them. "We can't keep this quiet any longer, so you may as well know." My voice is steady, even as my blood still burns.

"Seraphina has had a stalker. We've been hunting him, closing in. And now he's escalating."

The room is silent, all eyes locked on me.

Lucian takes over, his presence filling the space. "You've seen the proof. He's bold, reckless. That makes him dangerous. Which means until he's caught, every single one of you needs to be vigilant."

I add, "Safe routes. Security checks. If you see something, you don't question it—you report it. Immediately."

For a long moment, no one speaks. Then slowly, one by one, the Companions nod. The staff. The guards. Every face in the room hardens with seriousness.

The weight of it sinks into the room, heavy and sharp. Faces harden, fear tempered with resolve. They understand now—every single one of them—that this isn't rumor or paranoia. This is real, and it's in our walls.

That's enough for tonight. We've put them on guard. And the rest? That's on us.

The staff and Companions file out, voices hushed, heads bent together in tight whispers as they disappear into the hall.

Lucian's already pulling out his phone, pacing toward the head of the table. He taps once and waits.

The line clicks, and Jaxon Kane's voice comes through, dry as ever. "Well, well. For you to call me this early, it must be the end of days."

Lucian doesn't rise to the bait. His tone is iron. "There's a problem."

Something in his voice wipes the sarcasm clean. "What do you need?" Jaxon asks, sharp now.

"I need to know how someone got around our security. Tonight, Seraphina's dressing room was vandalized. Then the atrium. Red paint, pictures—he left a fucking show for us." Lucian's eyes cut to me, then back to the phone. "I want everything, Jax. How he did it. Who let him in. When. Where. If someone so much as blinked at the wrong moment, I want a name."

The room is quiet except for Lucian's low, controlled fury.

Because this isn't just about Seraphina anymore. The bastard walked into the heart of the Ledger and left his mark.

Declared war. And we're going to find out exactly how. And we're going to answer it.

Fifteen minutes crawl by, every one of them dragging nails down my spine. I check my watch, then my phone. Over and over. Like either will give me something I need— her voice, her face, proof she's fine. Nothing.

Jax keeps talking as he works, his tone clipped, focus razor-sharp. "Someone slipped a device into your building. Blacked out everything—cell signals, cameras, sensors. But it spoofed the feeds to look like everything was running. No alarms. No alerts."

My jaw tightens. "How long?"

"Minutes. No more. Had to be when the atrium was hit. But..." He exhales through his nose, frustrated. "Her room could've been trashed hours ago. Days, even."

I grit my teeth so hard my molars ache.

"I'll put my AI over it. Run full analysis on the body

language of your security. If anyone slipped, twitched, looked the wrong way—I'll find the anomaly—"

He cuts off mid-sentence. Silence stretches.

Lucian and I snap to alert at once.

"What?" Lucian's voice is low, lethal.

For a long second, nothing. Then Jax's voice comes back, tight, grim. "Seraphina's building just went dark."

The words hit like a gunshot.

My blood runs ice-cold, then hotter than fire.

"Fuck." My chair scrapes back hard, my hand already on my gun checking the clip, heart hammering like it's trying to crack my ribs open. "I'm going to her."

I'm a ball of fire tearing through the city, weaving through traffic, horn blaring, every red light nothing but an obstacle I don't see. My grip on the wheel aches, my knuckles white, my mind a reel of a million worst-case scenarios I can't shut off.

I call my men. No answer. I call her cell. Nothing. The silence on the other end guts me. I slam the heel of my hand against the steering wheel, the sound ringing sharp in the car.

Jaxon's voice is in my ear, steady, precise. "Building's still dark. No signals. No cameras."

"Fuck!" I roar, shoving the accelerator to the floor.

My car flies into her building's valet area, tires screaming as I slam it into park. I don't wait for the keys to be taken—just bolt inside, hammering the call button for her private elevator over and over like that'll make it faster.

The ride up feels endless, though it's less than a minute.

Every tick of the floor counter another nail through my chest.

The doors finally open. One of my men stands outside her door, calm as ever—until he sees my face. His spine straightens, hand twitching toward his weapon.

"She in there?" I nearly scream it, shoving past him before he can answer.

The door bangs against the wall as I storm inside.

And there she is.

Seraphina jumps, startled, shoulders jerking at the sound. But she's whole. Untouched. Just standing at her stove, kettle in hand, steam curling up as she pours water for tea.

"Jesus, Killian."

My lungs seize. Relief and fury collide so hard my knees nearly buckle.

"Building just came back up," Jaxon's voice cuts through my earpiece. "I'll stay on this. You stay with your girl."

I breathe hard, too hard, sliding down the wall until I hit the floor. My palms press against my eyes, pushing hard, like I can force the last five minutes out of my skull. The earpiece dangles loose until I rip it free and let it fall, clattering uselessly to the ground.

At the stove, her soft voice floats through the kitchen, casual, teasing. "Aw, were you worried about me, big man?"

She doesn't see me breaking. Doesn't hear the crack in my chest.

"Worried?" The word comes out shredded, my voice nothing but gravel.

That sound—broken, not me—snaps her attention

around. She spins, blue eyes wide, kettle forgotten on the counter.

"Killian?"

"Your systems went down," I rasp, forcing the words out through my throat. "I couldn't see you. I didn't know..." My voice gives out, jagged silence tearing through me.

I drag my eyes to hers, raw and unguarded.

"Worried? I was fucking gutted, Seraphina."

I don't mean for it to happen.

But the burn in my chest snaps, and before I can stop it, a single tear tracks hot down my cheek.

Her breath hitches. She sees me breaking.

"Killian..." Her voice is low, careful, like she's approaching a wild animal ready to lash out.

She comes closer, slow, hands lifted, eyes wide. "I'm here. I'm okay. You hear me? I'm okay."

My back presses against the wall as if I could disappear into it, shame clawing at me for falling apart in front of her. But then she's there—sliding into my lap, wrapping herself around me like she belongs there.

And fuck, she does.

Her arms anchor me, her heartbeat pounding against my chest. She presses her cheek to mine, letting me breathe her in—soap, tea, the sweetness that's all her.

Her lips brush the tear's salty path, and then her eyes lock on mine. Blue and endless. Pulling me back from the void that almost swallowed me whole just now.

Something inside me breaks open, everything I've been holding back, everything I've been burying under duty and silence. It spills out, unrestrained.

"I can't fight it anymore," I rasp, voice hoarse. "Christ, I've tried. Told myself this was a job. That I was just here to protect you. But it's a lie, angel. All of it."

Her fingers thread into my hair, her touch trembling but steady.

"I don't want to just guard you. I don't want to just fuck you. I want you. Every stubborn, beautiful, infuriating part of you." My chest heaves, raw with it. "I want nights where I fall asleep with you in my arms. Mornings where you steal the covers. I want the fights, the laughter, the goddamn forever. Only you. No one else. Never anyone else."

The last word tears out of me like a vow.

For a second, I can't breathe. Can't take back what I've said. Can't protect myself if she pushes me away.

Her answer comes first in her body—her mouth crashing against mine, desperate, claiming, her hands fisting in my shirt like she'll never let me go. The kiss is wet, salty from my tears and hers, but it's fierce, a brand seared into my soul.

When she finally pulls back, she rests her forehead against mine, breath shaking.

"Killian Shaw," she whispers, eyes shining as a smile breaks out on her beautiful face, "are you trying to tell me you love me?"

And just like that, I'm undone all over again—but this time, it's not despair dragging me under. It's her.

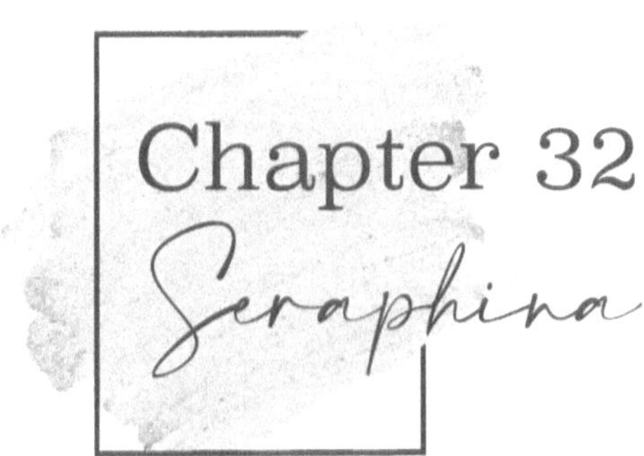

Chapter 32
Seraphina

"Killian Shaw," I whisper, eyes stinging with tears as a smile breaks over my face, "are you trying to tell me you love me?"

Something shatters in him. Not rage. Not grief. Something deeper, older—something that's been clawing to get out.

The next second I'm not on the floor anymore. He hauls me up like I weigh nothing, his mouth claiming mine, devouring me as if the words themselves lit him on fire.

We slam into the kitchen table, a chair clattering over, Killian's leather jacket dragged down with it. Neither of us cares. My hands are fisted in his hair, tugging, pulling, kissing him like I'll never get enough.

Clothes disappear in frantic motions—his shirt torn over his head, my jeans shoved down, his belt undone with trembling urgency. His hands grip me everywhere, greedy, desperate, shaking with the force of it.

And then his mouth is on me.

I watch, breath caught, as he lowers between my legs and ravages me like a starving man. His tongue moves fast, ruthless, flicking and circling until my thighs tremble. The sharp press of his piercing drags against me, sending electric shocks through my body. His mouth seals over my clit, sucking hard, pulling a cry from my throat.

"Oh—fuck, Killian—"

My nails scrape across his scalp, clutching him to me as if I could anchor myself against the storm he unleashes. His growl vibrates through me, low and primal—the sound of a man who refuses to stop until I'm wrecked.

The pressure builds fast, brutal, my body clenching tight as I throw my head back, eyes squeezed shut. Pleasure slams through me, my legs twitching helplessly around his head as I come apart on his mouth.

"Killian—oh God—"

He doesn't let up. Doesn't slow. He devours me through it, tongue relentless, sucking until I'm gasping, shaking, tears pricking the corners of my eyes from how hard it hits me.

When I finally collapse back against the table, chest heaving, I look down at him—his mouth slick, his eyes dark and burning into mine—and I know this isn't just sex.

This is surrender. For both of us.

He rises from between my thighs and crashes his lips to mine like the kiss itself is giving him life. I taste my release on him, feel the desperation in the way his hands clutch at my face, and I can't hold it in anymore.

I cup his cheeks, forcing him to see me, to hear me. "I

love you too, Killian. I've fallen in love with you—so fucking hard I don't ever want to stop falling."

His breath stutters against my mouth, gray eyes wide, raw.

"I've been dragging myself through dinners, looking for a partner, looking for the one I thought I needed…" My voice breaks, and I shake my head, a shaky laugh slipping out. "But he was here the whole time. You. It's always been you. I just had to stop lying to myself."

"Fuck, baby," he groans, low and guttural, and kisses me again, deeper, fiercer, like he'll never let me breathe without him. "I've been desperate to hear you say those words."

"Bedroom," I pant against his lips.

His answering growl vibrates through me.

"Now."

I tug on his shoulders, pulling him with me down the hall, kissing him with every step until he picks me up and carries me the rest of the way. My legs are still trembling, my body still thrumming, but I don't care. I push him back until he sits on the edge of the bed.

I drop to my knees, sliding my hands up his thighs until I'm at his zipper.

His breath hitches as I free him, his cock springing heavy and hot into my hand.

I look up at him through my lashes, my heart pounding. "I can't wait another second to taste you, Killian Shaw."

Then I take him into my mouth.

His head falls back with a groan, his fingers tangling in my hair instantly. I hollow my cheeks, stroking him with my lips, my tongue—every motion deliberate. Not just pleasure.

Worship. My way of saying all the things words could never hold.

He curses low, his hips twitching when I tug on his piercing, watching him pant for me. "Christ, angel—"

I take him deeper, until my throat closes around him, until my eyes water. He looks down, his face wrecked, and I want him to see it all—the tears, the need, the devotion.

I moan around him, one hand gripping his thigh, the other wrapping around the base of his cock, twisting in rhythm with my mouth. His groan rips through the room, primal, undone.

He tugs hard on my hair, his body shuddering as he fights control. "Fuck, Sera—don't stop. Don't you dare stop."

And I don't. I can't.

Because this isn't about getting him off—it's about answering him the only way I know how. With my lips, my tongue, my whole body bent to him. My confession given in gasps and moans, in devotion and surrender.

And if he ruins me for everything else, so be it. Because I'm his. Completely.

His grip tightens in my hair, his hips rolling shallow thrusts against my lips as if he can't help himself. His voice is rough, unraveling.

"You love this, don't you?" he rasps, breath coming harsh. "Being used by me. Taking every inch until your eyes water. Fuck—Sera—"

I swallow him down, greedy for it, greedy for him. His thighs tense under my palms, his body shuddering.

"Gonna come down your throat," he growls, broken and feral. "And you're gonna drink every drop, angel."

The warning is barely out before he jerks, groaning deep, guttural, as hot pulses of release hit the back of my throat. I don't let a single drop escape, swallowing him, sucking until he twitches against my tongue and every last moan of ecstasy is wrung from him.

When I finally pull back, licking him clean, his chest is heaving, his gray eyes wild as they pin me in place.

"Greedy little killer," he murmurs, voice wrecked.

Before I can answer, he's hauling me up, his mouth crashing into mine, the taste of him still on my tongue. He spins, tossing me back onto the bed. His knife tumbles onto the mattress beside me, gleaming under the lamplight as he strips the rest of his clothes away.

His cock is still hard, still pulsing, ready for more.

Honestly, the stamina on this man should be studied as a scientific marvel.

I lean back on the bed, bare and open, my knees bent and spread wide. Every inch of me is his to see, his to touch, to claim. I coax him with a hungry smile, my voice husky. "Come here, big man. I need you."

That's all it takes. His control frays, feral energy pouring off him as his gaze drops to the knife glinting on the mattress. His grin turns wicked.

He picks it up, twirling it once like it weighs nothing, like it belongs in his hand as much as I do.

"You're lying there naked for me, angel," he rasps, crawling up the bed until he looms over me. "Spread open like a fucking feast. And all I can think about is how you'll look with my knife against your skin while I take you."

My pulse hammers. Excitement crashes into a tremor of fear, winding me so tight I could snap.

He brings the tip of the blade to my throat, dragging it slow, deliberate, down the column of my neck. My breath shudders out.

"You scared?" he asks, filthy and taunting, his gray eyes locked on mine.

"Yes." My voice is barely a whisper.

"Wet?"

"Yes."

His smirk deepens, feral now. "That's my girl."

The blade glides lower, between my breasts, circling one nipple before flicking across it with the flat of the steel. My back arches off the bed, a moan breaking free.

"You trust me?" he asks, pressing the cool blade flat against my sternum.

"Yes," I breathe, every nerve ending on fire. "Always."

His eyes darken further, his grin sharp as sin. "Good. Because I'm gonna make you come with this knife against your skin. You'll scream for me while you feel how close I could cut you—and how much you fucking love it."

The edge grazes down my stomach, stopping just above my mound, and my hips lift, begging.

"Say it," he growls, pressing the blade flat against my thigh, close to where I ache for him. "Say you want this."

"I want it." My voice cracks, but it's strong enough. "I want you. All of you. Every way you'll take me."

His cock twitches against my thigh, thick and hot. His

free hand spreads me open, his eyes blazing as the knife hovers dangerously close.

"Filthy angel," he murmurs, the sharp tip of the blade brushing my swollen clit before he replaces it with his tongue. "You're mine to ruin."

He nips my clit between his teeth, his tongue piercing teasing across it. Not hard, but it's so fucking sensitive it nearly sends me into space.

My scream fills the room as fear and desire collide, and I know I'll never want anyone but him.

His mouth is relentless, tongue flicking and sucking at my clit, his piercing dragging over me until my thighs quake.

He shifts, pressing the cool handle to my entrance, sliding it in with a slow push that makes my breath catch. The stretch is sharp, shocking, filthy. My moan breaks into a scream when he adds two thick fingers beside it, fucking me open while his tongue works me ruthlessly.

"Killian—oh God—"

I buck against him, overwhelmed, his mouth devouring me as the handle thrusts deep, his fingers curling inside. The mix of steel, flesh, and his hot tongue is unbearable—intoxicating.

"Come on, angel," he growls against me, lips slick, voice rough between licks. "Soak my knife. I want to taste you all over it."

It shatters me. My body bows off the bed, groans ripping free as I come hard, squirting over his hand, over the handle, over his face. He groans into me, sucking harder, drinking me down as my release drenches everything.

When the spasms finally break, he withdraws the knife, glistening with my cum, and raises it above me.

"Lick it clean," he orders, voice like gravel.

I grab his wrist, my gaze locked on his, and drag my tongue up the steel. Slowly. Deliberately. Licking my release from the blade like I'm starving for it. His eyes go black, a guttural curse spilling from his lips.

"Good girl," he rasps, his dick resting hot and heavy on my pussy.

Then he shifts, settling back on his haunches between my spread thighs, his cock poised thick and hard. The knife gleams in his hand, his grin wicked as sin.

"Open," he orders.

My lips part without hesitation, breathless and trembling, and he slides the handle of the knife between my teeth. The taste of steel fills my mouth, the weight of it heavy on my tongue.

"Bite down, angel."

The command rumbles through me a second before his hands seize my hips and he drags me onto his massive cock in one brutal thrust.

I scream around the handle, the sound muffled, my body arching as he buries himself deep, hard, unrelenting.

He fucks me ruthlessly, pulling me down over and over, the knife handle locked between my teeth, every moan forced out of me jagged and raw.

Then he plucks it free, his eyes wild as he flips the blade, the tip gliding along my throat, slow and deliberate.

"God, look at you," he rasps, pressing deeper into me.

"Spread wide, stuffed full of my cock, trembling under my knife… you're everything I ever wanted to worship."

The blade grazes my throat, shallow, just enough to sting. His mouth is there instantly, sucking, soothing, claiming. He drags the tip lower, tracing the swell of my breast, cutting another shallow line near my nipple. His tongue follows, licking the bead of blood before pulling it into his mouth.

My groans are half pain, half pleasure—and all surrender.

He grips my ankles, spreads me wide, thrusting into me with brutal force. The blade is pressed into my palm now, his command low and raw. "Get yourself off, angel. Show me how much you love it."

I press the handle to my clit, circling frantically as he pounds into me. The pressure builds fast—violent, unbearable.

"Come with me," he growls, voice shredded. "Soak me again. Mark me as yours."

The climax rips me apart—violent, wet—flooding him as my body convulses. I scream his name, soaking his cock, the sheets—ruined by him, for him.

He roars my name as he comes with me, pulsing deep, holding me wide open as we fall apart together.

"Fuck, Seraphina, fuck."

His forehead drops to mine, his chest heaving against me, both of us shaking, slick with sweat and each other. For a moment it's just the sound of us trying to breathe.

Then his voice, raw and broken open: "I love you, angel. Christ, I love you."

Tears sting my eyes, but my smile breaks anyway—wide and unguarded. I cup his face, forcing him to see me. "I love you too, Killian. More than I ever thought I could."

The weight of it hangs between us—not fragile but solid, undeniable. His lips crush mine in a kiss that tastes like salt and heat and truth, sealing what we both already knew.

And for the first time, it feels like we've stopped running —from each other, from ourselves.

Chapter 33
Seraphina

T he dream is back.

Familiar. At least, I think it is.

"Sera!"

The voice cuts through the fog, sharp and echoing. My heart leaps. Stasia? It sounds like her.

"Seraphina!"

Another voice now. Different. Deeper. Killian. He's behind me. No—back the way I just came.

I freeze, breath catching. My arms stretch out in front of me, fingertips brushing against thick, wet air. The fog clings like cobwebs.

"Killian?" My voice comes out thin, shaky. It bounces back at me, distorted, whispering my name in a hundred directions.

I start forward, or at least what feels like forward. The ground beneath my bare feet is cold, hard. Stone, maybe. A corridor, shifting and endless. I can't see the walls, only the press of darkness hemming me in.

"Sera!" Stasia again, somewhere ahead.

I run. My lungs burn, and the fog curls tighter with every step.

A turn. Another.

My palms scrape against damp stone as I spin around corners, chasing the sound of her voice. But the path keeps shifting—dead ends, sudden walls where there shouldn't be any.

"Seraphina!" Killian again, closer now. Behind me.

I whip around, chest heaving. Nothing. Just shadows stacked on shadows.

And then I see something.

At the far end of the corridor: a figure.

He sits in perfect stillness, swallowed by the dark. But there's light—no, not light. A single, sharp spotlight, cutting down through the fog. It illuminates the thing in his hand.

A white rose dripping with blood so red it glistens.

I stumble back, slamming into stone. My throat closes.

No.

I turn and run again, faster, twisting through passage after passage. I can hear my sister, hear Killian, both of them calling me, but their voices are warping, dragging at the edges like they're being torn apart.

Another corner. Another hall, and he's there.

Closer this time.

The rose bleeds between his fingers, dark drops spattering the stone beneath him. His head is bowed, features swallowed by shadow.

"No..." My whisper cracks, breaks. I bolt again.

My feet slap against the ground, heart hammering

louder than my breath. The fog feels alive now, clawing at me, pulling at my clothes, my hair.

I whip around another bend—

He's there.

Closer still.

I can see his shoulders, the slope of his jaw hidden beneath the dark. The blood runs thicker now, spilling down his hand, slicking the stem of the rose until it drips in a steady rhythm to a white tile floor below.

Drip. Drip. Drip.

Terror claws up my throat. I can't breathe.

One more turn—one more chance to escape—

And he's waiting for me.

Right in front of me. So close I can feel his breath against my face.

The rose trembles in his hand. His head lifts.

Shadows cling to his face, but the blood doesn't. It flows freely, spilling down his cheek, over his mouth, dripping onto the flower below.

"...Sera?"

The word rasps out of him, wrong and broken.

Then his hand lashes out, gripping my throat like a vise.

My scream lodges in my chest, and I jolt upright, gasping for air, the echo of blood still dripping in my ears.

I shoot up in bed with a gasp, lungs burning like I never got enough air.

Beside me, Killian jerks awake too, his body tight, on guard in an instant. His arm flexes around me before he realizes I'm not under attack—I'm trembling, drenched in sweat.

"I know who it is." The words scrape out, raw. My voice doesn't even sound like mine.

He stills, steel-gray eyes snapping to me, and I know he believes me without question.

"The stalker." I pant. "It's him."

I fling the sheets off and pace, bare legs brushing against Killian's T-shirt—the one that hangs to my mid-thigh, neckline slipping off one shoulder. The cotton feels too soft, too gentle for the storm clawing inside my chest.

I grab my phone, thumb fumbling. It's before dawn, but Stasia will be on shift.

"It was the hospital," I whisper, more to myself than him. The words come in fragments, like the dream still owns part of me. Images flood back—the blood, the rose, the shadowed face whispering, not my name, but Sarah.

The line clicks after only two rings. "What's wrong?" Stasia's voice is panicked, sharp.

"The girl's name," I blurt. "What was the girl's name?"

There's a beat of silence. "What girl? Stacy?" She chuckles softly, but it's uneasy. "She was pissed at you—"

"No." My voice cracks. "The drunk driver. The couple. That night. What was the girl's name?"

Stasia exhales, thinking hard. "Sarah... something."

I knew it.

My heart slams harder. The more I try to pin it down, the further away it feels, like smoke slipping through my fingers.

Across the room, Killian has his phone pressed to his ear, already moving. His gaze never leaves me—stern, dark, like a hunter biding his moment. His voice is low, meant not to disturb me. "She says she knows who it is."

"Something like… Town… or…" Stasia trails off, then snaps her fingers on the other end. "Appleton. Sarah Appleton."

The name detonates inside me.

I look at Killian, wide-eyed. "Sarah Appleton. The hospital records from that night. The man she was with. It's him. The rose. The blood. Sarah. That's it. That's who it is."

His palm finds the side of my head, rough and grounding, but gentle all the same. His thumb strokes my cheek. "Good girl."

Then, to his phone, his voice dropping into that ruthless calm: "You pulling it up?"

A muffled answer hums through the line. He nods once and flicks the call to speaker.

Killian drops his phone onto the mattress and pulls me into his lap like I weigh nothing. I straddle him, knees digging into the bed on either side of his thighs.

"We'll hear it together," he murmurs.

His arms cage around my waist, solid, immovable. I loop mine around his neck, press my face against him, and breathe him in. His skin, his warmth—anything to ground me. My heart still races like I'm back in that maze, my throat so dry it burns.

On the speaker, Jaxon yawns, the sound muffled by rapid keystrokes. "Hospital records are such a piece of cake." He's half-talking to himself, his voice edged with concentration. "Doing a wide search for Sarah Christina Appleton."

Sarah Christina. Seraphina. Even her name is close. Too close.

"Shit."

Killian stiffens under me. "What?"

"She could pass for Seraphina easy," Jaxon says. "I'm sending you everything. Lucian too—he's on the way over."

Killian nods once, sharp, like Jaxon can see him.

"Got 'em," Jaxon mutters, keys clacking faster. "Caleb Ward."

The name is a shotgun blast. It ricochets through me—not because I know it, but because my bones do. My blood does. Every instinct inside me screams that's him. The shadows finally have a name.

"Pulling up employer and last known."

Silence for a breath. Then Jaxon curses. "You son of a bitch." He exhales hard, disgust curling in his tone. "Lucian's gonna be pissed. Just warning you now—maybe take the next week off to avoid his meltdown."

"What is it, Jax?" My voice cracks.

"He works at the Ledger. Right now. He's a janitor."

The air leaves my lungs in a gasp. My fingers tremble as I grab the rendering off the nightstand—the one we made just days ago. I cover one eye with my hand, staring at the sketch, my voice breaking into a whisper. "Oh my God."

Killian's phone pings.

On the screen—his picture. Real. Current.

It's him.

Nearly identical to the rendering.

Except for the black eye patch.

And I know—if it came off—I'd see it. That one blue eye that's haunted me every night since this began.

Chapter 34
Seraphina

FIVE YEARS AGO

The smell of burnt coffee and disinfectant clings to everything, even the cafeteria. Stasia and I sit side by side at one of the corner tables, both still in scrubs, both half-slumped from another night shift that doesn't seem to end.

Aurora's picture lights up her phone screen when she sets it down, and Stasia smiles like she can't help it.

"She's saying new words every day now," she says around a bite of her sandwich. "And we're gonna try potty training soon. Wish her auntie Sera was around more to see it."

There it is. The guilt trip. She doesn't even bother to make it subtle.

I pick at my salad, stabbing a tomato harder than necessary. "I'm trying, Stas. Between this and the Ledger—"

"You can't keep running yourself ragged." She gives me

that big-sister look, even though we're the same age. "You've been doing two jobs for how long now?"

I sigh, pushing my food away. "Long enough that I feel like I'm about to burn out. Some days I don't even know why I'm still here. The money over there is unreal."

I keep my voice low, though the cafeteria is mostly empty. "Yeah. They've asked me to consider going full-time."

"And?"

I shrug, but my chest feels tight. "I don't know. It's a totally different world over there. Glamorous, excess is everywhere, but…"

"But it's not this," she finishes softly, glancing toward the doors that lead back into the ER. "You're a damn good nurse, Sera. You'd be missed. And I think you would miss this too."

Before I can answer, the intercom crackles overhead, sharp enough to cut through the hum of fluorescent lights.

"Attention ER staff. Incoming ambulance, ETA five minutes. Three patients from motor-vehicle collision. One critical, two stable. Trauma team to Bay Two. Repeat—three patients incoming, one critical. Trauma team to Bay Two."

The room stills for half a beat. Stasia and I lock eyes.

Break's over.

We're already moving, tossing our trash, scrubbing sanitizer into our hands as we rush for the doors. My stomach knots, half from the food I barely touched, half from the dread that always coils before we see what the night is about to throw at us.

The sliding doors burst open, and chaos comes with them.

Stasia's already moving toward Trauma Two, where the critical will land. The staff surges forward as the first ambulance screeches up. They sprint beside the stretcher, barking questions, absorbing the medic's rapid-fire updates.

I catch only a glimpse as they disappear down the corridor—blood, mangled limbs, a face so destroyed it's barely human. My gut twists. I know the team will fight, will bleed themselves dry for her, but the truth presses hard in my chest. We're losing one tonight.

The second ambulance arrives right behind. This time, the patient is stable. A man. Middle-aged. His arm in a crooked splint, his face slack with alcohol and unconsciousness.

Of course. Figures.

The drunk who made the selfish choice... walks away with a broken arm. While a woman in a different bay fights for her life.

He's wheeled past me, met by a couple of staff who take him down a different hall. I swallow hard, bile creeping up my throat.

The third ambulance rolls in, siren fading, lights still strobing red and blue across the glass doors. The stretcher jolts as it's rushed inside, and I fall in step.

"Severe head trauma," the medic shouts. "Stable vitals, but disoriented."

The man is babbling, voice cracked and desperate. "Where is my fiancée? Where is she?"

The medic tries to keep him calm, but it's useless—he's thrashing, eyes wide with panic.

I grab a chart from the desk and step into his path. "I'll take him," I tell the charge nurse, and she nods, already dispatching another nurse toward Stasia's trauma.

We push the stretcher into a curtained bay, and I close it behind us.

"His name is Caleb," the medic mutters before he hurries out. "That's all we could get."

I move to his side, reaching for gloves. "I'm Seraphina," I say gently. "Do you know where you are, Caleb?"

He stares at me, confusion and blood clouding his expression. His hand shoots out, clutching me with terrifying strength.

"Sarah?"

His voice cracks, desperate, and before I can stop him, he's pulling me against him, sobbing into my shoulder.

"Sarah, thank God, I was so worried—"

I peel him back, forcing him down, my heart hammering. "No. My name is Seraphina. You were in an accident. You're at the hospital. If you can remain still—"

But he won't. He sits upright, refusing the bed, refusing the pillow. His head wound is grotesque—split wide from temple down the left side of his face, blood running so freely it soaks his collar.

He's probably going to lose that eye. He'll lose vision in it, at a minimum.

He's wearing a tux. "Where were you going tonight, Caleb?" I ask, trying to see if he can remember. Also trying to calm him so we can do our job.

In his hand, gripped like salvation, is a white rose. A boutonniere, maybe.

Only now it drips scarlet with every drop from his wound. The petals stained red, one by one.

"Sarah," he whispers again, kissing the flower with reverence. "Don't leave me."

My throat tightens, but I steady my voice. "I'm not leaving you. Call me Seraphina. We need to give you something to help, to calm you—"

He cuts me off, eyes glassy, wet. "Sarah Christina." He says it like a prayer. Like devotion. "I was going to propose."

Something twists painfully in my chest. I feel for him, I do. But we need to treat him, and he won't lie down.

He fixes me with a look that burns through the haze of blood loss. "You would have said yes, wouldn't you?"

The intercom explodes overhead, pulling the breath from my lungs:

"Code Blue, Trauma Two. All available staff to Trauma Two, immediately. Code Blue, Trauma Two."

That's Stasia's patient. The critical.

I jump up so fast the curtain rattles. "Prep him for sedation," I bark to the nurse sliding in behind me, already rattling through orders as I sprint for the doors.

"Sarah!" His voice cuts after me, ragged.

But I don't look back.

"Sarah Christina!" He screams it this time, the words splitting with desperation as I push through the doors and vanish into the chaos of Trauma Two.

The doors slam open, and the room is already a storm. Monitors shriek. Gloves snap. Voices collide in a rush of orders—IV, O2, epi, suction. Someone's counting vitals, another shouting for blood, another pushing a crash cart closer. The air reeks of antiseptic, iron, and sweat.

And in the center of it, she lies on the table.

Blonde hair matted dark, drenched with blood. So much of it I can't tell where the wounds end and her face begins.

"Get on compressions!" the attending barks, sharp and fast.

"Starting compressions!" I shout, already moving.

I slide into place, pushing past a nurse withdrawing bloody gauze. My palms slam down, hard and fast, over the sternum. Count—one, two, three, four—my arms locked, shoulders screaming as I drive her chest down an inch and a half at a time.

Across from me, Stasia works with laser focus. She's at the head of the bed, securing the airway, her voice tight as she calls for suction and adjusts the laryngoscope. Her brow is furrowed, sweat dripping down her temple, but her hands are steady. She doesn't see me staring at the patient's face.

Through the blood, through the gashes ripped open across her skin—I see us.

Stasia. Me.

The resemblance is gutting, but there's no time to freeze.

"Bag her!" Stasia shouts, and another nurse squeezes the valve, forcing air into blood-filled lungs.

The monitor wails. Asystole. Flat.

"Epi in," someone calls.

The syringe goes in. A fresh nurse takes over compressions, and I stagger back, breath tearing through me, my gloves slick with blood.

She looks like us. God, she looks just like us.

"Pulse check!"

Hands press against the neck, the groin. Silence. Nothing.

"No pulse."

"Resume compressions," the attending orders, but the words drag this time, heavy with doubt.

"I've got it," I say, and I'm already back on the chest. My palms drive into her sternum, rhythm sharp, almost frantic. Sweat drips down my temple, stinging my eyes.

"Push one of atropine."

The syringes empty, but the monitor doesn't move. That awful flatline screams at us, unbroken, unrelenting.

"She's been down thirty minutes," a nurse murmurs, voice subdued.

"We're losing her," another says, softer still.

The attending nods grimly. "Another two minutes, then we call."

But I can't stop.

My arms keep pumping, harder, faster, my breath tearing through me. Her blonde hair is plastered to her face, streaked in blood, but I can see her through it—see Stasia.

So much like Stasia.

I slam down again and again, refusing to stop, refusing to let her go.

"Seraphina," someone says. A warning.

I don't hear them.

It's my sister's face. It's mine. God, it could be her.

"Seraphina."

This time it's closer. A hand closes over my wrist, firm but gentle. I look up through my haze, and it's Stasia standing across the table, her eyes brimming but steady.

Her voice softens. "That's enough."

My arms falter. My gaze drops to the woman beneath me—the blood, the broken body, the slack jaw. My chest heaves, and only now do I feel the wet streaks on my cheeks.

I look back up at Stasia, and she's crying too.

The attending clears his throat. His voice is low. "Time of death, 03:27."

The words cut the room into silence. One by one, the staff step back, gloves snapping off, heads bowed. The storm dies.

And I'm left with blood on my hands, my heart splintered, and the image of my sister's face on a woman we couldn't save.

I scrub my hands raw in the sink, watching red swirl down the drain until the water runs clear. My arms are clean now, but the scrubs are ruined. Bloodstains splatter the fabric like some macabre painting. The smell of iron clings to me no matter how hard I breathe.

I press my back against the cold tile wall, sliding down, knees drawing up, and I let it out. The sobs. The kind you choke on, the kind that wrack through your chest and leave you empty.

"Hey."

Stasia's voice breaks through. She rounds the corner,

and when she sees me—sees the state I'm in—her expression softens instantly.

"What happened back there?" she asks gently, crouching down beside me.

I shake my head, wiping at my face uselessly. "She looked like you, Stas. Like us. And I—" My throat tightens. "I couldn't stop. I kept seeing you on that table. I couldn't let her go."

Stasia doesn't say anything at first. She just sinks down onto the floor next to me and pulls me against her. Her arms are warm, steady, and I bury my face in her shoulder like I used to when we were kids.

"She wasn't me," she murmurs into my hair. "She wasn't you either. We did everything we could."

"I know," I whisper, though the words feel like lies.

"We knew we weren't going to win that one, Sera. But we tried like hell."

We sit there, pressed together, the only stillness in a hospital that never stops moving.

The curtain whips back suddenly. A harried orderly pokes his head in. "Hey—where's the patient with the head wound? Guy from the crash?"

Stasia and I both blink. I frown, pushing up onto shaky legs. "What do you mean? He was sedated. There's no way he—"

But when I cross the hall into the bay, the bed is empty. The monitors still beep, cords dangling loose. The floor is smeared with footprints, a trail of red leading nowhere.

And on the mattress, where he had been sitting, lies a single rose.

White. Blood-soaked.

I stare at it until my vision blurs again. Not because of him, not because of the strangeness of it being left behind, but because I know—deep down—I can't do this anymore.

I can't walk into a trauma room and the patient's face becomes my sister's.

Another night like this, and it'll break me.

After that night in the hospital, Seraphina quit nursing. Said she couldn't do it anymore—couldn't look at a patient without seeing Stasia. Couldn't face another code where all she saw was her sister's face going slack. She tossed the rose he left behind in the trash, not realizing how significant it would become in her life.

The nurse had sworn he'd only turned his back for a second, prepping sedation, and the bastard was gone. Staff searched; security swept every floor. No sign of him.

And then the drunk—the one with nothing more than a busted arm, the one who killed a woman with his selfishness—turned up dead the next morning. No trauma, no struggle. Everyone thought the hospital missed something, botched the case. There was an investigation, but nothing stuck.

Now it makes sense. Caleb Ward could've slipped into

his room, found the man who killed his fiancée, and smothered him with a pillow while he slept. Simple. Quiet. Final.

But the story didn't end there.

Jaxon dug deeper, pulling records nobody else thought to cross-check. Turns out Caleb was picked up hours later, wandering the streets, covered in blood, half out of his mind. EMS logged him as a John Doe and took him to another hospital across town. He got treatment there—but a traumatic brain injury like his doesn't heal easy, and it's clear he never got himself much care after.

So, he unraveled. And in that broken place, Seraphina became Sarah.

The one who died on the table while Seraphina pressed the life out of her chest, begging her back. In his head, they fused.

It took him six months to track her down and get a job at the Ledger. And from there, he sank into her shadow—watching, waiting.

The notes came first. The flowers followed, close to the one-year mark of Sarah's death. Jaxon checked—it lined up exactly. And now we're staring down the five-year anniversary.

Makes sense why he's escalating.

Why he wrote TIME'S UP on the wall.

The anniversary is tomorrow.

But I'm not waiting for tomorrow. I'm not luring him out or playing defense while he circles.

This ends today.

When I left Seraphina with Lucian, I could read the look

on her face. The words hanging off the top of her tongue that she was battling to hold back.

Don't make me promise not to kill him, I told her. *Because I won't.*

She doesn't deserve a life of shadows. Doesn't deserve to wonder when he'll come again.

She deserves peace.

And I'm going to make sure she fucking gets it.

I park down the block, engine cut, lights off. Caleb's apartment squats in the middle of a row of tired brick buildings, the kind of place you only notice when the rot starts to show. Perfect cover for a ghost.

I don't walk straight in. I circle. Once, twice. Every alley, every doorway, every flickering light bulb above a cracked stoop. I wait, watching the windows. Fifteen minutes. Nothing stirs.

Everything is too quiet.

I move. Up the stairwell, testing each board before my weight hits it. His door is cheap, lock cheaper. I slip it in seconds.

The smell slams me in the face the second the door cracks open.

Sweet. Heavy. Wrong.

Rot.

The kind that settles into the walls and doesn't leave.

My grip tightens on the knife at my hip, but I already know I won't need it.

He's dead.

Caleb Ward sits slumped in a chair, jaw loose, eyepatch still strapped across his ruined face. His body has started to sag, skin pulling away, the stink of it thick enough to choke on.

But it isn't the decay that holds me frozen.

It's the knife in his chest.

My knife—or close enough. Same steel, same curve of the hilt, same balance I've carried for years. Except for the letter inlaid in the handle.

Not a K.

A C.

Cormac.

My brother.

The world tilts, bile stinging my throat. Caleb's been dead for days. Which means everything since—the roses, the writing, the games—wasn't him. It was Cormac.

He wanted me to find this. To know.

This isn't about Caleb Ward. It never was.

It's about me.

And about the war we started when Seraphina was taken. The day blood spilled in the street and didn't stop until my cousin hit the ground with Lucian's bullet in his skull. I fired the first shot. Lucian ended it.

Cormac hasn't forgotten.

He's not after Caleb. Not even after Seraphina.

He's after me. After Lucian.

But he'll use her blood to gut me. And he'll use the Ledger to burn Lucian's empire to the ground.

The knife in Caleb's chest isn't a victory.

It's a message.

And if he knows I'm coming here, that means I'm already too late.

Chapter 36
Seraphina

The penthouse feels too big without Killian.

I keep trying to distract myself, folding laundry that doesn't need folding, rinsing lettuce leaves that taste like ash when I chew them. My stomach's a knot, and every tick of the clock just makes it tighter.

Lucian hasn't stopped. He's been on the phone for hours, pacing the living room like a storm in a suit, his voice all steel and clipped orders. I've told him twenty times it's fine for him to leave, that I'm safe here with Finn and the others, but he won't hear it. Not after what happened at the Ledger.

The break-in cracked something in all of us. The impenetrable fortress wasn't so impenetrable after all.

Another call comes through. This time, he doesn't put it on speaker. He just lifts the phone to his ear, his posture shifting subtly as he listens.

I only catch pieces—Damien Wolfe's name, Manhattan tycoon, Lucian's old friend. My mind scrambles to keep up.

Damien developed the Ledger skyscraper. Lucian had pulled him in, along with the two architects who designed the building—Dante and Grant. He didn't just want blueprints. He wanted everything. The wiring. The ventilation. Every hidden artery that kept the tower breathing.

And right now, they're at the Ledger, leading the search, directing teams, making sure not a single corner is left unchecked. Jaxon is there too, buried in tech, digging into what caused the blackout—what gave Caleb Ward his opening to slip inside and vandalize the atrium.

Then Lucian's voice changes.

Lower. Darker.

My head snaps up. His eyes cut to me, sharp and steady, and in that moment I feel it in my bones: something is very wrong.

He lifts one finger to his mouth. *Don't talk.*

My throat tightens.

"Understood," he says into the phone, his tone so even it feels rehearsed. Then his gaze flicks to Finn, lounging in an armchair with a newspaper. Lucian snaps his fingers twice.

Finn is on his feet instantly, the paper sliding to the floor, his expression stone.

Lucian checks his watch. "Fifteen," he says, like it's code.

The call ends.

He motions with his hand—pen. Paper.

I scramble to the kitchen, pulling open drawers with shaking fingers until I find both and thrust them at him.

His hand moves fast, writing with a force that nearly tears the page:

– Penthouse is bugged

– Don't say anything

– Going to Ledger

He lays the pen down. That's all we get.

Finn nods once like it's enough. Like it explains everything.

But my mind is spinning, a million questions colliding all at once. *How long? Where? Who's listening right now?*

Lucian doesn't give me a second glance. He slips the note into his pocket, smooth as folding a handkerchief, and walks straight to the door. Quiet. Controlled. A man who leaves nothing behind but silence.

The door shuts, and I'm still standing in the kitchen with my heart in my throat when Finn clears his throat. His brogue is bright, cheery, almost jarring.

"How about some tea, lass?"

As if nothing is wrong at all.

"Yeah," I manage, my voice catching. "Tea."

My hands feel clumsy as I grab the kettle, fill it under the tap. The gush of water is too loud, too bright against the silence, but it gives Finn cover. He leans down, whispers something quick into the ear of one of the other guards. The man nods once and slips out as quietly as Lucian had left.

I want to reach for my phone, to text Killian, to tell him something is wrong. My fingers itch for it, but Finn is there, shaking his head before I can type a word. No. Wordless but clear. Anything electronic could be under watch too.

The kettle fills, and I set it on the stove, twisting the burner on. The blue flame sputters to life, but my insides are still ice.

I sit at the table, nails picking against each other until

they ache. My eyes drift, unfocused, until they land on Killian's jacket still slung over the back of a chair. Black leather, worn and heavy.

I want to put it on.

I want to bury myself in the smell of him, in the heat of it, pretend it's his arms wrapping around me instead of the empty silence pressing against the windows.

I didn't even realize I'd taken it until I was lifting it to my nose and breathing it in. Closing my eyes, I use it to cover my shoulders, tucking my arms inside and playing with the jacket's edge. The dread coils tighter inside me with every second that passes.

Like something is already on its way.

My fingers toy with a hard speck, like a small button in an odd location.

A thought gnaws at me.

Flowers.

Where are the flowers?

They'd been there all along—every note, every shadowed reminder. If it wasn't a rose pressed into my hand, it was one embossed on the corner of an envelope. A petal drawn in ink at the edge of a letter.

But these last few days...

Barrett Hall's vandalized car. The hair dumped onto silver platters. The atrium at the Ledger desecrated with spray paint and filth.

No flowers.

Not one.

I can't shake it. But the speck on Killian's jacket comes

off. It could have been a crumb of some kind, but as I stare at it on the tip of my finger, my pulse thunders.

"Hey, Finn?" I call, turning in my chair. "What's—"

The door bursts open.

Gunfire cracks, deafening.

The bullet tears into the stove behind me. Gas meets spark.

The explosion is just enough to rip me off my feet. The blast throws me hard to the ground. My ears scream with a high-pitched ringing that swallows every other sound.

I blink through the haze, through the smoke, and Finn is there, on the ground beside me.

A knife juts from the center of his chest. His eyes are wide, glassy, his mouth open as if to speak. His chest still moves—but not for long. My nurse's mind doesn't need a stethoscope to know he won't survive this.

My stomach flips, bile rising, but before I can crawl to him, hands seize me.

I'm rolled onto my back, the ceiling swimming above me. The light blocked out by a man.

He looks like Killian. Same sharp angles, same eyes. But these aren't Killian's eyes. They're colder. Hateful.

He smiles down at me, and it's not kindness—it's knives and promises of pain.

The ringing in my ears fades into static, and I can just make out his voice, distorted, heavy, like I'm hearing him underwater.

"Name's Cormac." His smile widens, cruel. "You've been keeping my brother quite distracted, haven't you?"

I'm tearing through Manhattan like the devil is on my bumper, one hand locked around the wheel, the other hitting redial again and again.

No answer.

Her number just rings.

Yesterday's memory won't let go—the blackout, her penthouse swallowed in darkness, my heart dropping into my stomach. Feels like that was a warning. A shadow cast ahead of tonight.

Now it's happening for real.

"Pick up," I growl, flooring it through another red light. Horns blare, brakes screech, but I don't stop. Can't. I'm closer to the Ledger than her place, but my gut's already twisting, screaming I'm behind. That I'm too goddamn late.

The phone in my hand vibrates, then shrieks.

A sound I never wanted to hear.

The Ledger app.

Its alert cuts through me like a siren, sharp and merciless. It only screams like that for one reason.

Code Black.

A Companion is dead.

My chest locks, vision tunneling for a second before rage burns the haze away.

No. Not her. Not Seraphina.

I slam my foot down harder, weaving through traffic like the city belongs to me. Every instinct I have screams blood. If Cormac laid a hand on her—if he so much as breathed her air—then I'll carve my way through New York until his heart stops beating.

I'm calling everyone.

Lucian. Straight to voicemail.

Finn. Nothing.

Her. Again. Still nothing.

Every second of silence tightens around my throat until I'm choking on it.

The app goes off again, louder this time, blaring like an air raid siren. My eyes flick to the screen on the dash.

CODE BLACK: All Companions report to a checkpoint. All Contracts are cancelled effective immediately.

The words blur as my pulse spikes. Cancelled contracts. Companions recalled. That only happens when blood's been spilled.

When someone's dead.

"No," I grind out, shoving the phone back to my ear. I call her again. Listen to the empty rings, to the void on the other side, until the sound almost suffocates me.

I can't breathe. Can't think.

I try Jaxon. This time, the line clicks open.

"Jesus Christ, finally," I snarl, but the moment he speaks, I know. His tone isn't clipped and efficient like it should be. It's low. Shaken.

"Killian..."

My stomach drops. "Don't waste time. Who was it?"

"They just... they just found the body."

My hands clamp around the wheel, knuckles bone white. "Where? At the Ledger?"

"Yes."

The word is a nail driven straight through my chest. I cut the wheel hard, tires screaming as I whip a U-turn into oncoming traffic. Horns explode, lights flash, but I don't stop.

"Is it her?" My voice rips out of me, raw. "Seraphina. Is it her?"

Silence.

"Jaxon!" I roar it so loud the phone nearly cracks in my hand. "Fucking tell me!"

On the other end, his breath stutters. "I—" His voice breaks. "Yes. Sienna found her."

The world tilts. The city smears past in a blur I can't see.

"I'm so sorry, Killian."

The words gut me. I feel the ground fall out from under me, my chest collapsing in on itself. Terror floods every vein, cold and merciless.

I can't lose her.

Not like this.

Not to him.

I make it there in minutes, the car screaming up onto the

curb, tires spitting rubber. I don't even cut the engine. I tear across the sidewalk, through the Ledger's revolving door like a missile with one target.

The lobby is chaos. Eve and Elena are crouched around Sienna. She's sobbing, face blotched and red, clutching at Elena like she's trying not to break in half. When her eyes land on me, she almost does.

The bottom drops out of my stomach.

"Where is she?" My voice is a roar, raw, already shattering.

Sienna shakes her head, tears streaming. "Killian—don't go out there."

"Where the fuck is she, Sienna!?" I boom, the sound echoing off marble and glass.

Eve's voice cracks. "Parking deck. Lucian is there." She's crying too, and my heart is about to detonate in my chest.

I run. Through the building, past security, slamming my palms against the bar of the heavy steel door that leads into the Ledger's private garage.

"Killian!" Jaxon shouts from behind me, but I don't stop.

The door crashes open and I see them.

Lucian, kneeling. His massive frame bowed in a way I've never seen, as if even he's crushed by the weight of it. A ring of security stands frozen around him, faces pale. And at the center, sprawled on the concrete, is a body covered by a sheet.

A sheet already stained through with blood.

Lucian rises when he sees me, hands outstretched like he means to stop me.

"It's not Seraphina, Killian."

I don't care. I'll plow through him, tear the world apart if I have to. I need to see.

"Move." My voice is a growl, feral.

Lucian doesn't fight me when I shove past him. My knees hit the concrete hard as I grip the edge of the sheet. My hands shake when I pull it back.

The sight beneath rips me apart.

It's not Seraphina.

It's Sylvia.

The decoy. The Companion we used to give Sera a night of peace at her niece's birthday. The blonde hair on those silver platters. The word LIAR sprayed in blood. They'd figured it out. Turned the game back on us.

Her face is nearly unrecognizable. Bruises, cuts, split lips. Her nails torn to the beds, jagged and broken like she clawed across the ground, fighting for her life. Her shirt rides up, showing a stomach carved open by stab after stab after stab.

Too many to count.

Like they kept going long after she was gone.

There's a blood trail from the back of a car across the concrete. She made it as far as the driver's side door before she collapsed. Before she couldn't crawl any farther.

My vision blurs red.

This has Cormac written all over it. His brand. His cruelty. Just like our father—he doesn't flinch using innocents to wage his wars. Collateral damage isn't collateral to him. It's the point.

And I know without a single doubt in my mind—he's planning on making Seraphina the next body I find.

Sylvia's hand looks wrong.

I don't notice it at first, not until I lean closer and see how tightly her fingers are curled, rigid even in death. Something has been forced there, shoved between them. I ease it free, the paper crinkling in my blood-slick gloves as I unroll it.

Two words stare back at me, written in thick black ink.

Time's up.

The same words that had been painted across the atrium wall yesterday.

The sound of the garage door crashing open behind me makes me whip my head around. Jaxon bursts in, his laptop already open, his face pale with sweat.

"We've got two problems," he announces, voice carrying over the heavy silence of the parking deck.

I push to my feet, the note still clutched in my fist, and shove it at Lucian. "And another message," I grind out, the words thick with rage.

Lucian takes it, his eyes scanning quickly before his jaw locks hard enough I hear the faint crack of his teeth.

Jaxon doesn't pause. He strides to the nearest car and slams the laptop down on its hood, the glow of the screen washing his face in cold light. "Seraphina's apartment has gone dark again. And—" his voice falters, just for a breath, "—there's already a 911 call about an explosion."

The air leaves my lungs.

For a heartbeat, all I can see is her on the ground covered in that sheet and it's enough to rip me in two.

I start moving without thinking. My body turns toward the door, toward the street, toward her. But Jaxon's voice cuts through, urgent and sharp. He grips my arm, holding me here.

"Killian, wait. We need you here."

I round on him so fast my vision tunnels. Both hands fly to his chest, and I push him back. "She's out there, Jax. Don't you fucking dare try to keep me here when she's—" My voice cracks, raw and violent, my chest threatening to split in two.

"We have a bigger fucking problem, Kill."

He spins the laptop toward us.

On the screen is a countdown timer, its numbers bleeding red, each second slipping away like a drop of blood.

Lucian steps closer, his shadow heavy beside me, but it's Jaxon's voice I hear. Flat. Grim.

"The whole building is wired to blow."

The words sink like stones into my chest, heavier with every breath.

I want to run to her. God, I want to tear out of here and find her before it's too late. But my legs won't move, caught between the love that has rooted itself so deep inside me it feels like my soul—and the reality that if I leave this building, the Ledger and everyone in it could be reduced to ash.

And somewhere in the city, my brother is watching. Laughing.

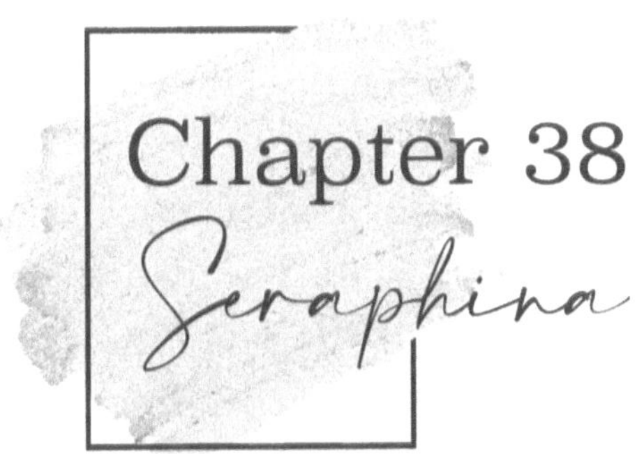

Chapter 38
Seraphina

The last thing I remember is the sting in my arm, the burn of a needle sliding under my skin before I could fight it off. The heaviness came fast—too fast. Not the haze of alcohol, not the slow drift of sleep. This was chemical. Precise.

Midazolam, probably.

I've given it enough times to know the sensation—the sharp drop, the way the world folds in on itself in seconds. A sedative, quick and dirty. The kind you use when you want someone compliant but not gone too long.

Someone took me. I blink and shake my head, trying to pull the memories forward.

Cormac.

The name slams into me, and suddenly the fog in my head feels heavier. My mouth is dry, my tongue thick. I try to shift, only to realize I can't.

My wrists are bound in front of me, rope biting deep, the coarse fibers grinding my skin raw when I test them. A gag stretches tight across my mouth, pressing hard into the corners of my lips, damp with saliva. A second rope winds around my torso, cinching me back against a chair so tight it forces my ribs to ache with every breath.

A quick look at my thumbnail makes my heart lurch. They knew I wore a tracking device there, must have scanned me to find it. It's been filed away.

Killian and Lucian won't have a way to find me, just like before. The irony of this being so similar to the situation that caused this war in the first place.

I draw in air, but it stinks. Ash. Damp stone. Something old, burned, and left to rot.

When my eyes finally focus, I see the ruins around me.

It's a cathedral—or it used to be. The skeleton of one, really. Charred stone walls loom jagged and broken, sections collapsed into heaps of rubble. The wall to my right has crumbled away entirely, daylight streaming in through the open wound, while another section has fallen behind the altar, leaving only a cracked crucifix still hanging against the blackened stone.

Most of the roof is gone. Only a section behind me remains, sagging timbers blackened by fire. This place looks as though it should have been condemned years ago. The fact that it still stands feels like some cruel trick of fate.

I twist harder, trying to work my wrists free, ignoring the sting as the rope scrapes deeper into my skin. Nothing gives. My shoulders tremble with the effort until I collapse back against the chair, breath ragged behind the gag.

And then I hear laughter. Voices.

Low, rough, echoing off the stone and getting closer.

I turn my head just as he enters, cigarette glowing in the shadows, a plume of smoke curling out as he exhales slow and deliberate, like he's savoring every second.

He looks enough like Killian that my chest wrenches, but his eyes are wrong. Harder. Colder. Empty in a way Killian's could never be.

"Well, well, well." Cormac drags on the cigarette again, letting the smoke spill from his mouth like he's drawing out the suspense. "Seraphina."

He says my name slowly, rolling each letter, as though he's testing it on his tongue.

"Glad you woke up in time." His voice carries a faint Irish lilt, heavier than Killian's but not so thick it masks the cruelty behind it. "Thought you were going to miss the big show."

His smile grows, and it's nothing but knives.

My throat works around the gag, desperate to form words, but all that comes out is a muffled sound. Still, he understands. He tilts his head, smoke curling from his lips.

"You're wondering about your guard, aren't you?" His tone is flat, almost bored. "Poor Finn. Loyal old dog. To some at least. Not his family, though."

He taps ash onto the stone floor, eyes never leaving mine. "Probably in a body bag by now, I would say."

The words hit harder than any fist. My eyes squeeze shut, a tear breaking free and sliding down my cheek.

He crouches in front of me, the shift of his weight making the chair creak beneath me. His face is so close now I can smell the smoke on his breath, the tang of nicotine and something darker.

"But you shouldn't worry about anyone but yourself... Seraphina."

This time, he spits my name like it tastes foul, like it's poison in his mouth.

His hand shoots up, fingers clamping down on my cheeks, squeezing until my jaw aches. He forces my face up, forces me to look into those cold, empty eyes that feel like they're burrowing into my skull.

The cigarette glows bright in his other hand as he brings it closer. Slowly. Too slowly. The burning tip aimed at my face.

"I have something special in mind for you."

My heart pounds against the ropes holding me. I try to stay still, try to keep my body from jerking back, but tiny whimpers still slip past the gag. The heat radiates off the cigarette as he hovers it closer and closer to my eye.

And I know—God, I know—he would do it. He'd blind me and smile while I screamed.

I force myself still, chest heaving, my lashes wet as another tear tracks down.

Then, just as suddenly as he started, he jerks the cigarette back. As though he's lost interest in the game. He sticks it between his lips again, inhales deep, and exhales like nothing happened.

His dozen men chuckle from their various positions around me.

The click of his lighter echoes as he checks his watch with a casual glance. Smoke curls into the ruined air.

"Mmm... three minutes." His voice is almost sing-song.

"Just enough time to let our little angel in on the festivities for the night."

I don't have time to wonder what that means before he moves again.

No warning as to what he does next.

The cigarette comes down hard against my thigh, searing through fabric, biting into skin.

The pain rips through me, white-hot, and I scream against the gag, thrashing in the ropes as the smell of my own burning flesh fills the air.

He presses it in, grinding it deeper.

The heat lingers even after he pulls the cigarette away, a molten ache burrowed deep into my thigh. My body shakes, breath tearing out of me too fast, too heavy. I try to pull it together, to compose myself, to give him nothing—but I can't stop the tears. Can't stop the wet streaks cutting down my cheeks or the sound of my ragged breathing through the gag. It feels like lava has been poured into me, boring straight through flesh to bone.

He crouches again, watching me tremble. His hand flashes up, fingers striking across my face in a sharp slap— not hard enough to split my lip, not hard enough to make me see sparks, but enough to jolt me. To pull my focus back to him.

"Listen." His voice is rough, low, threaded with something colder than cruelty. "This is important, burning angel."

The words dig into me. *Burning angel.*

My stomach drops as he leans in closer. "You should

know... you inspired me. Your name. And of course—our father's favorite way of settling debts."

The memory of Killian's voice crashes into me. *He burned down a church with his enemy inside.*

My chest seizes as the realization slams into me. This place—the charred stone, the blackened beams sagging above me—it's not just ruins. It's history. A grave. The very church their father burned, the walls still standing like broken teeth after swallowing his enemy and innocent children whole.

And before Cormac even says it, I know. This is what he has planned for me.

To let me burn.

His smile is thin, cruel. He grabs my chin again and forces my head to turn, to look past the collapsed wall.

"Before that, though—tell me. Any of those buildings look familiar to you?"

I choke on a gasp as my eyes fix on the skyline. Of course it's familiar. It's home. My home. Right there in the center of the horizon, tall and gleaming—the Black Ledger.

He doesn't need to explain. The vantage point is perfect. My stomach twists into a fist of ice.

"Beautiful, isn't it?" he says softly, almost reverent. "The perfect place to watch my own method of revenge. A little different than Father's. But just as permanent."

He nods to one of the men behind him. "Go ahead and let it go, Johnny. What's a minute early?"

The man pulls out his phone, taps the screen.

I can't move. Can't breathe. I'm tied to this chair, helpless, forced to stare through the jagged frame of collapsed stone at the city beyond. *My* city.

The Ledger's upper floors detonate with a roar that shakes even the bones of this ruined church, fire punching into the sky as if to burn out the stars themselves. More blasts march down the building, blowing out windows like an elevator of destruction riding straight to the ground.

My scream claws at the gag, strangled, useless—swallowed by the blaze ripping through the horizon.

Cormac exhales smoke like he's savoring it, his grin split wide, eyes alight with triumph. "There it is," he says, voice almost reverent. "Lucian Vale gutted our empire, so I've gutted his. The infamous Black Ledger, reduced to ash. Cleansing this rotten city of its whores and dogs by fire. Poetic, isn't it?"

The building hasn't collapsed. Through my tears, through the smoke billowing, the structure is there—but God knows if it will remain.

He turns back to me, his smile curdling, cruel. "And as for Killian..." He crouches close, his breath hot with nicotine. "My brother spilled family blood. Our cousin's blood. Before I take his life, I'll spill the blood that will carve the heart out of him. Yours." His eyes glitter. "He was so emotional when the children burned. I can only imagine how he'll beg when he learns the woman he loves was burned alive too. All for his sins."

My stomach lurches, bile clawing up my throat, but I hold his gaze, refusing to give him the satisfaction of seeing me break.

"And he was the one who walked in your penthouse and

planted my little device. Pretty ingenious, huh? He never even felt it when the kid stuck it on his jacket."

Cormac turns and spits. "And you know the tech giant that engineered it—well, reverse-engineered it, at least. Elijah Carter made a few modifications to the tech Lucian has been protecting the Ledger with. And we used it to bring it down."

There's a grumble of laughter from the surrounding guards.

"We also used it to shoot my big brother's falling angel right out of the sky. That tiny little *speck* you found on his jacket did it all."

He jerks his head, and one of his men steps forward, a knife flashing as he slices through the rope binding me to the chair. My hands are still tied in front of me, raw and burning, but my torso is free now.

Cormac grabs a fistful of my hair, yanking me to my feet. Pain sears across my scalp, and I claw at his wrist, desperate to ease the pressure, but his grip is iron. I kick, twist, dig my heels into the ground, but I'm outsized and outnumbered. He's not as big as Killian, but big enough.

They drag me through a doorway into the darker part of the church, where the stone hasn't burned as badly. The air is damp, colder. The corridor turns sharply before ending in a flight of narrow stone stairs, spiraling down into total black.

Every nerve in me screams *no*. I know with every shred of my being that if they take me down there, I'll never see daylight again.

I cling to the only thought that keeps me upright—that

somehow, by some miracle, Killian wasn't in that building when it went up. That he's alive. That he'll come for me. That he still knows his brother well enough to guess where he's brought me, even with my tracker destroyed.

The stairs yawn before me like a throat waiting to swallow me whole.

No.

I dig in, twisting, and slam both feet against the wall with all the strength I can gather. The force rockets me backward, my skull connecting with Cormac's nose in a sickening crunch.

His roar splits the air as his grip releases, blood spraying down his lips. I hit the ground hard, scrambling, wrists clumsy in their bonds, chest heaving.

But I'm not fast enough.

Before I can rise, his hand fists in my hair again, vicious.

"You little cunt," he spits, his words thick with blood and hate.

Then he hurls me forward—without care, without pause, without a shred of mercy.

I tumble, body slamming against unyielding stone, the world spinning as I crash down the dark staircase into nothing.

Chapter 39
Seraphina

The world tilts sideways as I slam into the stone landing. Air punches out of my lungs, ribs screaming with the impact. My shoulder takes the brunt, white-hot pain flashing through me, and I roll, only to crash into the next set of steps. Each jagged edge batters bone until I sprawl at the bottom, a heap of broken breath and throbbing limbs.

The room spins. My vision splits, then fuses again. The copper taste of blood blooms across my tongue, thick and cloying. I try to push up, but my elbow buckles beneath me, useless. My body feels like a marionette with its strings cut, limp and unsteady.

And then—

Boot steps. Slow. Unhurried.

Cormac strolls down the stairwell like he's coming for Sunday supper, not walking into the ashes of a tomb, not dragging me into hell. The harsh shadows hide the sharp angles of his face, his smile carved cruel and thin.

Several of his men trail behind, shadows hulking, weapons glinting. At the top, he jerks his chin without looking back.

"Keep watch up there. If any Ledger dogs come sniffin', don't let 'em past."

Their footsteps fade, leaving me with this devil and the monsters at his side.

I try to scramble back, nails scraping over the gritty stone, but one of the men hauls me up like I weigh nothing. My body jerks, protesting every tug and drag as they force me forward.

The air down here is damp, colder, carrying the smell of mildew and rot. The underbelly of the church.

And then I see it.

The pyre.

A lattice of wood stacked high, blackened already at the edges like it's been tested, waiting. In the center, a thick beam rises, jagged and cruel, prepared for a body to be lashed against it. My stomach heaves. My heart jack-hammers.

"No." The word mumbles through the gag, raw and broken. I thrash, kicking, clawing—anything—but it's useless against their grip. One of them slams a fist into my gut and the air rips out of me again.

Cormac laughs, low and mean.

"Don't waste your breath, love. You'll need it for screamin'."

I twist harder, panic clawing up my throat. My wrists burn where they tied them, using the rope to drag me closer,

closer. My mind races—Killian, is he alive? Did he make it out? He has to. He has to.

But Cormac leans down, his face close enough I can smell the whiskey and cigarettes on his breath.

"You know what I like best, Seraphina? Poetic endings. Even if my brother does come for you, he'll never make it to you in time. Not before the fire takes you."

My protesting scream rips through the stone belly of the church as they shove me forward—

—straight against the thick beam waiting for me.

Rough hands wrench my arms back, the coarse bite of rope grinding into raw skin. They bind me tight to the beam, my shoulders pressed hard against the splintered wood until I can feel every jag digging into bone. Each pull of the rope squeezes the air out of me a little more, cinching me down, making me part of the pyre.

Cormac prowls in front of me, his smile stretched wide, casual as sin. The flick of his silver Zippo clicks open, closed, open again—flame flaring before he snaps it out with a flick of his wrist. He toys with it like a boy with a new prize, waiting for his moment.

"Ledger, Ledger, Ledger," he muses, voice echoing off the stone. "All those fine ladies and gents blowin' to kingdom come. Wonder if they were still scrubbin' their faces in the spa when the fire kissed 'em. Or maybe mid-fuck upstairs—burnin' with their cocks still out. Ah, poetic, aye?" He laughs, sharp and cruel. His men chuckle too, low and mean, though their eyes keep darting to the flames dancing from his lighter.

My stomach knots. I jerk against the bindings, chest heaving, eyes scanning the dark corners of the basement. Dust. Stone. Broken pews, cobwebs strung like shrouds. Nothing I can use. Nothing to save me. The scant light comes from the crackling lighter and then—a crash above. Shouts.

We all freeze.

Boots pounding, voices raised, echoing down through the floorboards. Gunfire comes sudden and sharp, rattling the ceiling dust down into my hair.

Hope bursts inside me like oxygen.

Killian.

It has to be.

Cormac stiffens, then snarls, spitting orders over his shoulder. "Go! Don't let him near. Put him in the fucking ground!"

Two of his men rush for the stairs, weapons drawn, boots thundering upward. That leaves him. Him and three shadows lingering at his flanks.

Cormac turns back to me, grin returning slow and vicious. He steps close enough that I can feel the heat of the flame he coaxes to life again with his lighter, the tiny fire that promises so much worse. His eyes glitter with hate and triumph.

"Let's give him a proper welcome, eh?" He winks, almost tender in its mockery—

—and flicks the burning Zippo down into the dry kindling at my feet.

The pyre answers with a hungry roar.

The fire crackles—hungry, eager—curling up the brittle

edges of the stacked wood. Smoke begins to sting my eyes, acrid and sharp, searing my lungs with every gasp. The heat licks closer and soon will be chasing up my legs. The air is heavy with ash and the stink of old rot and burning mildew.

Cormac lingers, arms folded like he's watching a stage play instead of orchestrating my death. His expression is smug, satisfied, the flames mirrored in his eyes. "Beautiful," he murmurs, like this is art.

I wrench against the ropes until they tear my skin raw. My wrists are slick with blood, but the knots hold. My throat tightens around a sob. This is it. This is how I die.

And then—a sound.

Low. Rough. A growl that doesn't belong in any church, not even one blackened with sin.

The edges of the room seem to darken, a burst of shadow swallowing the meager light. Two flashes explode in the dark—gunfire—and one of Cormac's men drops with a wet grunt, body folding into the dirt.

Then he's there.

Killian.

He barrels into another guard like a battering ram, the two of them crashing into the stacked timbers. They go down in a brutal tangle of fists and fury. Another guard yanks his weapon free, muzzle sparking as shots ring out. Bullets ricochet, stone spits dust, the sound deafening in the close chamber.

"Get in there, you useless shite!" Cormac roars, shoving the gunman toward the fight.

Then his attention slides back to me.

He snatches a length of wood from the pyre, its end

already lit and spitting embers. With deliberate care, he thrusts it into the voids around me—dark corners of stacked timber that the fire hasn't yet touched. Flames crawl greedily over fresh fuel, climbing higher, closer, eager to swallow me whole.

Panic claws through me. I cough, lungs raw, heat blistering against my shins. My mind races for escape, for hope.

But maybe... maybe the stale, dank air of this basement will be my saving grace. Maybe the smothering dark, the lack of breath, will keep the fire starving—will buy me the seconds Killian needs.

If it doesn't—no. I can't think of that.

The fight crashes around me, violent and unrelenting. The guns run dry, and the men are fighting with their fists now.

Killian against two—fists and fury echoing like thunder in this stone tomb. Every time he swings, his gaze flicks to me—panic in his eyes, desperation carved into his face. He knows. He knows I have minutes, maybe less, before the flames devour me.

Cormac smirks, inspired by the discarded furniture littering the open room, and heaves a tall cabinet into the blaze. It topples with a crash, wood splintering, glass doors shattering as it slams against my side and the stacked timber around me. The fire leaps higher, swallowing greedily. The sharp edge of glass punches deep into my thigh.

My scream tears out but dies against the gag, strangled and useless.

I look down, chest heaving, and see the shard—long, jagged, buried to the hilt in muscle. My hands tremble so hard I can barely keep focus, but I know. I can use it. It missed anything vital. It's sharp. It's hope.

I push everything else—the fire, Cormac, Killian—to the back of my mind and fix on the shard. My fingers close around it, slippery with sweat and soot. I pull. My body jerks in revolt, pain blazing up my thigh, so raw it steals the breath from my lungs. My muffled scream burns my throat, tears flooding my smoke-stung eyes.

I can do this.

I breathe steady through my nose, force my hands back. Fix my grip and pull.

The torment is white-hot and searing, but I wrench it free, careful not to let it slip from my shaking hands. The shard drips with my blood, slick and red, but it's mine. It's salvation.

I twist it against the ropes binding my torso—sawing, sawing. Each drag slices my palms open further, blood mixing with soot, the shard threatening to slide loose. I grit my teeth, hold on, force it down, again and again.

"Cormac!" Killian calls out to his brother.

I look up—his gray eyes lock on mine just as a fist crashes into his gut, folding him over, another smashing across his face. The men seize his arms, holding him wide open.

It works. Cormac stops throwing things into the fire and steps toward him.

I can't hear his words over the roar of fire, but I see the grin. The promise.

I can't stop. I can't let the fire touch me, can't let him fall. The flames crawl higher, licking at my arms, singeing my skin. My clothes will catch soon. Once they do, it's over.

I saw harder, sobs shaking me, tears blurring my vision. I don't look away. Can't. Even as the fire sears closer, even as Killian bleeds. I keep sawing, desperate, frantic—

Until the rope gives with a snap.

It slacks, falling away from my torso. My arms wrench upward, pushing the coil higher until I can duck and slide out from under it. My wrists are still bound tight, skin flayed raw, but I'm free of the beam.

The fire rages behind me, heat blistering at my back. The cut in my thigh throbs with every movement, blood slicking my leg, but I can move. I stumble, eyes searching—anywhere to jump, to roll, to throw myself clear of the pyre before it swallows me whole.

The toppled cabinet becomes my salvation. Its splintered side juts just far enough from the pyre to give me a foothold.

I steady myself, rope-burned wrists clumsy, thigh screaming with every move. My balance falters, but I push. Jump.

The injured leg drags me down like an anchor. I don't make the distance I need. My lower leg plunges into the fire, heat searing through denim as flames clutch hungrily at my calf. Pain tears a scream from my throat as I roll, slapping frantically until the blaze dies, leaving scorched patches across my jeans.

But I'm out. Free.

I rip the gag from my mouth, chest heaving, lungs

aching for air. My voice rips raw, louder than the roar of the fire.

"Killian!"

Two of Cormac's men hold him wide, his arms stretched, his face bloodied—his lip split, blood running in a dark line from his brow down the scar carved there years before.

He looks up when he hears me.

And something changes.

The pain is still there, but beneath it is iron. Determination. Rage sharpened to a single point.

He surges, using their hold against them, and drives his boot into Cormac's chest. The impact cracks like thunder, sending his brother flying backward toward the furnace he created.

He doesn't stop.

An elbow smashes into one guard's face, the crunch of breaking bone echoing in the chamber. The man howls, blood pouring from his ruined nose. Killian turns his head, slamming his skull into the other man's with brutal precision. The guard reels, dazed, and Killian's fist follows, crushing across his jaw and sending him stumbling.

The man staggers. Trips over debris. Falls—

And I move before I think.

The shard is still in my hand, slick with my blood. I raise it high and chase him down, the world narrowing to fire, smoke, and survival.

When his body slams against the concrete, I drive the glass deep into his neck. It slides through flesh and sinew, crunching against the ground beneath as it bursts out the other side. The shard shatters, jagged edges cracking, blood flooding hot over my hand.

The man jerks once, twice, then goes still.

I stay there, shaking, breath ragged, staring at what I've done.

And when I lift my head, my eyes lock with Killian's across the smoke and fire.

Chapter 40
Killian

Freedom's at my back.

Between me and the woman I love are two men that need to die, and a fire that wants to take her from me.

The church won't last much longer. Flames crawl up the toppled cabinet Cormac shoved into the pyre, climbing the wall, licking at the ceiling. Smoke thickens—choking, turning every breath into a burn. The beam Seraphina was tied to glows at its base, embers spreading upward. When the fire reaches the ceiling joists, the whole goddamn place is coming down.

And then—Cormac's scream cuts through it all.

He's rolling, back a sheet of flame, arms flailing. The stench of burning flesh hits me like a hammer. One of his men tears off his jacket, beating at the fire, smothering the blaze before it eats him alive.

It gives me my second.

I take the steps fast, sliding to my knees at her side, next to the bastard she just killed. She's shaking, sobbing, blood everywhere.

"Killian." Her voice cracks, breaking me open.

She's hurt. Bad. Her thigh is pouring blood, her wrists torn raw from the ropes.

I need her gone. I need her safe so I can put my brother in the ground where he belongs. Because after what he's done to her—after what I've just seen—I'm not walking out of here without making him bleed.

Touching her is like life coming back to me.

My knife's in my hand before I even think, slicing through the bindings on her wrists. She collapses into me, arms tight around my neck, sobbing my name, kissing me like I'm the only thing tethering her to this earth. I kiss her back hard, smoke and salt and blood between us.

"Go. Find Lucian. Get out of here," I rasp, but she shakes her head.

"Not without you." Her hands cradle my face, eyes fierce even through tears. "When you go, I go."

Fucking stubborn, beautiful angel.

Her leg is bleeding like hell. I rip my shirt over my head, tear a strip free, and bind it tight around the wound. She hisses through her teeth but doesn't pull away. I knot it fast, my hands slick, furious at the blood soaking through already.

"Please, baby," I growl. "Get out of here."

Her grip only tightens. Her eyes, red-rimmed and wet, don't waver. "Not without you."

Behind us, Cormac coughs out a laugh, hoarse and

mean, singed but not dead. "That all you got, brother?" he jeers, spitting blood, voice echoing through the chamber. His man beside him looks ready—fists clenched, eyes locked on me like he's hungry for another round.

I look back at her.

She's everything.

I take one more kiss—hard, hasty, desperate—before I rip myself free. "Don't get killed," I command, fire in my voice.

She smirks, even through the smoke, even through the blood. "You too."

The sound of it is a battle cry in my chest.

I rise, knife in hand, ready to end this.

I let them hold me before. Let them think they had me. Gave Cormac his shot at glory, his chance to drag me away from her, because I knew—if I kept their eyes on me, it bought her seconds to get the fuck off that bonfire.

And it worked.

Now it's different. Now it's two-on-one, and I'm not holding back.

The first man comes at me fast, fists flying. I catch his punch on my forearm, twist, and drive my elbow into his jaw. Bone cracks. He staggers, but the second slams into my ribs with a blow that makes my chest explode with fire. I spin, fist hammering into his gut, lifting him off his feet.

It's brutal, ugly—blood and sweat slicking the stone floor, every strike fueled by one thought: get her to daylight.

I'll kill Cormac in this fire or under the sun, but she's getting out.

The heavier one catches me across the jaw with a hook

that rattles my teeth. I stumble, spitting blood, and he rips free of my grip. He grins, thinking he's got me.

He doesn't see her.

Seraphina steps out of the smoke, a length of wood in her hands, the end aflame. She swings it with everything she has. It cracks across his face, embers exploding, fire biting into flesh. He screams, clawing at his eyes.

"Move!" I bark.

She drops—instinct sharp as a blade. My knife is already in the air, spinning end over end, and it buries itself in his face with a wet thud. He drops like a stone.

One left.

Cormac.

But the fire's part of the fight now, raging hotter, feeding on the wreckage, stealing the air from our lungs. Smoke claws its way into my chest with every breath. The wood above us groans, splinters—

Cracks.

She hears it too, and her eyes snap up. The ceiling is about to come down.

She doesn't hesitate. She wrenches my blade from the corpse, hurls herself toward me just as the world caves in.

"Fuck—"

I catch her, drag her in, wrap myself around her as stone and timber crash down, the roar of destruction swallowing everything.

Smoke billows, choking, smothering. For a heartbeat, there's nothing but fire and weight and her trembling body pressed into mine.

When it settles, I lift my head, coughing hard, eyes burning. The only way out—the stairs beyond this burning room —is buried under rubble. Flames eat it greedily, chewing through splintered beams, climbing higher, hungrier.

Across the debris, Cormac rises—hair singed, face streaked with soot—but his smile is pure malice.

"Looks like we're all gonna die in here, brother." His voice is hoarse, broken, but his grin is wide. "Difference is, you'll go first. I'll slice your little angel to ribbons while you watch her bleed out. Then I'll join Father in hell, and we'll drink to your ruin."

I stare at him through the smoke, chest heaving, rage boiling hotter than the fire around us.

"You won't touch her, Cormac. Not a fuckin' hair."

I bare my teeth in something that's not a smile.

"You want hell? I'll walk you there myself."

I put her behind me, her small hand pressing my knife into my palm.

Good girl.

"Look for a way out, baby." My voice is rough, smoke-burned. I don't take my eyes off Cormac.

He peels off what's left of his singed shirt, tosses it into the fire like a challenge. His chest heaves, blackened skin blistering, but his grin is all venom. Each breath burns deeper, smoke turning our lungs to ash. Seraphina coughs behind me, and I hear her stumbling through rubble. She's weak from blood loss, weaker from the smoke. Time's running out.

If it comes to it, I'll sleep easy with her in my arms—so long as my brother rots here in the ashes.

He rips a burning beam from the floor and flings it at

me. It sails wide, sparks raining, but I'm already moving. He charges, and I catch him by the throat and the waistband, twist with his momentum, and drive him face-first into the wall. Stone cracks with the impact.

I knee him in the gut. His breath bursts out ragged. My boot slams into his ribs and he staggers, but I don't give him room. My hand fists in his hair and I slam his face into stone again, pulling him back to see the ruin I've made of him— blood streaming, teeth broken, eyes wild.

I grip the knife, knuckles white, and my fist crashes into his face once. Twice.

His body goes slack, dead weight in my hold, but I don't stop.

Again. Again. Again. My knuckles split, blood slicking the blade's handle, but I keep going.

"This is for every drop of blood you spilled."

Crack.

"For every woman you hurt, every soul you ruined."

Crack.

"For our mother."

Crack.

"And this—" my fist drives down one last time, his face unrecognizable now, "—this is for touching my angel."

I feel the moment bones give way—shatter under my strikes. The second shards drive into his brain. The wet gurgle in his throat is the only sound left before he goes still.

I spit beside his body, chest heaving, knuckles raw and dripping.

Cormac. My brother. My curse.

Dead at last.

The fire's a living thing now—gnawing, clawing, roaring as it devours what's left of the church. My chest heaves, lungs ripping raw with every breath, but all I can think about is her.

She's in the corner, slumped against stone, her face pale and streaked with soot, eyes half-lidded. Blood runs down her thigh, soaking the strip of cloth I tied, and each cough wracks her whole body.

I can't let it end like this. Not with her. Not here.

I grab a beam splintered from the collapse, thick and heavy, and stagger to the wall. I swing it hard—smashing stone, wood, anything that might give. Again. Again. My muscles scream, arms shaking, but the wall doesn't yield. Each strike steals more of my strength until my knees threaten to give.

Behind me, she chokes—a ragged cough—and when I turn she's sliding down the wall, her body folding in on itself.

"Angel—" I drop the beam, scrambling to her. Her skin's cold under the soot, her body trembling against mine.

Her lips part, voice breaking. "I tried…"

My throat closes, but I force the words out—rough and raw. "You did more than try."

Her hand trembles as it lifts, brushing weakly against my cheek. Her lips barely move, the whisper fragile, fading. "Go…"

I shake my head and kiss her, desperate, pouring everything I am into her mouth. "Not without you." My voice cracks as I press my forehead to hers, holding her close.

"When you go, I go," I whisper into her ear, tears racing down my smoke-stung cheeks.

I clutch her tighter, willing my strength into her frail body, vowing I'll never let her go. Not here. Not like this.

And then—a crash on the other side of the wall. Another. Louder. Closer.

The wall a few feet away shudders, dust spilling in a cloud. Then the blade of an ax punches through stone and mortar, sparks flying.

Hope surges hot through my veins.

Another ax. And another. Three blades tearing the wall apart from the other side. Lucian. Jaxon. Damien.

"Hold on, angel," I murmur, cradling her face, forcing her eyes open. "They're here. I won't let you go—not now, not when we're so close."

Her lashes flutter, her body weakening against me. I pick her up, clutching her tight, whispering into her hair. "Stay with me, baby. Breathe. Just breathe."

The hole widens with every strike, daylight spilling through in fractured beams.

"Back away!" Jaxon's voice roars through the smoke.

I turn, shielding her, just as the pew smashes through—ripping the wall wide. Fresh air blasts in, feeding the fire, flames roaring higher, but the hole's big enough.

I hunch low, shield her with my body, and force us through.

Lucian's there, his hands gripping my arm, dragging us out. "We're not dying today." He says it like he can control it.

Jaxon grabs her legs, easing the weight from me. Damien

doesn't hesitate—he's already heading for the stairs. "Here!" he shouts.

We run. I stumble, coughing blood, vision blurry, but I keep her in my arms, limp and too quiet. Lucian and Jaxon flank us, half carrying, half dragging me forward.

The stairwell's a furnace, flames snapping at our backs. Damien carves the path ahead, driving us upward—step after step—until we're out.

I collapse to my knees on the lawn, still clutching her. Smoke billows black into the sky, the church crumbling behind us, fire lighting the ruins in a hellish glow.

The helicopter's already there, blades chopping the air, howling over the roar of the fire. It's how they got to us so fast.

Jax and Lucian haul me to my feet, each gripping an arm. Lucian's voice cuts through the ringing in my ears. "Just a little farther, buddy."

Damien's already climbing into the cockpit, flipping switches, hands sure and steady. The rotors scream louder, wind blasting the grass flat.

Jax moves in first, arms outstretched to take Seraphina from me. My body revolts. The second I let her go, I nearly break in two. She's limp. Lifeless. Her eyes closed, skin ghost-pale beneath the soot and blood. My heart stops just looking at her like that.

I scramble in after them—faster than my battered body should allow—and take her back into my arms before I fall apart. I rock her against me, my lips against her hair, words spilling out in low, frantic tones.

"Stay with me, angel. Please, baby—please. I love you.

You can't leave me." I stroke her matted hair and kiss her temple. "Please don't leave, angel. I need you."

"I need you."

The helicopter lifts—engines screaming, blades hammering the sky as the ruined church burns below us.

And I hold her tighter, praying to gods I don't believe in that she's not dead.

Chapter 41

Stasia made sure her trauma team was waiting on the helipad. The blades hadn't even slowed before they were there—scrubs, masks, hands reaching, voices commanding, the urgency sharp and precise.

I stepped out with Seraphina in my arms. Stasia froze—just a beat, just long enough for her face to break wide open. Her entire soul cracked in front of me, shattering as she saw her twin limp in my hold. Pulse there, but weak. So goddamn weak.

She swallowed it down, steel locking over her grief as training took over. "Here—on the stretcher."

I laid Seraphina down, my hands shaking so bad I nearly missed the rails. Stasia climbed on top without hesitation, sealing an oxygen mask over her mouth, squeezing the bag, forcing air into her lungs.

"Go, go, go!" someone shouted.

I ran with them, pushing the gurney down the corridor, my chest burning like I'd dragged the fire inside with me.

We burst into the elevator. Hands shoved me back, hard against my chest.

"You can't come further," one of them barked.

The doors started to close. I locked on Seraphina's face until the last possible second—her pale skin beneath the mask, chest barely rising. Then I looked at Stasia. Just before the doors sealed, she met my gaze and gave one sharp nod.

I won't let her die.

The world tilted. My knees buckled. Hands caught me, steering me into another elevator, into another room. Oxygen. IV. Cold water down my throat. They checked everything—lungs, ears, eyes, skin where the smoke had clawed its way in. Ice packs pressed to burns. Needles stitching torn flesh across my knuckles, over my brow. My fists twitched with every pull of the thread, because all I could see was Cormac's face breaking under them.

Lucian didn't leave. Sat still as stone in the chair across from me while we waited.

Damien and Jaxon took the Wolfe Industries helicopter back. Eve and Sienna came with clothes, made me wash up in the sink until the water ran black. They even packed a bag for Seraphina. For when she wakes up.

Because she will wake up. She has to.

And thank Christ—Finn's okay.

They brought him in hours ago, carried on a stretcher with a blade sunk deep in his chest. Cormac had shit aim, missed the heart by inches, punctured a lung instead. He's stable now, stitched up, Nora glued to his side. One less ghost to carry.

But still—it's her. Always her.

I couldn't eat. Couldn't close my eyes. Couldn't stop pacing outside the doors she'd gone through.

Minutes. Hours. I don't know. Time didn't exist anymore.

Eventually, my body forced me into a chair. My head fell into my hands, fingers dragging through the rough scrape of my beard. My chest ached so hard I thought my ribs might crack.

Then Lucian moved.

He knelt in front of me, his hand heavy on my shoulder, grounding me. "Hey." His voice was quiet, steady. "I already told you. No one from our family dies today."

My throat closed. My eyes burned, and no matter how I swallowed, I couldn't force words out. Guilt clawed higher, drowning me. Broken fragments slipped through. "It's... my fault. Should've—"

Lucian's grip tightened. His other arm came around me, pulling me down like a brother. "Don't. Don't fucking do that to yourself." His voice sharpened—not with anger, but steel. "You didn't do this."

Tears burned, hot and relentless, streaking down my face. The smoke still clung to me, like I'd never left that fire. I shook my head, but Lucian pressed closer, his words driving in deep.

"If it weren't for me—"

"You got her out, Killian. You. She's alive because you never stopped. Don't let him take that from you."

I choked on a sob, raw and jagged. My fists curled, stitches pulling, blood seeping through fresh bandages.

Lucian just held tighter.

Finally—fucking finally—the door cracked open.

Stasia stepped through.

Her chin wobbled. Her mouth tried for a smile, but her eyes flooded, her face crumpling. Tears broke fast and hard, shoulders shaking.

"She's going to be okay," she sobbed.

For a second, the world stopped. I had to process the words she just spoke.

Then they hit me like a tidal wave. I was on my feet, dragging her into me, crushing her against my chest.

"She's going to be okay," Stasia repeated, muffled into my shirt.

And for the first time since I saw her strapped to a pyre—

I could breathe.

Chapter 42

Killian

A month. That's how long it's been since I carried her out of the fire.

The first week was hospitals—IVs, oxygen, her thigh stitched shut, skin bandaged where ropes and glass bit deep. When they finally said she was stable enough to leave, I thought she'd want her penthouse.

Instead, her weak hand clutched mine, her voice glassy with drugs and exhaustion. *"Can we go to your place?"*

It gutted me, hearing that plea. She didn't need to explain. Too much had gone down in her apartment—ghosts in every corner. But pride bloomed sharp in my chest. She felt safe in mine. She said it was warm there.

So I took her home.

For the next three weeks, I didn't let her lift a finger. I waited on her day and night. Held her when she slept, which was most of the time at first. Watched her strength creep back inch by inch.

She'd laugh and swat me when I scooped her up instead

of letting her hobble on crutches. I only did it a handful of times, but I never let her forget—I'd carry her anywhere if she asked.

Stasia brought the kids once. I turned the couch into a giant bed so they could pile under blankets for a movie. Daniel hung in the kitchen with me, talking woodwork while I made enough snacks to feed an army.

When she tried to read, the bandages on her palms made turning pages hell. So I read to her. Should've checked the titles—half were smut wrapped in innocent covers. I started highlighting passages, saving ideas for when her body could take what her eyes kept asking for.

One night, after a particularly filthy oral scene, she shoved the covers down, legs spread. *"Killian, if you don't eat my pussy right now, I may die of arousal."*

And fuck, I did. Careful. Tender. Slow—because every time I closed my eyes, I still saw her limp in my arms, soot-covered and silent. That memory kept my hands soft even when I wanted them rough.

Now—today—a storm batters the windows, rain slashing in sheets, thunder rolling heavy. We've been curled on the couch all day, drifting between old records, bad movies, and the dog-eared book I've been half-reading, half-mocking just to make her laugh.

I clear our dishes and sink down beside her.

"Come sit on your throne," I tell her, patting my lap.

Her mouth curves. "Your smart mouth or your fat cock?"

"Take your pick," I murmur, my hands already sliding to her hips. "Both are yours."

She swings a leg over, straddling me. My palms find her

ribs, her waist, the swell of her ass. I harden under her, and she gives me one slow roll of her hips—promise, threat, tease.

"You feeling up to tomorrow?" I ask, thumbs stroking circles under her shirt. "Touring the rest of the Irish territory."

"You mean *your* territory," she counters, eyes glittering. "Now that you sit on the Irish throne?"

"It's always been my throne," I tell her, voice low. "Just like you've always been mine… to watch, to guard, to own."

She huffs a laugh. "Did I just trade one stalker for another?"

"Angel," I drag my knuckles up her spine, "I've always stalked you. Just did it in plain sight—with no plans of ever letting you go."

I peel her shirt off. Braless. Nipples tight in the cool air. I pinch, suck, bite until she gasps and bows into my mouth.

"Now you'll be my Irish queen," I growl, "my ruined little killer. My cockwhore, begging me to own you."

"Why don't you stop talking and show me how you'll ruin me, big man?"

Challenge accepted.

"Strip," I command.

She rises slow, peeling herself bare. Heat flushes her throat, her chest, her thighs. I slide my knife free, press the flat of the blade to her slit. It comes away slick.

"Already drooling for me, you filthy little slut." I lick the metal clean, tasting her, then grip her throat and kiss her hard as I walk her backward down the hall.

"Lay on the bed. Head off the edge."

She obeys, throat a pale vulnerable line over the mattress. I strip, cock heavy above her lips.

"You want it, don't you?"

"Yes."

"You want me to fuck your mouth—own your throat."

Her swallow is audible. "Yes."

"Then beg."

Her fingers stroke my length, wet from her pussy. "Please, sir. Feed me your cock."

Sir. Goddamn. That one word snaps chains off me.

"That's my girl."

I slide deep, hitting the back of her throat. She gags, hands flying to my thighs. I hold her there just a beat. "Breathe through your nose." I ease out, then drive back in, teaching her rhythm, praising between thrusts.

When she steadies, I lean down, tongue lapping her clit. I fuck her mouth while I eat her pussy, greedy for every sound she makes. Her orgasm floods my tongue, her throat spasming around my cock. I groan, haul her up, kiss her deep—her release still wet on both our mouths.

"On all fours."

She goes, ass high, wrists sinking into the sheets. I cuff her ankles to the footboard, spreading her wide.

"Spread like a good whore."

She trembles but obeys. I murmur against her ear, "If your leg hurts, you tell me. Promise me, angel."

"I promise, sir."

Good girl.

I slick my fingers, press into her ass—one, then two, then three, stretching her slow. She moans into the sheets, drool wetting the pillow.

I slap her pussy lightly with a thick dildo. "Suck it."

She takes it deep, gagging, eyes watering as I finger her ass open. When I pull the toy free, I grind it over her clit. "Ask for it."

"Please, sir," she sobs. "Stuff me full. Use everything."

"Atta girl."

I push my cock into her ass, slow but relentless, while I slide the toy into her pussy. She's filled everywhere, obscene and perfect. I pound her, cock and silicone working in tandem, until she breaks apart screaming, squirting all over the sheets.

I don't stop until I'm spilling in her ass, snarling her name.

But I'm not done.

I unclip an ankle, flip her onto her back, hook her good leg high and slide into her cunt in one savage stroke.

"Yes, sir—fuck me," she cries out, back arching.

I pound her open, ass-to-pussy, branding her throat with my palm. "Dirty girl. Took me in your ass and now you're sucking me into your cunt. You love being my slut. Say it."

"I love it—I love being your slut."

"Fucking good girl."

I drive harder, until her walls convulse around me and

my seed floods her again. I stay buried, choking on the sight of her—ruined, trembling, radiant.

I soften my grip on her throat, press a reverent kiss where my thumb left her pulse hammering.

"My enemy took you, and I came for you. Killed for you. Claimed the Irish to rule with you. But you—" I angle her face to mine, voice rough, "—you're the only throne I'll ever bow to."

Her pupils blow wide. She bites my lip, hard enough to draw blood. *"You killed for me,"* she whispers, hips rolling to take me deeper, *"but I'd burn for you."*

I groan into her mouth, tasting copper and heat. *"Then take me with you, angel—because you're mine. This life, the next. You go, I go. Forever."*

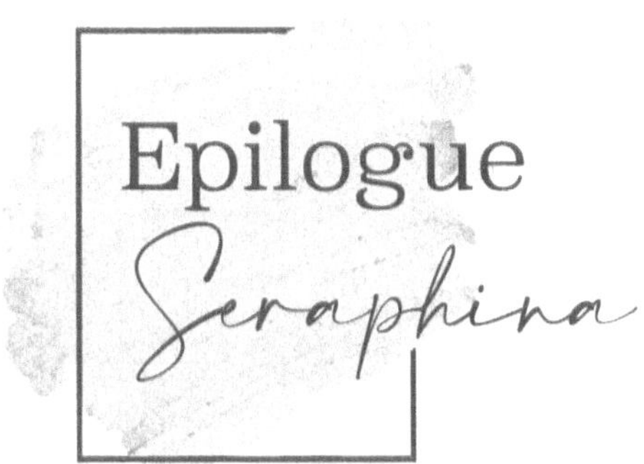

Epilogue
Seraphina

The wedding was beautiful. Simple and golden, the kind of day that feels like it should be bottled and kept forever. Cassidy was radiant, her smile brighter than the lights strung between the beams of the barn. And Jaxon—God, there has never been a groom prouder or more in love. He barely looked away from her all night.

Now, as the music hums low in the background and the stars blink awake over the horse farm, we gather around a large, round table—the Ledger family, a band of misfits who never belonged anywhere, yet somehow belong perfectly together here.

I tilt my fork toward Elena, unable to hide my grin. "This cheesecake, Elena … I'd kill for another slice."

From the corner of my eye I see Killian's faint smirk at my comment, and I elbow him.

Eve nods vigorously. "Forget 'kill'—I'd maim. This is dangerous."

Across the table, Sienna would probably agree if she weren't too busy lifting a bite to Lucian's mouth. He takes it, lips brushing her fingers before his gaze softens. That steel-cut man of ice and shadow—smiling, but only for her.

On the other end, Damien, Grant, and Dante are knee-deep in a discussion about the new Ledger high-rise, gesturing with their glasses as if sketching blueprints in the air. Since the old tower's top was blown apart, the rebuilding has become the obsession of the men who thrive on empire.

"So," Damien finally leans back, his sharp gaze sliding to Lucian. "What's next for the Ledger?"

Lucian's mouth curves, the corner of it tugging upward as his attention drifts to Sienna. "We've got a few things in mind."

Sienna, ever the quiet thunder at his side, adds, "Seraphina has inspired a new venture at our U.K. office."

Killian's brows lift, surprise flickering across his face as he angles toward me. "Oh yeah?" His tone is warm, teasing. "And what's that, then?"

Lucian cuts in smoothly. "The Black Ledger Matchmakers."

I laugh under my breath, shaking my head. "What? Brides for sale. A billion each."

Grant leans forward, smirk lazy. "Or grooms. We're equal opportunity here."

The laughter swells just as Jaxon and Cassidy approach. She doesn't even bother with her own chair, simply folding into his lap like she belongs there—which, clearly, she does.

Eve leans in with a wicked grin. "God help us all when

those two start having children. That Kane gene pool doesn't need reinforcements."

Damien snorts, dry as bone. "Please. Knowing Jaxon, he'll have an algorithm shitting out little replicas in no time."

Cassidy flushes crimson while Jaxon only smirks, tightening his hold on her waist.

Horror flashes across Eve's face like she's just seen a head explode. "Oh my God, no."

Jaxon's smile turns feral. "Well, since you brought it up …"

Cassidy glances at him, eyes sparkling, and then back at us. "We're pregnant."

The table erupts—cheers, shouts, congratulations flying in every direction. Glasses clink, chairs scrape, hands reach across to touch, to hug, to celebrate.

Everyone except Eve, who looks positively green. "I can't believe you're spawning."

Elena laughs, nudging her best friend. Children and relationships have never appealed to Eve.

Elena twines her fingers with Damien's, her engagement ring flashing in the light. "Hey, children wouldn't be so bad."

Damien's smile could power all of New York; his gaze is locked on her. "Trouble, if you gave me a little brunette baby girl, I'd give new meaning to the word spoiled."

Her breath catches, lips parting just before he leans over to claim them in a quick, tender kiss.

Cassidy clears her throat, tugging a small velvet box

from Jaxon's tuxedo jacket. "I have a little surprise—a wedding-day gift for my husband."

Jaxon takes it, suspicion written all over his face. He flips it open—and instantly goes pale. "Am I looking at what I think I'm looking at?"

Cassidy just nods, laughter bubbling from her chest.

"Twins?" His voice cracks.

"Yes," she says, delighted, and that's all it takes. He surges up, scooping her into his arms by the bottom and spinning her in wild circles, both of them laughing breathlessly before he sets her back down for a kiss that has the whole table cheering louder. Cassidy's mother watches from where she's sitting, happiness glazing her eyes.

The joy is contagious. Elena wipes at her eyes with a napkin; Eve gapes in disbelief, muttering, "This is worse." Someone orders more champagne.

By the time Jaxon sits again, Cassidy perched happily in his lap, the ultrasound photo is already making its rounds. Eve stares at it like it might bite, then shoves it into Sienna's hands, who gazes down at it with a smile before passing it on.

"Overachiever," Jaxon announces, arms spread wide. "What can I say?"

"Actually, it's the mother who's the overachiever," Eve shoots back with a smirk.

Lucian's gaze flicks to Sienna, voice smooth as smoke. "She'd have to be, to put up with him."

The laughter rises again, echoing through the rafters.

Jaxon lifts his glass, Cassidy's hand tucked tight in his.

"You guys better get your empires back in order. There are nieces and nephews on the way."

"Oh, we'll be ready." Lucian raises his glass in answer. "With the Italians under the Ledger."

Killian's arm curls heavier around my shoulders; his own glass rises. "And the Irish under me."

Lucian's smile sharpens, final and sure. "We'll rebuild, and come back stronger than ever."

He looks around, taking in this odd assortment of people who have become a family, and pushes to his feet, lifting his glass higher, his voice rich with pride and power. "To the Ledger. To family. To our future."

Everyone joins in, voices overlapping, glasses clinking, the sound rolling like thunder.

Killian leans over to kiss me, slow and certain, and I rub my nose against his when we part. My whisper is for him alone. "And here's to my final contract, big man."

His glass tips toward mine, eyes holding me captive. "You're damn right—and I'll prove it with every breath, angel."